MY HEART
and other
BLACK HOLES

MY HEART and other BLACK HOLES

Jasmine Warga

BALZER + BRAY

An Imprint of HarperCollins*Publishers*

Balzer + Bray is an imprint of HarperCollins Publishers.

My Heart and Other Black Holes
Copyright © 2015 by Jasmine Warga
www.epicreads.com

Library of Congress Cataloging-in-Publication Data
Warga, Jasmine.
My heart and other black holes / Jasmine Warga.—First edition.
  pages cm
  ISBN 978-0-06-232467-2 (hardcover)
  ISBN 978-0-06-239112-4 (international edition)
  Summary: "Sixteen-year-old Aysel's hobby—planning her own
death—takes a new path when she meets a boy who has a similar plan
of his own"— Provided by publisher.
  [1. Suicide—Fiction.] I. Title.
PZ7.1.W37My 2015   2014021982
[Fic]—dc23   CIP
                                                              AC

Typography by Torborg Davern
15 16 17 18 19 CG/RRDH 10 9 8 7 6 5

First Edition

In memory of Aidan Jos Schapera,
who loved life and taught the rest of us how to

The real voyage of discovery consists not in seeking new landscapes, but in having new eyes.

—MARCEL PROUST

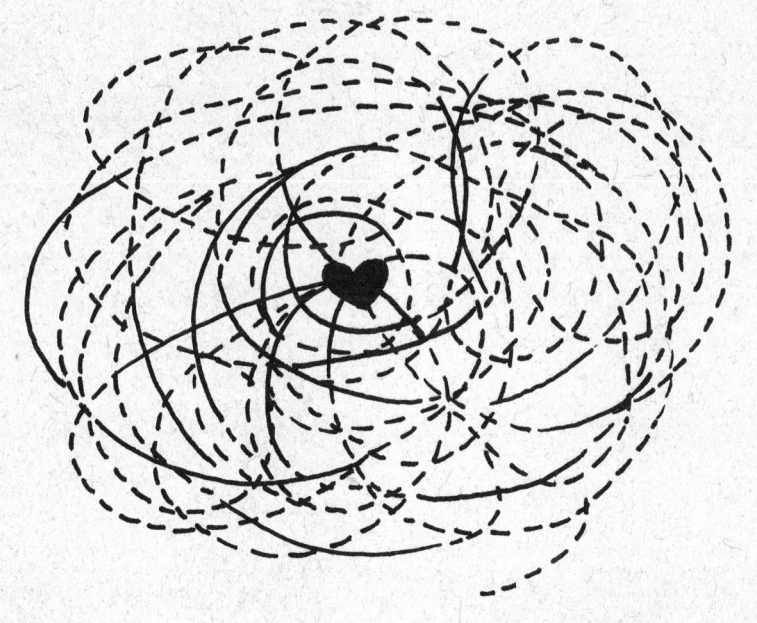

TUESDAY, MARCH 12

26 days left

Music, especially classical music, especially Mozart's Requiem Mass in D Minor, has kinetic energy. If you listen hard enough, you can hear the violin's bow trembling above the strings, ready to ignite the notes. To set them in motion. And once the notes are in the air, they collide against one another. They spark. They burst.

I spend a lot of time wondering what dying feels like. What dying sounds like. If I'll burst like those notes, let out my last cries of pain, and then go silent forever. Or maybe I'll turn into a shadowy static that's barely there, if you just listen hard enough.

And if I wasn't already fantasizing about dying, working at the phone bank at Tucker's Marketing Concepts would definitely do the trick. Lucky for them they're off the hook in terms of liability because I have a preexisting condition.

Tucker's Marketing Concepts is a telemarketing firm located in the basement of a dingy strip mall and I'm their only employee who wasn't alive to witness the fall of Rome. Several gray plastic tables that were probably bought in bulk from Costco are arranged in rows, and everyone gets a phone and a computer. The whole place smells like mold mixed with burnt coffee.

Right now, we're conducting a survey for Paradise Vacations. They want to know what people value more on vacation—quality of food and beverage or quality of hotel rooms. I dial the next number on my list: Mrs. Elena George, who lives on Mulberry Street.

"Hello?" a scratchy voice answers the phone.

"Hello, Mrs. George. My name is Aysel and I'm calling from Tucker's Marketing Concepts on behalf of Paradise Vacations. Do you have a moment to answer a few questions?" I lack the singsongy delivery of most of my fellow workers. I'm not exactly TMC's star employee.

"I told y'all to stop calling this number," Mrs. George says, and hangs up on me.

You can run, but you can't hide, Mrs. George. I make a note on my call log. Looks like she's not interested in a two-week vacation to Hawaii with a time-share opportunity. Sorry, Paradise Vacations.

Making more than one phone call without a break in between is too much for me, so I turn to face my computer. The only perk of my job is the free, unrestricted internet access. I double click on the browser and log back on to Smooth Passages, my favorite website of the moment.

"Aysel," Mr. Palmer, my supervisor, snaps, mispronouncing my name as always. It's Uh-zell, not Ay-zal, but he doesn't care. "How many times do I have to tell you to stop playing around on your computer?" He gestures toward my call log. "You still have a lot of numbers left."

Mr. Palmer is the type of person who could change his whole life if he just once went to a different barber. He currently has a bowl cut, the type more typically found on gangly sixth-grade boys. I want to tell him that a crew cut could really bring out his jawline, but I guess he's pretty happy with Mrs. Palmer so he's in no rush to reinvent himself. Nope, no midlife crisis for Mr. Palmer.

I hate to admit it, but I'm a little jealous of Mr. Palmer. At least he can be fixed, if he wants to be fixed. A few scissor clips and he'll be brand-new. There's nothing that can fix me.

"What?" Mr. Palmer says when he catches me staring at him.

"You have nice hair." I swivel in my chair. I guess I lied,

my job has two perks: free internet access and I get to sit in a spinning chair.

"Huh?" he grunts.

"You have nice hair," I repeat. "Have you ever considered wearing it in a different style?"

"You know, I took a risk, hiring you." He waves his wrinkled finger close to my face. "Everyone in this town told me you were trouble. Because of your . . ." He trails off and looks away.

Because of your father, I complete his sentence in my head. The inside of my mouth fills with the sour, metallic taste I've come to know as humiliation. My life can be neatly divided into two sections: before my father made the nightly news and after. For a moment, I allow myself to imagine what this conversation would sound like if my father weren't my father. Mr. Palmer probably wouldn't speak to me like I'm a stray mutt raiding his garbage can. I'd like to think he'd have more tact, but no one wastes their tact on me anymore. But then it hits me, the thought I try to squeeze out of my mind. *You wouldn't feel any different inside.*

I dip my chin to my chest in an attempt to shake that thought. "Sorry, Mr. Palmer. I'm on it."

Mr. Palmer doesn't say anything; he just looks up at the three giant shiny banners that were recently hung on the office's back wall. Each one of them features Brian Jackson striking some sort of pose—arms crossed over his chest, arms thrown above his head in victory, arms pressed at his side midsprint. He's been Photoshopped to have perfect skin, but there was no need to alter his ashy-blond hair or bright blue eyes. And I know from passing him in the halls at school that his calf muscles really are that large. At the bottom of each giant banner, the words HOMEGROWN IN LANGSTON, KENTUCKY, AND OLYMPIC BOUND are scrawled in red block text.

The banner doesn't say anything about the first boy from Langston who almost qualified for the Olympics. But it doesn't have to. As I watch Mr. Palmer study the banner, I know he's thinking about that boy—the first boy. Almost anyone who sees Brian Jackson's sweaty brow and muscular calves can't help but think of Timothy Jackson, Brian's older brother. And anyone who sees the banner and then sees me will definitely think of Timothy Jackson.

Finally, Mr. Palmer peels his eyes away from the poster and turns back to me. He can't look me in the eye, though. He stares over the top of my head as he clears his throat. "Look, Aysel. Maybe it would be best if you didn't come in tomorrow. Why don't you take the day off?"

I press my elbows into the table, wishing I could melt into the gray plastic, into an unfeeling synthetic blend of polymers. I feel my skin starting to bruise under the weight of my body and I silently hum Bach's Toccata and Fugue in D Minor. My mind fills with dark and heavy organ notes and I imagine the organ's keys arranging themselves into the shape of a ladder that leads to an empty quiet place. A place away from TMC, away from Mr. Palmer, away from everyone and everything.

Mr. Palmer seems to misinterpret my silence as confusion, not complete and utter mortification. He stretches his hands out in front of him, wringing them out like he just washed them. I inspire that feeling in most people—the desire to wash their hands clean. "As you may know, tomorrow we're going to be making calls on behalf of the city of Langston to try and increase attendance at Saturday's rally for Brian Jackson." Mr. Palmer's voice quivers a bit and he sneaks a quick glance back at the banner, as if Brian Jackson's focused athletic countenance may help him muster the courage to continue.

Brian's magic must rub off on Mr. Palmer because he finds his voice again. "Brian's coming home for the weekend from training camp and the city wants everyone to show him a warm welcome. And as much as I know you would like to help, I'm afraid some of our customers might feel uncomfortable with you inviting them to the rally because, well, because of your father and . . ." His voice lowers and he continues talking, but he's stumbling over his words and I can't really understand what he's saying. It's something of a mixture between an apology, an explanation, and an indictment.

I try not to laugh. Instead of focusing on the absurdity of

how I am apparently too unappealing to even operate as a telemarketer, I choose to zero in on Mr. Palmer's word choice of "customer." I don't think the people we harass on the daily consider themselves to be customers, but rather victims. And thanks to my dad, I'm pretty good at making everyone feel like they could be a potential victim.

Red-faced and flustered, Mr. Palmer walks away from my desk and begins strolling the other rows. He asks Marie to stop chewing gum and he begs Tony to please refrain from smearing hamburger grease all over the keyboard.

Once Mr. Palmer's a safe distance from my desk, I open Smooth Passages again. In the simplest terms, Smooth Passages is a website for people who want to die. There are tons of these websites. Some are fancier than others, some are more niche oriented for people who have a specific method they prefer, like say suffocating, or they're for a certain type of person, like depressed injured athletes or some shit like that. I still haven't found one dedicated to the unwanted daughters of psychotic criminals, so for now Smooth Passages is the place for me.

Smooth Passages' website is plain, no flashy or cheesy HTML work. It's black and white. Classy. That is, if a website dedicated to suicide can be classy. There are message boards and forums, which is what I mostly look at. Recently, I've become really interested in this one section called Suicide Partners.

The problem with suicide, which most people don't realize, is that it's really hard to follow through. I know, I know. People are always yammering on and on about how "suicide is the coward's way out." And I guess it is—I mean, I am giving up, surrendering. Running away from my black hole of a future, preventing myself from growing into the person I'm terrified of becoming. But just because it's cowardly doesn't guarantee it's going to be easy.

The thing is, I'm concerned that my self-preservation instinct is too high. It's like my depressed mind and my very-much-alive body are in a constant struggle. I worry about my body winning out at the last minute with some jerky impulse and then I'll end up having done the deed only halfway.

Nothing scares me more than a failed attempt. The last thing I want is to end up in a wheelchair, eating pulverized food and being watched around the clock by some sassy nurse who has a not-so-secret obsession with cheesy reality TV.

And that's why lately I've been eyeing the Suicide Partners section. I guess the way it works is you find some other sad excuse for a person who lives pretty nearby and you make your final plans with them. It's like peer pressure suicide, and from what I gather, it's pretty damn effective. Sign me up.

I scan some of the postings. None of them are a good fit for me. Either they're way too far away (why do so many people in California want to blow their brains out? Isn't living by the ocean supposed to make you happy?) or they're just the wrong demographic (I really don't want to get mixed up with some adult who's having marital troubles—stressed-out soccer moms are not for me).

I contemplate composing my own ad, but I'm not really sure what I'd say. Also, nothing seems sadder than reaching out, trying to find a partner, and then getting rejected. I look over my shoulder and see that Mr. Palmer is a few rows away. He's massaging Tina Bart's shoulders. He's always massaging Tina Bart's shoulders. Maybe he isn't as happy with Mrs. Palmer as I thought.

Mr. Palmer catches me staring at him and shakes his head. Flashing him my sweetest grimace, I pick up the phone and dial the next number that's on my log: Samuel Porter, who lives on Galveston Lane.

As I'm listening to the familiar ring of the phone, I hear my computer beep. Damn. I'm always forgetting to mute the volume.

Laura, the middle-aged lady who works next to me and wears lipstick that's too bright for her jaundiced complexion, raises her eyebrow at me.

I shrug. "I think the software is updating," I mouth to her.

She rolls her eyes at me. Laura, apparently, is a human bullshit detector.

Mr. Samuel Porter doesn't answer his phone. Guess he's

not craving piña coladas. I hang up the phone and click back to Smooth Passages. Looks like it beeped because someone posted a new message in the Suicide Partners forum. It's titled "April 7th." I open it:

> I'll admit I used to think this was stupid. The whole point of killing myself is so I can be alone forever so I never understood why I'd want to do it with someone else. But that's changed now. I'm nervous I'll chicken out at the last minute or something. There are other things, too, but I'd rather not get into that here.
>
> I only have a few requirements. One, I don't want to do it with anyone who has kids. That shit is too heavy for me. Two, you can't live more than an hour away from me. I know this might be hard since I live in the middle of nowhere but for now I'm sticking to that. And three, we have to do it on April 7th. That date isn't negotiable. Message me for more information.
>
> —FrozenRobot

I check FrozenRobot's stats and try not to judge the screen name. But, FrozenRobot, really? I understand that everyone on here is a little bit, okay, a lot emotional, but still. Have some dignity.

FrozenRobot is apparently a he. He's seventeen, so only one year older than me. That's fine. Oh, and he's from Willis, Kentucky—that's about fifteen minutes away.

A surge jolts through my bones and I vaguely remember that this is what excitement feels like. FrozenRobot has perfect timing. Maybe, for the first time in my life, I'm lucky. This must be a sign from the universe—if the only time you get lucky is when you're planning your suicide, it's definitely time to go.

I read the message again. April 7, that works for me. Today is March 12. I can maybe last another month or so, though lately each day feels like an eternity.

"Aysel," Mr. Palmer says again.

"What?" I say, hardly paying any attention to him.

He walks so he can stand behind me and taps my computer screen. I try to minimize the window. "Look, I don't care what you do in your free time but don't bring it to work. Got it?" His voice sags like an old couch cushion. I'd feel bad for Mr. Palmer if I had any pity saved for anyone else but me.

I'm going to go out on a limb and guess that Mr. Palmer isn't familiar with Smooth Passages. He probably thinks I'm looking at some heavy metal fan site or something. Little does Mr. Palmer know, I like my music soft and instrumental. Didn't his parents ever teach him not to buy into stereotypes? Just because I'm a sixteen-year-old girl with unruly curly hair who wears dark striped shirts every day doesn't mean I can't appreciate a nice violin solo or a smooth piano concerto.

Once Mr. Palmer walks away, I hear Laura scoff. "What?" I say.

"Don't you have the internet at home?" Laura asks, frowning at me. She's sipping the complimentary coffee, and the plastic mug's rim is stained with her god-awful berry burst lipstick.

"Don't you have a coffee maker at home?"

She shrugs, and just when I think the conversation is over, she says, "Work isn't the place to be fishing for dates. Do that on your own time. You're going to get the rest of us in trouble."

"Right." I look down at my keyboard. There's no use explaining to Laura that I'm not searching for a date, or at least not that kind of date.

I stare at the pieces of cheese crackers that are stuck in the spaces between the F and G keys, and that's when I decide— I'm going to message back FrozenRobot.

He and I have a date: April 7.

WEDNESDAY, MARCH 13

25 days left

The only class I really like is physics. I'm no science genius, but this is the one class that I think may have some answers to my questions. Ever since I was little, I've been fascinated by the way things work. I used to take apart my toys, studying how all the little pieces fit together. I would stare at the independent parts, picking up an arm of a doll (my half sister, Georgia, has never forgiven me for the autopsy I gave to her Prom Date Barbie) or the wheels of a car. Once, I dismantled my father's alarm clock. He came in and found me sitting on the faded beige carpet, the batteries rolling around by my sneakers.

"What are you doing?" he asked.

"Breaking it so I can learn how to fix it."

He put his hand on my shoulder—I remember his hands, big, with long thick fingers, the type of hands that make you feel both scared and safe at the same time—and said, "You know, Zellie, there are enough broken things in the world. You shouldn't go around breaking things just for the fun of it." The clock stayed dismantled for years, until I eventually threw it away.

Anyway, physics at least feels useful to me. Unlike English, where we're reading poems by depressed poets. Not helpful. My teacher, Mrs. Marks, makes this big production out of trying to decode what the poets were saying. From my perspective, it's pretty clear: I'm depressed and I want to die. It's painful to watch all my classmates tear apart each line, looking for the significance. There's no significance. Anyone who has actually been that sad can tell you that there's nothing beautiful or literary or mysterious about depression.

Depression is like a heaviness that you can't ever escape. It crushes down on you, making even the smallest things like tying your shoes or chewing on toast seem like a twenty-mile hike uphill. Depression is a part of you; it's in your bones and your blood. If I know anything about it, this is what I know: It's impossible to escape.

And I'm pretty sure I know a lot more than any of my classmates. Listening to them talk about it makes my skin crawl. So for me, English class is like watching a group of blind squirrels try to find nuts. Mrs. Marks will say, "Let's take a look at this line. Here the poet John Berryman says, 'Life, friends, is boring.' What do you think he meant by that?" My classmates all clamor, shouting out ridiculous things like "He didn't have anyone to hang out with on Saturday night" or "Football season was over so there was nothing good to watch on TV."

It takes all the restraint in the world not to stand up and scream, "He was fucking sad. That's it. That's the point. He knows that life is never going to get any different for him. That there's no fixing him. It's always going to be the same monotonous depressing bullshit. Boring, sad, boring, sad. He just wants it to be over." But that would require me to talk in class, which would violate one of my personal rules. I don't participate. Why? Because I'm fucking sad. Mrs. Marks sometimes gives me this look, like she knows that I know what John Berryman meant, but she never calls on me.

At least in physics my classmates aren't desperately trying to make uncomplicated shit complicated. Nope, in physics, we're all trying to make complicated things uncomplicated.

Mr. Scott writes an equation on the board. We're learning about projectile motion. We're studying the properties of an object in motion that's under the influence of gravity only. There are all these variables like the angle the object is launched from and the initial velocity.

My eyes gloss over. Too many numbers. I start to day-dream about gravity. Sometimes I wonder if gravity is the problem. It keeps us all grounded, gives us this false sense of stability when really we're all just bodies in motion. Gravity keeps us from floating up into space, it keeps us from invol-untarily crashing into one another. It saves the human race from being a big hot mess.

I wish gravity would go away and just let us all be a big mess.

Unfortunately, that's not the answer to the question Mr. Scott is asking.

"Aysel, can you tell me the highest point the football reaches?"

I didn't even know the object in the problem was a foot-ball. I give him a blank stare.

"Aysel," Mr. Scott prompts. He pronounces my name in the accent he probably cultivated about a billion years ago when he took high school Spanish. The problem is my name isn't a Latina one. It's Turkish. You'd think Mr. Scott would've connected the dots by now.

"Uh," I mumble.

"'Uh'? Miss Seran, 'uh' is not a numerical answer." Mr. Scott leans back against the whiteboard.

This makes the class laugh. Mr. Scott clears his throat, but it's no use. He's already lost control. I can hear their whispered insults, but it all sounds like a mumble of hisses to me. And no matter what it is that they're saying, it can't be worse than what I imagine at night when I lie in bed wondering if it's physically possible to claw away your own genetics.

The bell rings. Mr. Scott fumbles to assign us homework. Most everyone in the class leaves before they can write down the assignment. I stay seated and carefully jot it in my notebook. Mr. Scott gives me a sad smile and I wonder if he's going to miss me when I'm gone.

Once the classroom is empty, I get up and leave. I walk down the hallway, my eyes glued to the dirty tiled floor. I force myself to pick up speed. The only thing worse than going to gym is being late for gym—I'm not really in the mood to run extra laps. Coach Summers is always talking about how running will strengthen our hearts so we can live longer. No extra laps for me, please.

This is my least favorite part of the day. And it's not because I'm anticipating the horrors of sit-ups and dodge ball. No, I hate this part of the day because I have to pass by the memorial—the monolithic testament to my father's crime.

I always try not to look, telling myself to keep my head down and turn the corner. But I can't help it, I glance up and take it in. I feel my breath catch in my throat. There it is, the gleaming silver plaque, dedicated in memory of Timothy Jackson, former state champion in the 400-meter dash. The plaque is the size of a large serving dish, and it hangs on the wall right outside the gym, reminding everyone that Timothy Jackson was going to be the first person from Langston to make the Olympics, but he died tragically at the age of eighteen.

What the plaque doesn't say, but might as well, is that my father is the reason Timothy Jackson is dead. Yup, my dad is the stellar individual who slashed the Olympic dreams of the whole town. Every year on Timothy's birthday, the news runs a special just to make sure no one forgets about him. It's been three years since Timothy died, and believe me, no one is close to forgetting about it. Especially now, since Brian Jackson is about to qualify for the 400-meter dash. Yes, the exact same event. Brian's trying to fulfill the dream his older brother was never able to attain—the local media can't get enough of the story, my school's hallways can't get enough of the story.

I force my feet to move past the plaque and I walk into the gym, curling my hands into fists at my sides. As the sun glints off the polished wooden court, I wonder what my classmates are going to do with all their hate and anger and fear once they don't have me here anymore.

I can't wait until they don't have me here anymore.

WEDNESDAY, MARCH 13

25 days left

When I get home from school, I see Mom seated at the kitchen table. Our kitchen is narrow and tiny, and if I were to spread my arms out, I could touch each mint-colored side wall with the palms of my hands. Mom's thumbing through bills, her neck craned in concentration, but when she hears the door, she turns to look at me. And there it is. The same facial expression she's greeted me with for the past three years. It's a cross between a wince and a frown.

Until three years ago, I used to spend the weeks with my dad and the weekends with my mom. But then after my dad got locked away, Mom had no choice but to let me live with her and Steve.

Before my father's crime, my mother used to look at me with a combination of love and longing, like I was a mirror into her past life, a bittersweet memory. Her dark almond eyes would glaze over, she'd tilt her head forward and her straight light brown hair would fall over her thin shoulders, and she'd squeeze my hands tightly, like if she gripped me hard enough, I'd transport her back in time. It was almost like I was her permanent bruise. Not a painful bruise, but a tender one made of melancholy memories.

I didn't mind that. I secretly relished being the vehicle to her past life, her connection to Turkey and my father and her youth.

That all changed three years ago. Everything did. Now I live with her, Steve, Georgia, and Mike. She'd never say it, but I am an intruder in their happy home. An infestation. I've gone from being a bruise to an open festering wound. Evolution isn't always a positive thing.

"You're home early," she finally says. Every day, her accent becomes less and less Turkish and more and more southern. Actually, "southern" would be the wrong word for it. People in Kentucky don't have southern accents. They have bluegrass accents. Their accents are distinctly less charming than southern accents. Think less *Gone with the Wind*, more Colonel Sanders. I've worked hard not to develop one. But now I wonder—if I'm never going to turn seventeen—what was even the point of mastering how to speak normally.

"I don't have to work today." I don't mention that I was told not to come in because I would make the customers "uncomfortable." Mr. Palmer is nothing if not the king of euphemisms. He and my mother would probably get along splendidly, considering my mother refers to what happened with my father as "that unfortunate incident." Or used to refer to it that way. Recently, she's been pretending like it never happened. As if simply not talking about something makes it disappear. Newsflash: It doesn't.

Georgia marches into the kitchen. She drops her pom-poms on the scratched wooden table. Her honey-colored hair is slicked back in a high ponytail. "You're going to be at the game tonight, right?"

She's asking Mom, not me. I'm invisible.

Georgia is my half sister. We have the same mom, but you'd never know it from looking at us.

"I'm going to try my best to make it," Mom says. Translation: Hell will freeze over before Mom isn't at the game. Georgia's only a freshman, but she's on the varsity cheer squad. Apparently, that's a big deal. Though it seems to me that unlike other sports where JV and varsity are determined by skill level, in cheerleading, JV and varsity are determined by cup size.

"It's the play-offs," Georgia reminds her. Her tone is

calm, the tone of someone who is used to being in control, used to getting what she wants. Georgia's good at that. She's always been a schemer. When everything went down with my dad, some of the heat fell on her too, but she somehow managed to use it to her advantage.

I remember one day, a few months after my dad was officially convicted and locked away, I saw Georgia talking with a boy in the hallway. I hid around the corner so I could spy on them. I was ready to intervene if she needed my help, but the thing about Georgia is she's never needed my help.

"Yeah," Georgia answered the boy's question, which I'd been too late to overhear. She nervously fingered the shell necklace I'd given her for her birthday two years ago. "Aysel's my sister, but he's not my dad."

"But did you ever meet him?" the boy asked Georgia, his voice eager. I stared at the back of his head, tufts of light corn-colored hair, and guessed it was probably Todd Robertson, a boy from my grade who everyone thought resembled the leading actor in that summer's popular vampire romance movie. Georgia was in sixth grade at this time, but from the way her eyes glossed over as she stared up at Todd, I guessed she knew exactly who he was.

I watched Georgia wrinkle her nose as she considered his question. "Yeah, a couple of times."

"You did?" Todd pressed, clearly hopeful that Georgia had some kind of inside scoop.

"Oh yeah," she said. "He was basically family." Todd leaned closer to her.

"I can tell you some crazy stories if you want," she added, in a flirtatious promise.

I remember being furious that she was willing to trade our family "secrets" for popularity, but I've finally learned to let it go. Georgia is Georgia, I know what to expect. Anyway, you can't really blame someone for surviving.

The same can be said for my former friends, not that I ever had that many. Most of the ones I did have scattered as fast as they could once the news of my dad's crime traveled through the halls of school, but some of them actually tried to stick by me. Especially Anna Stevens, my former best friend. When everything happened, Anna tried her best to comfort me, but I pushed her away. I knew it would be the best thing for her to disassociate herself from me, even if she didn't. I like to think I did her a favor in the end.

Georgia sashays around the kitchen table and takes a seat. "I think we have a really good chance of winning tonight. Could be historic. You have to come, Mom!"

There's a long pause in the conversation. Mom takes a deep breath and then says, "Why don't you come with me?"

I look behind me, certain that Mike, my younger half brother, must have walked in, but it's unlike Mike not to make his presence known. He's always bouncing his basketball inside, even though Mom has repeatedly told him to stop. I don't mind it, though.

"Are you talking to me?" I ask with perfect seriousness.

Georgia doesn't say anything, but I can see her face twist up like she just chugged rotten milk. She'd never insult me in front of Mom, but she's doing everything she can to signal that she doesn't want me to come. What can I say? I have a gold-star rating in the embarrassment department.

"Yes, I'm talking to you," Mom says, and I detect a slight quiver. Sometimes I'm convinced even my own mother is afraid of me.

"Thanks for the invite, but I have a lot of homework." I walk over to the cupboard and grab a chocolate-chip granola bar. It's weird, I know. But sometimes, I'm ravenous. It's almost as if I want to eat as much as I can to fill up the empty void inside of me. Other days, I can barely bring myself to nibble on a piece of toast.

But even if today I can muster an appetite, I'm mostly taking the granola bar for show. I don't want to give my mom more reasons to worry about me. I know she's not-so-sneakily studying me for signs, searching for any clues to my questionable mental state. I'm doing my best to hide it all from her. Once I'm gone, I don't want her to feel guilty thinking there was something she could have done.

"Good luck tonight." I give Georgia a fake wave and then head up the stairs to my room. Well, our room. But since she'll be at the game, it's my room for tonight. Once I get to our room, I crawl into my bed. I pull the charcoal-gray comforter over my head and pretend like I'm in the middle of the ocean, waves crashing over me, my lungs filling up with water, the whole world turning black. I try to imagine my potential energy turning into kinetic energy turning into nothing. As I hum Mozart's requiem, I wonder what it will feel like when all the lights go off and everything is quiet forever. I don't know if it will be painful, if in those last moments I'll be scared, but all I can hope is that it will be over fast. That it will be peaceful. That it will be permanent.

April 7, I think to myself. Soon enough.

Sometimes I'm convinced it's a sign of my own insanity that I still feel comforted by classical music when it was my father who first introduced me to it. He loved it. Bach, Mozart, you name it. The clunky cassette tapes were among the few things he brought with him when he came to America. When I was younger, he used to pop a tape into his old boom box that he kept on the counter at his convenience store and would tell me a story of his childhood, playing chess with his father on a smooth board made of alabaster stone or measuring people's feet at the shoe store his uncle ran. While he talked, I would dance around the store, moving clumsily as the notes rose and fell with the tempo.

Then one day he forced me to sit. "Really listen, Aysel," he urged, his dark eyes wide and focused. "All the answers are in this music. Do you hear them?"

So I'd listened and listened. Straining my ears in an attempt to memorize every note. I never really heard the answers, but I nodded like I did. I didn't want my dad to get mad and turn the music off, or lock himself in his bedroom for hours like he sometimes did. With my dad, you always had to tread lightly, like you were walking on icy pavement—it was so fun when you were gliding, but it was very easy to slip.

I squeeze my eyes shut and force that memory out of my mind. I roll around in bed, humming Mozart's requiem over and over again, and I'm able to find only one answer in the notes: April 7.

The walls of our old frame house are thin, and I can hear Mom and Georgia rattling around in the kitchen. I imagine them hugging. Georgia wrapping her arms around Mom's thin waist and Mom running her fingers through Georgia's shiny ponytail. The two of them fitting, interlocking, like mothers and daughters are supposed to. Fitting in a way that I never have. My edges have always been too sharp, my grooves too deep.

That's what they should write on my tombstone: Aysel Leyla Seran, the Girl Who Never Fit.

And since I've never fit, not really before my dad lost it, and certainly not after, Mom's life will be so much better without me. When I'm gone, she won't have to be reminded of my dad every time she sees my angular nose or curly black hair. Or my round cheeks and dimples. I know it's my dimples that get to her the most. Luckily, they're only really noticeable when I smile, and it's not like I've been doing a lot of that lately.

Without me, my mom won't have to stay up at night, worrying that the criminal gene, the murderer gene, was passed to me and that any day now, I'm going to blow up the school or something awful like that. I know she can't live through it all again—the police, the media, the gossip. I know she doesn't want to think about it, but deep down, I can see her struggling with her fear and her doubt. Her sideways glances and cautious probing questions are all her way of determining just how much of a mental case I am.

I want to say that I know for sure that I'm different from my dad. That my heart beats in a different rhythm, my blood pulses at a different speed. But I'm not sure. Maybe the sadness comes just before the insanity. Maybe he and I share the same potential energy.

All I know is that I'm not going to stick around and find out if I become a monster like my dad. I can't do that to my mom.

I can't do that to the world.

WEDNESDAY, MARCH 13

25 days left

The only good thing about Georgia cheering at the basketball game is that I have the house to myself, which means I can use the computer. Normally, I can't ever use the computer. Or at least I can't use it without unwanted supervision. Our household has only one computer and it's from the Ice Age. It runs slower than a three-legged dog and its keyboard is sticky from all of the fruit punch Mike has spilled on it.

Though Mom thinks Steve is the man of her dreams— wealthy, successful, honest businessman—the truth is Steve works on the line down at the Sparkle toothpaste factory.

Sparkle, manufacturer of second-rate toothpaste and mouth-wash, basically keeps Langston's economy running. Sure, Steve's gig on the line is an honest living and he has so far managed to keep himself out of prison, which is more than you can say for my dad. But it doesn't mean that Steve can afford to buy all of us our own laptops, so we're stuck with this clunker.

But tonight, the clunker is all mine.

I log on to Smooth Passages. It takes about ten minutes to even load the home page; Steve doesn't believe in paying for high-speed internet access, either. Once I'm finally logged in, I see I have a message from FrozenRobot:

> If you're really serious about this, we should arrange a time and place to meet. But you have to be serious. I don't want a flake.
>
> —Roman

I can't believe someone with the screen name Frozen-Robot is accusing me of being a flake. Looks like his real name is Roman. I'm not sure how much better that is than FrozenRobot. I resist the urge to make a *Julius Caesar* joke.

I type back to him, sans Shakespearean jeers: *I'm as serious as a heart attack. No, but seriously, I'm not a flake. Like I said, I'm from Langston. Where should we meet?*

I hang around the website a little longer. According to the

boards, Suicide Partners ElmoRains and TBaker14155 took the plunge. I don't know how SovietSummer231 obtained this information, but hopefully FrozenRobot and I will have the same kind of success. I shiver and swallow the hard lump in my throat. God, this whole thing is so twisted. I stare at the living room ceiling. I wonder if I would have the guts to string myself up. If I could muster the courage, I wouldn't need to deal with this Smooth Passages business.

The clunker makes a sound similar to a doorbell. My shoulders jerk forward and I see FrozenRobot responded to me. Looks like he's not out at any play-off games either. I open the message:

> How about tomorrow night at 5:30? We can meet at the root beer stand off Route 36. Do you know where that is? It should be pretty close to you. I'll wear a red hat so you know who I am.
> —Roman

I'm a little weirded out that FrozenRobot aka Roman wants to meet in such a public place. I guess that means he's not a serial killer or rapist or anything. Then again, I'm not sure it'd be so bad if he was a serial killer. At least I'd get it over with quickly. Unless he's one of the types who's into torture. That'd be no good. I don't want a long death; I want an instant one. I'm a coward like that.

I tell him that 5:30 tomorrow at the root beer stand is fine. I get off work at 5:00 tomorrow, so I'll just lie to Mom and tell her I'm working late. It'll be easy. I don't really like FrozenRobot's choice of venue, but I don't want to start the whole thing off by being difficult. The root beer stand is popular with kids like my sister. It gets really crowded after football and basketball games. Cheerleaders share ice-cream floats and basketball players scarf down chili cheese fries. Vomit.

It goes without saying it's not my scene. Not that anywhere is my scene.

I log off the computer and head back upstairs. I pull my physics book out of my backpack. It's strange, but the closer I get to death, the more I want to learn. I guess I don't want to die a complete dumbass. I open my notebook and scribble down the problems at the end of the chapter that Mr. Scott assigned.

We're starting our unit on the conservation of energy. According to Mr. Scott, energy cannot be created or destroyed—it can only be transferred. Potential energy can turn into kinetic energy and then back into potential energy, but the energy can't ever just go away. This doesn't make a lot of sense to me. I read over the first practice problem again: "A sky diver has a mass of 65 kg and is standing in a plane that is 600 meters off the ground. What is the diver's potential energy before jumping from the plane?"

My pencil shakes in my hand and I fight the urge to chew on the eraser. The thing is, it's not the sample problem that's bugging me. I know what formula I should use, and my handy calculator can do the math for me.

But the issue is I can't figure out what happens to all that energy when we're gone if it can't be destroyed. My stomach churns at the thought.

I write down my own practice problem: *Aysel Seran, 16 years old, is hanging from the ceiling at a height of 7.5 feet. She weighs 115 pounds. How much potential energy does she have? What happens to all that energy when she dies? What does it get turned into?*

Does a dead body still have potential energy or does it get transferred into something else? Can potential energy just evaporate into nothingness?

That's the question I don't know the answer to. That's the question that haunts me.

THURSDAY, MARCH 14

24 days left

I don't have my own car, but I do have a car that I'm allowed
to use to get to and from work. The old Ford Taurus smells
like stale fast food and has torn seats, but the engine is still
chugging so it's good enough for me. Steve bought it a few
years ago from a buddy of his. It's going to be Georgia's car
when she turns sixteen. The good news is I won't be around
to have to share it with her.

Pulling out of TMC's parking lot, I take a left and head
toward Route 36. The road is bumpy, full of potholes. No one
here wants to pay taxes to repair it. It's kind of sad because
it could be a really scenic road since it borders the river. Not

that the Ohio River is anything to brag about. It's muddy and polluted and tainted with an awful history, but no matter how gross looking a river is, there's always something magical about it because it moves. Rivers are never stuck.

When everything with my dad first happened, I used to imagine floating down the Ohio. I fantasized that I'd build a raft and drift aimlessly downstream to where the Ohio meets the Mississippi, and there I figured some nice family would take me in. I used to picture them as a childless couple that would be so happy to have a young girl. They wouldn't know who my father was or what he did. They would love me; they would make the bad feelings go away.

I never built that raft. And now I know that no one is going to make the bad feelings go away.

As I continue down Route 36, I think about how this road connects Langston to Willis. Connects me to Frozen-Robot, whoever he is. It's impossible to tell when Langston turns into Willis—the only thing separating them is this stretch of worn road, framed by the muddy river on one side and crabgrass on the other. Both Langston and Willis are podunk little towns, filled with old rickety houses, rotting wooden benches, and rusted Civil War monuments. They both have a gas station, and it was a big deal last year when Langston got a Wal-Mart. And they both advertise themselves as charming, trying to lure travelers to stop and have a soda at the old diner on Main Street or take their picture next to the large bronze fountain that sits in front of the courthouse. But no one ever comes to Langston or Willis intentionally. They're places you cross through, not places you visit.

As the root beer stand comes into view, I notice it looks fairly crowded. Langston High didn't have a game tonight, but maybe Willis did. I park my car in the gravel lot and sit in the front seat for a few minutes. I take a couple of deep breaths and pull at the collar of my striped shirt. My heart pounds against my rib cage—a sensation that I would have thought is more typical of first-date jitters. Not that I've actually ever been on a real date, unless you count a fifth-grade rendezvous at the mall where my supposed date ate too many Cheetos and rubbed the orange dust all over my brand-new shirt.

But I shouldn't be nervous. This kid is obviously a loser, just like me. We both need each other. I sneak a quick glance at myself in the mirror and then feel like an idiot for even caring what I look like. It's not like I'm auditioning to be FrozenRobot's girlfriend.

A tap on my window startles me. I jump forward in my seat, my chest pressing against the steering wheel. I see a boy about my age staring at me. He's wearing a red cap. He leans over and taps the window again.

I roll it down.

"ALS0109?"

That's my screen name from Smooth Passages. I should say something, but my mouth feels like it's full of cotton. I blankly stare at him.

He clears his throat and casts his eyes downward. "Oh, sorry. I guess I have the wrong person."

"No," I manage to squeak out. "I'm Aysel."

He scrunches his eyebrows together, making a wrinkled star in the middle of his forehead. He takes off the red cap and holds it at his side.

"ALS0109," I explain.

His lips pull into a half-moon of a smile. I don't think I've smiled in three years. FrozenRobot should rethink his life choices. Maybe he's not as depressed as he thinks he is.

"You aren't flaking out already, are you?" he asks, peering into my car. I wonder if he notices all the discarded fast-food bags on the floor.

What would give you that impression? I think, and grip the steering wheel. I'm half tempted to press the accelerator and leave. I wasn't ready for this. This kid is not what I expected at all. Not. At. All. He's not a scrawny, pimple-faced boy who looks like he's never seen the sun in his life. No. FrozenRobot doesn't look so frozen. He's tall, basketball player tall, with buzzed chestnut-colored hair and deep-set hazel eyes. Thin, but not in the awkward, wimpy way. I guess he's what you'd call lanky. Goofy lanky even, maybe. But still. He's definitely not what I'd imagined.

"Hey," he says. "I told you I didn't want a flake." He shakes his head. "I knew this shit would happen. Especially when I found out you were a girl."

I pull the key out of the ignition and open the door, almost hitting him with it. Oops. "What the hell is that supposed to mean?"

"Well, you have to know the statistics. Like guys actually do it and girls just talk about it."

I glare at him. "That's some sexist bullshit. And if you're such a hard-ass, why'd you even create an account on Smooth Passages? Why do you even want a partner?"

He recoils. "Whoa, I wasn't . . ." He trails off and scrunches his facial features together like he's thinking about what I just said. "I'm not a sexist." He looks down at his white sneakers. "And I'm definitely not a hard-ass."

"You sure sounded like one."

"A hard-ass?" He looks up at me and grins. His hazel eyes are brighter than they should be. This is all wrong.

"No, a sexist." I don't return his smile.

"Look," he says slowly; his voice is low and soft. "I'm fine with you being a girl. Really. I'm cool with girls."

"You're cool with girls?" I repeat in the most deadpan way possible.

"You know what I mean."

"I don't think I do."

He frowns and turns his cap over in his hand. "I'm really

sorry. Can we start over?"

"No," I say quickly. "We can't start over."

His frown grows and he shuffles his feet. His posture was always slightly hunched, but now he starts to sink even deeper into himself.

I watch him squirm for a second longer and then say, "But I'm willing to hear you out if you have a good explanation for why you need a partner."

He sighs and puts his cap back on. He grips the bill and folds each side down, casting a shadow over his face. "Yeah, I'll explain everything. I just thought maybe we could get a table and we could talk about it while we eat." He pauses and stares at me a little too long for my liking. "Unless you've already decided I'm a total ass and are ready to bail."

I consider this for a moment and then shake my head. "I'm not ready to bail, at least not yet. And besides, I'm not going to leave before I get some cheese fries." I walk away from him toward the root beer stand. He jogs to catch up with me. We trudge along in silence toward the counter where you order.

The root beer stand, which I think is officially named Tony's, but everyone around here just calls it the root beer stand, is run out of a trailer. You order at the counter and the food is prepared inside and then they bring it out to wherever you choose to sit. There's a carnival-style tent that has several picnic tables under it, but on really busy nights, it's almost impossible to find a seat.

I order first. I get cheese fries and a strawberry milk-shake. I take my plastic number 7 and find a seat at a picnic table in the back. I watch FrozenRobot order. He seems to know some of the other people here. He's nodding at them and saying hi. Weird. If FrozenRobot has so many friends, why does he want to off himself?

I should probably start referring to him as Roman, but that feels too personal. It's easier for me to think of him in terms of his screen name. Besides, he doesn't look like some-one who would want to kill himself—he's obviously still concerned with his appearance. His hair looks like it's been recently cut, and yeah, he's dressed casually, a hoodie and track pants, but they're the hip kind of athletic wear. Basi-cally, Roman seems like someone who would date Georgia or wave from a float at the Homecoming Parade. Not some-one who fantasizes about throwing himself in front of an eighteen-wheeler.

A queasy feeling builds in the back of my mouth and I wonder if this is all a sick joke orchestrated by my sister. I shake that thought out of my mind. Georgia isn't interested enough in what I do to waste energy organizing something like this. At least I don't think so.

FrozenRobot starts to walk toward me, but two other guys stop him. Both of them are on the taller side, but not as tall as him. They're patting him on the back and he's nodding, like he agrees with what they're saying.

I watch him and wonder if I would want to kill myself if I were like him. Someone with friends, someone whose existence made people happy. But deep down, I know that none of this, at least for me, is about any of that.

I used to play this game where I would bargain with myself: *Maybe if the whispers about Dad stop, maybe if Mom starts to look at you again like a normal daughter, maybe if you can guarantee you won't turn out like Dad.* But it's that last one that kills the whole deal.

There's no way to guarantee it, especially when I know for sure that there is something wrong with me. Something broken. What people never understand is that depression isn't about the outside; it's about the inside. Something inside me is wrong. Sure, there are things in my life that make me feel alone, but nothing makes me feel more isolated and terrified than my own voice in my head. The voice that reminds me that there's a high likelihood I'll end up just like my father.

I bet if you cut open my stomach, the black slug of depression would slide out. Guidance counselors always love to say, "Just think positively," but that's impossible when you have this thing inside of you, strangling every ounce of happiness you can muster. My body is an efficient happy-thought-killing machine.

On my worst days, I let myself wonder if my dad had the same black slug inside of him. If that's why he did the horrible things he did. Maybe there's a fine line between suicide and homicide. It's those kinds of thoughts that horrify me. It's those kinds of thoughts that make me think that I can't even wait until April 7. I need to get rid of the slug; I need to get rid of me.

"Hey," FrozenRobot says, putting his plastic number 8 next to my plastic number 7. Eighty-seven. I wish there was some significance to that. Recently, I've tried to find significance in everything. Like I'm waiting for the universe to give me the nod, saying, *Yes, you are free to exit now. Be on your way.*

He adjusts the numbers so they stand up straight. Maybe he's searching for meaning in them, too. Or maybe he's just OCD.

"You're popular here," I say.

He cringes. "I used to be."

"Looks like you still are."

The waitress brings out my fries and milkshake. She smiles at FrozenRobot and I swear she even bats her eyelashes a little.

Once she's walked away, I notice he's blushing. "See? Popular."

"Not me." He hands me the ketchup. "Someone I used to be."

I dump some of the cheese fries out on a napkin and shove one into my mouth. It's probably impolite to eat before he gets his food, but I don't think FrozenRobot is choosing his Suicide Partner based on manners.

Soon enough, the waitress comes back with his food. He ordered a cheeseburger, fries, a chocolate milkshake, and a side of jalapeños. Before the waitress walks away, she gives him another flirtatious smile and his cheeks flush red again.

I take a sip of my milkshake and make a face. The strawberry is more sour than I would've guessed, but the milkshake feels nice and cool in the back of my throat.

"Don't," he says, giving me a look after the waitress is gone.

"I wasn't going to say anything."

"I'm not what you expected. Am I?" He pops a fry into his mouth. It's a forced gesture, though. Too quick. He doesn't really want to eat. I know that drill.

I don't answer his question. Instead I ask one of my own. "Am I what you expected?"

He stares at me for a few seconds. "Honestly, no. But that's a good thing."

"I must have been at least a little like what you expected since you stalked me out in the parking lot."

He makes a pained expression, scrunching all his features together. He reaches out and grabs a couple of jalapeño peppers, tossing them straight into his mouth.

"What?" I raise my eyebrows.

He continues to crunch on the jalapeños. The peppers look like they came from a jar and their juice is dribbling all over his fingers. He winces slightly when some of the juice crawls into a scratch he has on his left hand.

"C'mon. Tell me," I prompt. "How did you know it was me?"

He looks up from the peppers and says, "I don't want to offend you."

"Seriously?" I say in a harsher tone than I intended. I take a loud slurp of my milkshake in an attempt to lighten the mood. I don't want him to think I'm mean. At least not yet. If he thinks I'm too mean, he might pick some other depressed freak over me.

He pulls the seeds out from one of the peppers and places them on his tongue. He swallows them, and as they slide down his throat, he doesn't make an expression, even though I know his mouth must be on fire. Finally, he says, "You just look like you want to die. You look really fucking miserable."

He stares at me and I stare back at him, a blank expression plastered on my face. The poor guy squirms on the picnic table bench and then looks down at his white sneakers. His head dips toward the ground, his chin pressing against his chest, and I can see that the back of his neck is freckled and has turned red.

It takes me a second to process what he said and then I burst out laughing. Laughing makes my throat feel sore. I take another gulp of my milkshake.

He raises an eyebrow at me. "I'm awful, right?"

I shake my head. "You're honest. I like that. And now you know I'm not a flake."

He shrugs and fiddles with the zipper on his sweatshirt. "I don't know that. All I'm saying is you definitely look like someone who wants to die, but I'm not entirely convinced you're going to be able to pull the trigger."

I frown. "Well, that's why I signed up for this. I want some . . . encouragement." I stare at his hoodie. It says UNIVERSITY OF KENTUCKY BASKETBALL across it in big, black block letters. "Teamwork. Moral support. Those are sports terms, right?"

His eyes drop to his sweatshirt. "I don't play anymore."

"I didn't ask you that."

"Yeah, I know," he says. "But I guess I get what you mean. You think it's going to be easier this way than on your own."

I rest my body weight on my elbows and lean toward him and channel our waitress's confidence. "So are you the man for the job? Are we going to do this thing together or what?" It's not like me to be so aggressive, but for some reason I feel the need to push FrozenRobot to choose me. I need to be assertive. I can't remember the last time I was assertive.

He shifts on the bench and picks at his cheeseburger. He tosses his tomatoes aside. I still haven't seen him take a real bite of it. "I'm not sure yet."

"What do you need to know?"

"More about you, for starters."

"Like?" I say.

"What kind of name is Aysel?" He pronounces it correctly. I try not to look impressed.

"Turkish."

"Are your parents Turkish?" he asks.

I nod. I don't tell him anything else about my parents. I also avoid giving him my last name. My mom is in the process of trying to legally change my last name to match her new one: Underwood. But that change hasn't gone through yet, and the last thing I want is for FrozenRobot to Google me and find out about my dad. No matter how screwed up FrozenRobot is, I doubt he'd want to tie his suicide dream to mine if he knew the truth about my family history.

"Do you speak Turkish?"

I shake my head. My dad never taught me to speak the language. Sometimes I'd gather the courage to ask about Turkey, and if he was in a good mood, he'd tell me about the narrow streets of his old neighborhood where he would play soccer with his friends in the evenings. But when he was having a bad day (and his bad days were more and more frequent toward the end), he'd snap and tell me to stop asking questions. He'd say that I was lucky to have been born in America because I would never have to move halfway across the world just to find a job.

And my mom, well, she's tried everything she can to erase her roots. My parents separated when I was less than a year old, and ever since she hooked up with Steve, she's tried to pretend like she's a homegrown white American gal. She's lighter than me, so if it weren't for her slight accent, she'd be able to pass no problem. I look decidedly more foreign than my mom because I inherited Dad's darker coloring.

"Is this making you uncomfortable?" FrozenRobot asks while he chews his burger. He doesn't seem to enjoy the burger as much as the jalapeños. It's like he's forcing himself to chew it and he does it slowly, nibbling at it, bit by bit.

"No," I say. "I just don't get why you're so hung up on my ethnicity. I'm not interrogating you."

He gives me a smile. I don't get this kid. "I'm just curious because I think Aysel is a cool name."

"You can have it, if you want."

"Funny," he says, but he doesn't laugh.

"Why April seventh?" It's my turn to ask a question.

"That's when it happened."

"When what happened?"

"The reason I want to die. It happened a year ago, on April seventh." He clenches his jaw and looks away from me.

"And I'm guessing you aren't going to tell me what happened?"

Before he can answer, the two guys from earlier come over and sit down next to him. "How's it going?" one of them says to me while the other slaps his back.

"I didn't know you were seeing someone, Roman," the

backslapper teases. "What does Kelly think?"

Kelly? Don't tell me FrozenRobot has a girlfriend. I give him my best what-the-hell look.

"Guys, this is Aysel." He returns my look with a pleading one. I'm not exactly the Nicest Person in the History of the Universe, but it's not like I'm going to blow up FrozenRobot's spot. Still, it's fun to watch him sweat. I keep my face frozen in a neutral expression. I'm outfrozening FrozenRobot.

"And Aysel, this is Travis and Lance." There's a slight tremble in Roman's voice, and I notice he has a small patch of freckles around his nose that have turned progressively redder since his friends came over.

"You go to Willis?" Lance asks. He wiggles his sandy-blond eyebrows at me.

"We would have noticed her if she went to Willis," Travis says in a slimy voice.

The tone of his voice is enough to make me lose interest in my milkshake. It goes without saying that if I did go to Willis, Travis definitely wouldn't be interested in me. The boys who go to my school who are like Travis and Lance definitely don't notice me. At least not in a good way.

"Don't scare the girl," says Lance. Lance apparently has a softer touch with the ladies. He looks more like a heart-throb than Travis, with his boy band shaggy haircut, big blue eyes, and broad shoulders.

There's a few seconds of awkward silence.

"She goes to Langston," Roman reluctantly offers.

"Wait, so if you go to Langston, you must know Brian Jackson, right?" Lance asks, widening his blue eyes. I hold my breath as I stare at him, trying to determine whether he's already connected the dots.

"Oh, so is that how y'all know each other? From Brian?" Travis says as he leans toward Roman, stealing some of his fries.

Roman and I exchange glances. "Uh, no," he says. "We met last week."

We did? "Where?" Travis asks. He sneaks another glance at me. I can tell he knows something's off. I swallow and send a little wish to the universe: *Please don't screw me on this. Please don't let them figure out who I am.*

"Down by the old playground. At the court," Roman says, and I make note of the fact that this kid can lie like a pro. His words are smooth and strong.

Travis erupts, tossing his arms up in the air. "I knew it, man! You still want to play. I told you Coach would definitely put you back on the team. You have to stop beating—"

"Can we not talk about that here?" Roman says, his voice suddenly chilly.

"Seriously, man," Lance says as he also grabs some of Roman's fries. "Why would you bring that up?"

Travis's face reddens. I didn't know boys like him ever felt uncomfortable, but I guess some things can even make types like him squirm. I'm learning so much about the male gender today. "Sorry," Travis mumbles, and he looks away from the table. A smile returns to his face as he checks out our waitress. "Suzie looks good, though, right?"

"She seems like she's doing well," Roman says in a matter-of-fact tone. He turns to me. "Suzie's our waitress. She goes to our high school."

I nod like I understand what's going on, but I'm pretty sure I'm missing all the subtext.

Travis elbows Roman. "But, for real. I think she's still into you."

Lance looks at me and then at Roman and then back to Travis. "Have some respect, man."

I'm about to tell him that Roman and I are not what he thinks. The idea of it almost makes me laugh again, and I swallow down some more of my milkshake. I slosh the strawberry around in my mouth, running my tongue over my teeth. I don't care how unattractive it looks.

Lance comes to the rescue again, breaking the awkward silence. "So wait, do you know Brian Jackson?"

I try not to visibly sweat. I pick at my fries, keeping my eyes focused on the ketchup. I can't look at any of them right now. "Not really."

"Isn't he like famous though now?" Travis says. He reaches out and slaps Roman on the back again. "That could've been you, man."

Roman grumbles something and I can't help myself from asking, "What do you mean?"

Lance's eyes awkwardly dart from Roman to me and then back again. "Can I tell her?"

Roman clamps his hand on the back of his neck and turns his face so he can stare off in the distance. "Do whatever you want."

Another uncomfortable silence.

"Roman used to play select basketball with Brian. Do you know what select basketball is?" Lance says.

I have a general idea, but I shake my head so I can get more details about FrozenRobot's connection to Brian Jackson. My head feels like a car alarm just went off inside it—all beeps and sirens. I try to steady my mind by mentally conjuring the beginning of Wagner's "Ride of the Valkyries."

"Are you humming?" Travis says before Lance can continue to explain exactly how Brian and Roman know each other. He starts to laugh, but Roman shoves him.

"Don't be a jerk," he says, glaring at Travis. His hazel eyes flash with anger, making them look more golden than green.

Blood rushes to my cheeks and I look down at the picnic table. There's a puddle of ketchup next to my fries. I wonder if FrozenRobot would be so defensive of me if he knew about my dad, and then I wonder why FrozenRobot is defending me at all. I can feel them all staring at me, but FrozenRobot's eyes feel different from Travis's or Lance's. Their eyes burn my skin in the same way as my classmates' eyes—they are greedy to uncover my secrets, to see inside. FrozenRobot's eyes are soft and patient. He knows what he'll find if he digs deeper. There's no rush to unpack my insides. He understands there is nothing special about emptiness, nothing interesting about depression.

I gather the courage to look up at him. He gives me a slight smile and I'm pretty sure I've found my Suicide Partner.

His friends are silent, watching him. Even though he claims he used to be popular in a past life, it seems like he's pretty damn popular in this one. He drums his hands against the top of the table. "Brian and I used to be friends when we were little. We played basketball together, on a team you had to try out for. A travel team—we'd play games in Louisville and Cincinnati and Lexington. Then, as we got older, Brian and I would work out together. Run and lift. Nothing exciting." Roman scratches the back of his neck again, his eyes turning cloudy and hard to read. "Now, he's a big shot. Olympic bound or whatever. We don't talk much." He stares straight at me. "Not that interesting, is it?"

Lance seems convinced that something is going on between Roman and me and tries to help his friend out by adding, "The point is, our boy here is mad athletic."

"Yeah, if Roman had stuck it out, he'd probably be attending UK next year on a fat scholarship for basketball,"

Travis adds. He puts his arm around Roman, like a proud brother or something, but Roman shrugs him off.

"Knock it off," Roman says, shaking his head and staring at the ground. "Aysel doesn't care about that stuff."

Translation: There's no need to impress this girl. I'm not trying to sleep with her, I'm trying to die with her. Neither Travis nor Lance seems to pick up on that undertone, though. Instead, both of them raise their hands in the air and start saying, "My bad, my bad." As I watch them, I know I should be thinking that they're such lemmings, going through the exact same motions at the exact same time, but instead, all I can think is how I've never been that in sync with someone else. I wonder if FrozenRobot used to be in sync with them but somehow fell out of orbit.

I wonder what happened to make him fall out of orbit. What happened that turned him from Roman, star athlete and friend of Olympic hopefuls, into FrozenRobot, tragic boy haunting suicide websites.

I stare at him out of the corner of my eye. His head is bent down, his shoulders hunched. He's studying the one jalapeño seed he has left, moving it around the paper plate with his finger. Slowly, he raises it to his lips and swallows it.

We're all watching him and finally he mumbles, "Well, it was good to see you guys, but I think Aysel's going to give me a ride home now. See you around later, okay?"

"Okay, dude." Travis squeezes Roman's shoulders. "Take

care of yourself. We're here for you."

"Let's hang out sometime soon," Lance adds. "I'd love to shoot hoops with you down at the old playground. It'd be like old times."

"Right," Roman says, his voice cold. "Just like old times." He gets up from the table and tosses the remainder of his food in the garbage can.

I give Travis and Lance a weak wave and follow Roman. I dump my fries, they're almost finished anyway, but I keep my milkshake. "So I'm giving you a ride home?" I whisper, hoping Lance and Travis don't hear me.

"Yeah. I don't drive."

"Aren't you seventeen?"

He gives me that same half-moon smile he flashed me when we first met. "You stalked my profile."

"I wanted to make sure you weren't a soccer mom or something," I say, and head toward my car. I don't add that I wish his profile had advertised his connection to Brian Jackson. I never would've agreed to meet.

Once I unlock the car, I toss the junk that's in the passenger seat to the back. I leave a few of the greasy fast-food bags on the floor in front of the seat. I figure he can just put his feet on them. Whatever. It's not like he's going to reject me because I'm messy.

He gets in and taps his hands on the dusty dashboard. "Nice ride." His sneakers crunch against the old bags.

"Looks like you maintain it, too."

I ignore his comments and put the key in the ignition. The engine makes a sputtering noise. I jiggle the wheel and we're in business. I pull out of the parking lot and then look over at him. He's staring straight out the windshield, his head tipped toward his chest. His hazel eyes are wide but empty. For the first time, I can really see it. FrozenRobot isn't playing around; FrozenRobot wants to die.

The black slug lives inside of FrozenRobot, too.

THURSDAY, MARCH 14

24 days left

For a while, we drive in silence. I'm a little nervous that FrozenRobot is going to open the car door and launch himself out onto the gravel road. I'm not sure the impact would kill him, but it'd still put me in a sticky situation.

When he reaches for the radio dial instead of the door, I take a shallow breath of relief. He chooses Georgia's favorite station—the one that plays the same top five hits on repeat. All the songs seem to be about getting trashed, wearing glittery short dresses, and dancing the night away. I make a face.

"What?" he says.

"I don't get you. You seem like such a—"

He makes a motion, crossing his arms in the air like a letter X, which I take to mean "shut up" and so I do. The one thing I'm pretty good at is following orders. Wait, I guess that's not true. I never follow Mr. Palmer's orders, though most of the time I at least try to pretend like I do.

Roman turns the radio off. "Sorry. I didn't know you were such a music snob."

"I'm a nothing snob," I say.

"Not a snob and not a soccer mom," he says. "You have a lot going for you."

"Right," I say, and then test the waters. "A lot of potential wasted on April seventh." Potential energy. I wonder if FrozenRobot ever thinks about the physics of death.

"Here's to that," he says, pretending to raise a drink in the air. "Cheers." I guess the songs on Georgia's radio station are a good fit for his interests.

We bump along the road for a little bit longer in silence. I reach for the radio dial and turn it to the classical music station. He doesn't comment on my music choice. The landscape slowly becomes hillier. We reach a sharp curve in the road and turn away from the river, heading toward the rolling hills. The grass is still brown and dry from the winter and most of the trees are still barren. Spring is running late this year. I roll down the window a little and the moist, cool air slips into the car. On certain days, you can smell bourbon in the air, the sweet rye scent coming from a distillery that's a few miles away, but today, I only smell mud and damp grass. The wind slaps against my cheeks and I resist the urge to look over at him, keeping my eyes focused on the road.

"I can't drive anymore because of something that happened last year," he finally volunteers. "That's why you're always going to have to drive. I had my mom drop me off earlier at the root beer stand. She was so thrilled that I was leaving the house for the first time in months to meet a friend." He gives me a look. "I told her you were a new friend. My mom is psyched."

So his parents are worried about him. That's kind of bad. That means heightened supervision. But I guess that's why he needs me, his trusted Suicide Partner. "Got it," I say. "Well, do you think you can at least give me directions so I know where to drop you off?"

He pauses and his bottom lip twists, like he's debating whether to talk or not.

"What?" I prompt.

"Can I ask you for a favor?"

My first task as his partner. Something inside me sways like a rocking chair in an empty room—it's both lonely and comforting. "Sure. What is it?"

"Can we stop at the fishing supply store on Main?"

I wrinkle my nose. "The fishing supply store?"

"Yeah. I need to pick up some earthworms."

I blink and sneak a quick glance at him. He's staring

straight ahead. His face muscles are relaxed, there's no sign that he's joking. "Um, okay," I say. "Just tell me how to get there."

"Stay straight on this road until it comes to the fork by the bridge. Then stay left and you'll be on Willis's main drag. The fishing supply store is on the right corner of the intersection between Main and Burns." FrozenRobot's voice is calm and steady as he delivers the directions. It seems like he's a regular at the fishing supply store. Weird.

I tighten my grip on the steering wheel and try to focus on the music. The radio station is playing Mozart's Symphony no. 40, but even the crisp, minor-key violin notes aren't able to distract me. "Why do you need earthworms? Are you big into fishing or something?"

He makes a sound that's something between a grunt and a laugh. "No."

Evidently, FrozenRobot is not a man of many words. "No?"

"No, I'm not into fishing." He squirms, moving his body so he can be closer to the passenger-side door. His knees knock against the dashboard and I consider suggesting that he could move his seat back if he's uncomfortable, but I don't.

"Okay. Then I don't get it. What am I missing?"

"Huh?"

I guess he's really going to make me spell it out. "Why do you need earthworms if you aren't into fishing?"

"For my pet turtle," he says like I should have known all along that he had a pet turtle. Like that's a reasonable assumption to make about people. Maybe Willis, Kentucky, is the pet turtle capital of the United States.

At first, I'm thrown off that he has a pet. He doesn't seem like the type to have an animal, and if he did, I'd guess he was a golden retriever person or something. He seems like that all-American, basketball-playing, hamburger-eating, dog-loving type. But then my throat tightens as the fact sinks into my mind. *He has a pet.*

I say it aloud. "You have a pet."

"I have a pet," he says, and then like he knows what I'm thinking, he looks over at me. "But don't worry. That's not going to stop me."

I take a deep breath and stare at my dirty floor mat. A crunched Coke can is wedged in the back corner. Its metallic surface reflects the sunlight, making it look like it's winking at me.

"You should keep your eyes on the road," he says.

"Excuse me?"

"Keep your eyes on the road."

"I heard you," I say in a tight, pinched voice. "But if you want to die, why do you care whether I focus on the road?"

He sucks in his breath, and out of the corner of my eye, I see his broad shoulders slump, making him look like a moose that was just shot and wounded by a hunter. "I want to die, but I don't want to hurt anyone else."

"Fair enough." I grit my teeth and stare straight ahead. I don't tell him about the Coke can. He'd probably think that was a safety hazard.

I steer the car around the fork FrozenRobot described, staying to the left like he instructed. My car glides down Willis's main drag. It's full of painted Victorian-style houses that have been transformed into cutesy businesses—the Creamy Whip, an ice-cream shop; the Fried Egg, a breakfast diner; Suds and Bubbles, a Laundromat.

"What's your turtle's name?"

"Captain Nemo," he says, and then adds, "I didn't name him."

I don't press the issue. The anonymous person who gifted Captain Nemo his name hangs in the air like an unopened envelope. We both know a letter, a story, is inside, but right now neither one of us is brave enough to break the seal.

As we approach a blue house that has fish stickers in the window, I slow the car down. There's a sign in the front lawn that reads "Bob's Fishing Supply & Co." I park in an empty place across the street.

"I'll run in," Roman says.

I start to take the key out of the ignition, but he shakes his head. "You can stay here."

Before I can say anything, he's already left the car and is slowly jogging up to the front door of Bob's Fishing Supply

& Co. He's moving with more urgency than I've seen him move all day. Back at the root beer stand, he was kind of lethargic, sluggish.

He must really love that turtle. My heart feels clogged, constricted, but slowly the feeling fades. I pat my stomach. *Good job, black slug.* As I wait for him to come back, I close my eyes and listen to the music. They've started playing a bit from Tchaikovsky's *Swan Lake*. It's not my favorite. It's too light, too pretty. It has too much longing.

I don't like songs about wanting things. I like songs about letting go, saying good-bye.

Before I know it, FrozenRobot is back, clutching a paper cup in his hands. As he squeezes back into his seat, I say, "You better not spill those."

"Why? Because you keep your car so clean?" His lips twitch, inching into a sloppy smile. The boy really has a smiling problem. Especially for someone who has the nerve to accuse me of being a flake.

I frown. "Because it would be gross."

"Fine, fine. I'll make sure they don't spill."

I pull the car out of the parking space and continue down Main. "So where's your house?"

Roman gives me directions and then at the end says, "How can you listen to this stuff?"

I gesture toward the radio. "This stuff? This stuff is the stuff of genius." I wish Tchaikovsky wasn't on and I could defend something more powerful, like one of Bach's toccatas, but still. *Swan Lake* is worlds deeper than whatever glittery pop ballad he'd wanted to listen to.

"There's no words," he says.

"That's kind of the point, and it's funny that you of all people should complain about that."

I feel him shift his weight in the seat again. His legs bump against the side door. "What do you mean?"

"I mean, you just don't seem like a big fan of words yourself. So I thought you'd appreciate the lack of lyrics."

He cranes his neck to look at me. I can feel his eyes on my face—they're still soft, no burn—but I can feel them nonetheless. "I like other people's words. They fill me up."

"Like words about getting trashed and grinding on the ladies?"

He snort-laughs. "No. That's just noise. I like that, too, though. Helps me forget."

"Forget about?"

"It. Why I want to die."

We enter his neighborhood. It looks similar to mine, same old frame houses, except the yards in his neighborhood look better maintained. There's no spotty crabgrass or dandelion patches.

"I don't get you." And it's true. It might be the most honest thing I've said to him all day. I don't get why he's looking to be filled up, looking to find things in music. When I listen to music, I'm searching for a place to hide, a place to escape my emptiness.

I can see him fiddling with the earthworms. They bounce up and down in his lap and he tries to keep the cup as steady and secure as possible. I wonder why he bothers to be so careful with creatures that are about to die.

He doesn't say anything, so I push it further. "I don't understand why you want this, why you want to be a part of this."

"Are you asking why I want to kill myself or why I don't want to do it alone?"

"Both," I say, chewing on my bottom lip. "Honestly, I don't really care why you want to kill yourself." That's a lie, but I don't want to tell him why I want to die so it seems only fair not to make him spill his reasons. "I just need to know you're not a flake."

He lets out a cold laugh. "Oh, so now you're concerned about flakes?"

"I saw all your friends. I need to make sure this isn't some sick prank." What I don't say is: *I need to make sure this isn't a setup since you know Brian Jackson.*

"Friends?" He spits the word out in disgust. "Those people aren't my friends."

"I'm not really an expert, but they sure seemed like friends."

"Look, you don't know what you're talking about so you

should shut up," he says. The sun is hanging low in the sky, splashing light inside the car, making his hazel eyes glow golden. I wish they would go back to being greener. He didn't look so mean, so angry, when they were green.

"That's not a very nice thing to say."

He tilts his chin upward, as if to signal that he's not going to apologize. "Take a left here." He motions toward a small street off Southwind, the main street in his neighborhood. "It's the red house on the right."

It's a rickety old house like mine, but the wooden siding looks better maintained and someone's clearly been gardening in the front yard. There's a freshly mulched flower bed, and even though nothing has bloomed yet, I imagine that come June, it's going to be full of lilies and marigolds. A butterscotch-colored mailbox sits at the end of the driveway and there's a sign affixed to it that says FRANKLINS'.

"Cute," I say.

"My mom tries," Roman says as he gets out of the car, balancing the cup of earthworms in his left hand.

I guess all moms try. "Wait," I say. "So are we going to do this thing or not?"

He walks around to the driver's side. I roll the window down all the way.

"Yeah. I'm in, if you are," he says.

"I'm definitely in," I say. "But I just don't get it."

"Get what?"

64

"Why you need me."

As if on cue, the front door to his house opens. A short, plump, middle-aged woman skips down the front steps. Her hair is the same chestnut color as Roman's, but it's graying. She's wearing a cooking apron and flower-print clogs. If I were making a tourism brochure for Willis, Kentucky, which thank God I'm not, I'd put this lady on the front cover. She's the human embodiment of the town.

"Roman!" she says, giving us both a little wave. It's a beauty queen pageant wave. Most of the older women around these parts have perfected that move—stiff wrist, slow turn. "Roman!" she repeats. "Introduce me to your friend."

My whole face burns and my stomach clenches and unclenches like a fist. It's not like I feel guilty—after all, it's not my fault her son wants to kill himself. But I didn't exactly want to meet his family. This is the soccer mom problem I was trying to avoid. Two strikes against FrozenRobot—a pet turtle and a loving mom. If I were pickier, I'd say he had too much baggage. But considering my situation, I'm in no position to be choosy.

"Um, Mom," Roman says, his voice uneven. He takes a few gulps of air, his Adam's apple visible in his throat. "This is Aysel."

Real smooth, FrozenRobot, real smooth.

"Aysel," she says, raising her eyebrows. She reaches her hand in through the open window. I know I'm failing the

"Southern Manners Test" right now. I should step out of the car and curtsy if I want to have a chance in hell of her approving of me. But I don't need her to approve of me. It's not like I'm asking for Roman's hand in marriage. And anyway, there will be no me to approve of in a month.

"Nice to meet you." I weakly return her handshake.

"Aysel's a beautiful name," she says. I've learned over the years that "Aysel's a beautiful name" is the tactful substitute for "What the hell kind of name is Aysel?"

"It's Turkish." I scan her face for any reaction. Mostly, I'm interested to see if the stories of my father have had the same staying power they do in Langston. If there's a possibility that Roman or his friends or his mother know about my dad and what he did. I'm pretty sure my dad is the only Turkish person to have made headline news in these parts of Kentucky. And recently, since Brian Jackson has been all over the news, the references to my dad have become more and more frequent. If she makes the connection, she doesn't show it. Her heart-shaped face maintains the same genuine smile.

"Your family lives here in Willis?" she asks.

"Langston," I say.

"I have some friends that go to House of Grace in Langston. Do you go there?"

She wants to know if I go to church. Clever. I have to admit I appreciate this woman's nerve.

"My mom goes to St. Columbia." It's not a lie. Mom, Steve, Georgia, and Mike all go to church every Sunday. I sometimes go, but I haven't been in a while. Right after I moved in with them, Mom used to force me to go, but she's given up that fight. Mom is good at giving up on fights. I'm sure everyone at church has noticed my absence. They probably whisper about how I'm taking after my devil father.

Roman's mom's eyes brighten at the mention of St. Columbia. She places her hands on her wide hips and leans in toward me, crouching down by the window. The smell of her hair spray fills the car. "I hear that's a nice church. I went to their Christmas pageant a few years back. Their choir director is really spectacular, yeah?"

I don't know anything about St. Columbia's choir director. I'm not sure how many different ways there are to sing "Away in a Manger" or "Silent Night," but I nod like I'm in agreement with her, like I'm a normal human being having a nice conversation about my church, like I'm not a ticking time bomb of a monster. "My sister sings in the choir."

This really makes her happy. Her smile is wide and straight, nothing like Roman's crooked, almost hesitant one. "Oh, how great! I'm always trying to get Roman to be more involved with the church. It's nice to see young people worshipping the Lord."

I resist the urge to roll my eyes. To be fair, I don't really know anything about my sister. We haven't had a real conversation in about two years, but I'm pretty sure she's not worshipping the Lord. She doesn't have the time to worship anyone other than herself. "She's really into singing in front of people." I don't mention that Georgia also loves the sound of her own voice.

Roman's mom's smile is getting so wide, I'm scared her face is going to break in two. She spins to face Roman. "Aw, you picked up food for Captain Nemo."

He hunches his shoulders, rounding his back, like he's trying to hide the cup of earthworms from her. Whatever physical disguise he's trying to assemble isn't working. "Yeah, we picked them up on the way back from the root beer stand."

She beams at me. "That's so lovely!"

I nod at her, not sure what I'm supposed to say. I stop myself from asking who named Captain Nemo. Maybe it was her. She seems like a pet person.

It's quiet for a couple of moments, and then Roman clears his throat and shuffles his feet. "Hey, Mom," he says. "Can you give Aysel and me a second?"

His mom looks confused, and then a strange, fevered look washes over her face. The type of face people make after they've just completed a triathlon or climbed to the crest of a mountain. She's beaming at me, like I'm this Christian angel here to rescue her forlorn son. She thinks she understands, but she definitely doesn't. She has no clue whatsoever. Poor lady.

"Sure, I'll see you inside, sweetie." She takes off his baseball cap and runs her hand through his short brown hair. She hands him back his hat, and as if in exchange, he hands her the earthworms.

"Can you take these with you? I'll feed him when I come in," Roman says.

"You got it." She handles the cup with care, like the worms are some kind of precious cargo.

Before she turns to go, she gives me one last smile. "It was so nice to meet you. You should come over for dinner sometime."

"Uh, that'd be great," I lie.

As she walks away from us, she calls over her shoulder, "I'll even look up some Turkish recipes. I'll make you some traditional food." She grips the plastic cup with both hands, cradling it, and then hurries toward the front door, her clogs clicking against the driveway's asphalt.

I've only eaten Turkish food a couple of times before, when my dad had some friends from out of town visiting. One of their wives took over the kitchen, and I remember the aroma of oregano and olive oil and sumac filled up the whole house.

"So that's why I need you," Roman says.

"Your mom?" I say. "She seems nice."

He shakes his head at me, his lips pulled in a thin line. "Right. Nice, but way overprotective. I'll need help getting away from her so we can, you know . . ."

That's one of the tricks of teenage suicide. You have to be able to get away from your guardian's watchful eye long enough to make sure you're really gone before someone finds you. Nothing's worse than someone cutting you down from the rope before you've actually suffocated or pulling you out of the car before the carbon monoxide has done its job. Looks like Roman has figured out he can't off himself at his own homestead; Mama Roman would be all over him.

"And you don't have transportation," I add. He needs me to get to his dying place. I'm not used to being needed. I kind of like it. I wish the black slug inside me would eat that feeling. Liking things is dangerous.

"That too," he admits.

"Why not ask Travis or Lance?" I wink at him. "They can both drive, right? You could just ask them to drop you off at the bridge near Main. Tell them you're taking a trip. A very long trip."

He glares at me. "I don't think anything about this is funny, Aysel." He makes a line in the grass with his sneaker. *Way to make me feel like hell, FrozenRobot.* "Sorry," I say.

"Can you hang out on Saturday?"

"Hang out?" I don't think in the history of my entire life I've ever "hung out" with someone. Even when I was friends with Anna Stevens, our get-togethers always had a purpose—collect and catalog fall leaves, build a model airplane, watch a PBS special on African beetles.

"You know what I mean. Like get together to plan this thing," Roman says. He tosses his baseball cap back and forth in his hands and finally puts it back on.

It's a funny thing, but for a moment I pretend that we're planning something other than our joint suicide, like a bank robbery or a prank or even something simple like a presentation for English class. I imagine that we are two normal teenagers, that I'm really going to come over and let his mom cook Turkish food for me, that we'll spend the evening listening to music and laughing while watching stupid videos on the internet.

I take a breath and I feel my rib cage expand. Nope, we're not normal teenagers. Yes, the black slug is still there, devouring any happy thoughts I allow myself. "Saturday night works for me. I'll put it in my calendar as Death Day Planning."

He smirks. No half-moon smile this time. He pulls his cell phone out of his pocket. "We should exchange numbers."

There's something poetic about the fact that the first boy to ever ask for my number is the same boy I'm going to die with. I bet John Berryman would have had a field day with that. Actually, probably not—he would likely find it very boring.

I give Roman my number and then add him as a new

contact. I put him under FrozenRobot. He squints at my screen.

"What?"

"Why'd you put me under that?"

"It's easier to think about you like that."

He shakes his head at me again. "You should stop trying to make this easy. Nothing about this is going to be easy."

I know, FrozenRobot. I know.

Mr. Scott is tapping his foot on the linoleum floor like he's auditioning for a role in *Waiting for Godot*. The bell rings and he springs into his spiel. "Today is one of my favorite days of the year."

I look at the date. Pi Day was yesterday. I wonder what else could get Mr. Scott so geeked out.

He frowns as his eyes scan the class. We're all slouched at our desks, most of us trying to pretend like we aren't spending every second staring at the clock.

Mr. Scott sighs. "Doesn't anyone want to know why I'm so excited?"

"I do, Mr. Scott," Stacy Jenkins says. She flips her shiny auburn hair and gives him her token suck-up smile.

"Anyone else?" he prompts, and the class groans.

"I'm glad to see how enthusiastic the young minds of the future are." His attempt at sarcasm falls flat. We all continue to look at him with glossy blank stares, our mouths slightly open. I bet if someone filmed Langston High's classrooms and then compared the footage with film taken of mouth-breathing sea creatures, the similarities would be striking.

"What's going on, Mr. Scott?" Stacy coaxes. I don't admire many things about Stacy, but I have to admit it takes some ovaries to talk to your physics teacher like he's a puppy. Mr. Scott doesn't seem to mind, though.

"Today I assign my world-famous physics photography project."

The class groans again. Projects are the worst.

"You'll each be assigned a partner."

More groaning. Scratch what I said before. Group projects are the worst.

"Oh, come on," Mr. Scott says, smiling. "My students always love this project."

"What do we take photos of?" Stacy asks as she twirls her pencil between her fingers.

"Patience, Stacy. I'm about to explain that," he says, and for the first time ever, I sense a bit of irritation in his voice.

I wonder if Mr. Scott dreamed of being a physics teacher when he was our age. I doubt it. I bet he thought he'd land a fancy job at NASA or something. Poor guy. I can think of few fates worse than teaching the young minds of Langston, Kentucky.

Mr. Scott continues, "You are going to take five photographs in the real world that represent the principles of the conservation of energy theory. The photographs must be related to a theme of your choice."

"Theme?" Tyler Bowen interrupts.

"Yes. Theme," Mr. Scott says. "In the past, I've had students use basketball as a theme. All of the photos were taken at a Langston High game. Other past themes have been amusement parks, dogs—"

"Like shopping could be a theme?" Tanya Lee volunteers.

Mr. Scott winces and then quickly returns to his neutral facial expression. "In theory, you could take all your photos at the mall."

Tyler Bowen raises his hand. This is new, him raising his hand instead of simply blurting out whatever's on his mind.

"Yes?" Mr. Scott points at him.

"Do we have to take the photos ourselves or can we just pull them off the internet?"

Another wince. "Good question. You must take the photographs. A big part of your grade is going to be—"

"That's not fair," Stacy protests. "This isn't photography class." Stacy isn't as good as Georgia at masking her whines as valid arguments, but I'd still give her an A for effort.

"You aren't going to be graded on the quality of the photographs per se," Mr. Scott says quickly. "But I'm going to expect that you'll . . ." He trails off. "Hold on. I might as well pass out the worksheet that better explains the project before I continue rambling."

The class mutters, a mixture of groans and sighs. Mr. Scott's face reddens and he fumbles with the worksheets. "Does someone want to help me pass them out?"

No volunteers.

"Aysel?" he says in a pleading voice.

"Uh, sure." I stand up from my desk even though I would rather eat staples than interact with my classmates. I don't make eye contact with anyone as I pass out the worksheets. No one seems that interested in looking at me either. Every time I reach someone's desk, I sense the person stiffening their back, holding their breath, willing me to go away. Part of me wants to shout that they don't have to be afraid of me, but another part of me, the bigger part of me, holds it in because I'm not so sure.

Once I'm back at my desk, Mr. Scott continues explaining the project. He tells us that he expects us to mount our photographs on white parchment paper and then organize the photographs into a booklet. Each photograph is expected to have a detailed written explanation under it, describing the history of the principle and the formulas that correspond to it. We'll be graded on the clarity of our photographs, our descriptions, and our explanations of the physics principles involved. We'll also earn points for how well organized our booklet is and the creativity of our theme. Additionally, if we don't have access to a digital camera, we can borrow one from the library. Mr. Scott is leaving little room for excuses.

"So now all that's left is to choose partners," he says, clasping his hands together. "I think the most fair thing to do is pull names out of a hat."

As predicted, the class erupts with protests.

"That's totally not fair," Stacy says.

"Yeah," echoes Tanya. "We should get to choose our own partners. Especially since our grade depends on them."

Mr. Scott scratches the back of his neck, his eyes twitching. "In the years that I let people choose their own partners, I got unoriginal themes and uninspired photographs. In years where the partners were chosen at random, I got much more creative work. I think it has to do with pushing students out of their comfort zone."

The class continues to argue with him even as we all write our names on small sheets of notebook paper and hand them to him. He grabs the Cincinnati Reds cap he has on his desk and puts all the names inside it. As he calls out the pairings, the groans and sighs become louder.

I clench my teeth and wish I'd been smart enough not to hand in my name. Maybe then I would've gotten to work alone. Even better, I wouldn't have to listen to my partner throw the World's Biggest Fit once they find out they're stuck with me.

"Aysel Seran," Mr. Scott announces as he pulls my name out of the hat.

The class goes silent.

"Your partner will be Tyler Bowen," Mr. Scott says cheerfully, completely oblivious to my social leprosy.

"Oh God," Stacy says. She reaches out to pat his shoulder. "I'm so sorry, Ty."

Tyler's face darkens like someone just murdered his mother. I guess given my family history I shouldn't joke about that. I almost feel bad for Tyler. I know that any association with me is bad news for him socially. But the thing is, our project is due on April 10, so in the end it doesn't matter.

I'll be gone before we have to turn it in.

SATURDAY, MARCH 16

22 days left

The last ten minutes of my shift at TMC are always the slowest. I debate calling the next person on my log, but that would mean I actually care about being a good employee, which I don't. Instead, I play around on Smooth Passages.

I read more of the postings in the Suicide Partners section. It's strange how some people post multiple times. I wonder if they didn't like the people who responded to them, and then I wonder if someone other than me responded to Roman. *Did he pick me over someone else?* The thought makes my stomach flip in a way I'm not used to. Mostly because never in my life have I been picked when there was another alternative. Though, if I'm being completely honest with myself, Roman probably didn't have any other choices. Willis, Kentucky, is the middle of nowhere. Lucky for him, Langston is only fifteen minutes west of nowhere.

"I told you to stop checking dating websites when you're at work," Laura grumbles.

"Why do you care, anyway?" I quickly minimize the window before she can get a better look at the website.

She picks at her chipped pink nail polish. "I don't care. Though I have to tell you I think you're only going to find straight-up weirdos on there."

She has no idea how right she is. "Thanks for the advice." I do my best to maintain a straight face, but I can't. Laura shakes her head.

"Don't blame me when your computer gets a virus." She points at my screen.

"I'll make sure to inform Mr. Palmer that the straight-up-weirdo website was all me." I give her a wink before I pick up the phone, trying not to laugh, and dial the next number on my list—Earl Gorges, who lives on Rowan Hill Drive.

"Hello?" a deep voice answers the phone.

"May I please speak to Mr. Earl Gorges?"

"Speaking," the voice says.

"Hi, Mr. Gorges, this is Aysel Seran, I'm calling from Tucker's Marketing Concepts on behalf of Fit and Active

Foods. I'd like to ask you a few questions."

"Go to hell," he says, and hangs up the phone.

I turn to Laura. "That man just told me to go to hell."

This time it's her turn to laugh.

I decide to take the long way when I drive to pick up Roman. My hands start to tremble as I pull onto Tanner Lane. I've avoided this street as much as possible since everything with my dad happened. Tanner Lane sits on the outskirts of town, home to only the recreational center and a few run-down shops. As I drive down the road, I let myself glance to the left.

And then I see it. My dad's old convenience store. The shabby gray cement building doesn't look any different now that it's abandoned, which says more about its past state than its current one. The town keeps talking about tearing it down. Apparently some developer bought it and plans to turn it into one of those fancy gas stations where you can treat yourself to a slushie of any color, buy a hot pizza, and fill up your tank. All you could get at Dad's old store was a candy bar, a cup of coffee, and the newspaper.

I know I should be eager for it to be torn down, hungry to see the memory crumble. Maybe if the scene of the crime no longer exists, people will start to forget. But I know that's not true. And even if it were, I don't want to see the building go. For better or worse, it's my childhood.

I stare at the building and remember sitting inside, behind the counter with my dad. We'd share a Snickers bar and listen to Bach. He'd tell me how when he was younger, he used to fantasize about learning how to play the piano. He said that once he made enough money at his store, he was going to pay for me to take piano lessons. He was going to send me to a fancy music camp. I guess things didn't exactly go the way he planned.

The parking lot is empty. I pull my car up to the building and turn off the engine. I step outside and run my hands over the familiar concrete blocks. I walk around on the front curb and search for the place where I pressed my palms in the wet cement of the sidewalk when I was ten.

When Dad first discovered what I'd done, his eyes blazed with anger and the vein in his forehead bulged, but then he stared at the tiny handprints and back at me and finally burst out laughing. He flung me over his shoulder and said, "I guess it's fine, Zellie. This way everyone will know the place belongs to you."

I squeeze my eyes shut and put my hands into the old imprint. They're too big to fit now, but it still feels like more of a fit than anywhere else in the world does. I tilt my head toward the sky and slowly open my eyes. The sky is gray and still, like it's holding its breath. I hold my breath too and wait for the pressure building in my throat to fade. It doesn't.

"I miss you, Dad," I whisper as I turn my eyes back to the

cement curb. "I know I shouldn't, but I do."

My phone beeps and I see a message from Roman. I tell him I'm on my way and I jump back into the car. When I reach FrozenRobot's house, I text him to come outside. I don't want to have to face his mom. But when the door opens, I see Mrs. Franklin standing there. She walks toward my car at a brisk pace.

I take a deep breath and roll down the window.

"Aysel," she says, her voice tight, "I'm so glad you're here."

It doesn't sound like it. I nod at her because I'm not sure what I'm supposed to say to that.

"Roman didn't get out of bed yesterday and refused to go to school. But he just told me that he's planning to go out with you. Is that right?" She squints at me like she's trying to determine what my allure is. Poor woman. She has no idea that it's not me that holds the appeal: it's death.

I nod again. "Yeah. We're going to hang out." I try to keep my voice neutral, afraid that even the slightest shake in my voice will give our true plan away, the real reason for our hangout.

"Where?" She puts her hands on her hips. I sink farther into my car's seat. I hadn't prepared for an interrogation.

I'm fumbling around for an answer when Roman comes up behind his mom. "We're going to the playground."

Her gaze darts from me to him and back again. A worried

look crosses her face and she pinches her lips. Then she smiles slowly, but it's a weak one. "Are you going to play basketball?"

I look to Roman for the answer. His shoulders are hunched, as if he can barely stand to hold himself up, like he's uncomfortable with his own height. But he's one of those people who can never be invisible, even if they want to be. "Yeah. I'm going to teach Aysel how to shoot." He slowly gestures toward me, his hands clumsy and sluggish. I wonder if he used to talk with his hands, but now he's out of practice. "You're looking at the next basketball superstar."

I force myself to smile and can only imagine how awfully fake it looks. "He claimed he could teach a cat to shoot, so I gave him a harder student. Me."

Mrs. Franklin laughs, but I still sense a bit of hesitance. "Okay, well, you kids have fun. But Roman . . ." She puts her hand on his shoulder and her pink lacquered fingernails glint in the glow of my car's headlights. "Will you call me if you're going to be out late?"

"Yeah, no problem, Mom." He gives her a weak hug and I look away as she runs her fingers through his short buzzed hair.

She waves at us as she walks back into the house. Roman slides into the passenger seat and we sit for a few moments in silence.

"Nice to see you, too," I say.

"I told you to stop making jokes."

"That wasn't a joke." I turn back on the engine. "So are we really going to hang out at the playground?" I use his same words from the other day. "Hang out" sounds so much less morbid than "Where should we go to plan our joint death?"

"Sure. The old playground sounds good." He stares out the window and seems even more distant than he was when I first met him.

I steer my car down his street and take a left turn onto Main. "You forget that I'm not from Willis. I don't know what you mean by the old playground." Maybe he's the type of person who turns his lies into truths in his head. Like just because he told his friends we met at the old playground, somehow the universe made that true.

"Keep going this way and then take a right turn onto Possum Run."

Only in Willis, Kentucky, would that be the name of a street.

"You had me at Possum Run," I say.

He glares at me.

"Okay, okay. I'll be serious."

"You're freaking me out," he says.

"Why?"

"With the jokes. You seem serious about this whole thing, but then whenever you start to talk about it, you're all light-hearted."

I let out my laugh. The same one that comes out whenever I'm talking to Laura. It's high-pitched and strangled.

"See?"

"Sorry. I laugh when I get nervous."

"Why are you nervous?"

I take the right turn onto Possum Run. "Because you're interrogating me about my motives. Besides, I once read that a side effect of depression is an overwhelming desire to make stupid jokes."

He frowns.

"I'm serious."

"I don't think that's true."

"Look it up."

"Okay, I will." He crosses his arms over his chest and looks out the window. "So are you going to tell me or what?"

"Tell you what?" My car bumps over a pothole on Possum Run.

"Why you want to do it."

I see the playground on the left side of the street. The "old playground" apparently consists of a rusted swing set, a cracked basketball court complete with a metal chain basket, and three rotting picnic tables. It looks like it used to have a sandbox, but at some point, I guess, the sand got replaced with gravel. Soda cans and plastic potato-chip bags are littered across the muddy grass. In some ways, the playground feels more like a graveyard. Like it's a decrepit testament to faded memories, better times. Maybe that's why Frozen-Robot likes it so much.

I park the car and look over at him. His knees are folded up and knocking against the dashboard, but he doesn't seem to mind. His hazel eyes are wide as he studies the playground.

"You haven't told me why you want to. I didn't know that we were planning on sharing with one another," I say. My lungs constrict, a warning not to reveal any information that I'm later going to regret having shared.

He opens the door and gets out of the car. I stay seated for a few seconds longer and squeeze my eyes shut. I know it contradicts the whole idea of having a Suicide Partner, but a giant part of me doesn't want to tell FrozenRobot my reasons. I don't want him to start looking at me the way the other kids at my school do, like I'm a ticking time bomb. I like that Roman thinks he and I are similar. I like having someone relate to me. I don't want to ruin that.

And worse, with his connection to Brian Jackson, I don't think he'd take what my dad did lightly. Sure, he might not still be close to Brian, but it all feels very uncomfortable considering my dad is responsible for the tragedy that's haunted Brian's family—the very reason his brother didn't make it to the Olympics. No way I can tell Roman about my reasons. I'm not going to risk him bailing on me.

All he needs to know is that I'm ready to die. That should be enough.

He taps on my window. I get out of the car and lean against it.

"Sorry," he says. "I can be an asshole sometimes. Ever since . . ." He trails off and cups his hand over his eyes as he gazes up at the sky. The sun has almost set, so I don't know why he's so worried about shading his eyes. Maybe it's just a habit. It's funny—the things we do out of habit.

"Ever since?" I prompt him.

He walks over to one of the picnic tables and sits on top of it. I take a seat next to him and breathe in the scent of damp, decaying wood. The sky is a hazy indigo. March sunsets are always like that in Kentucky. It's like the sky has too much moisture to produce any color that isn't some variation of blue.

"Ever since she died."

"Who died?" I don't miss a beat before I ask. It's probably not polite, but I figure none of the normal social rules apply to my and FrozenRobot's relationship.

"My sister. My little sister. She was only nine years old."

I bite the skin around my thumbnail and stare at Roman's profile. He's pulled his knees to his chin, folding himself up like a camp chair. "That's young." For a brief moment, I think of Mike. He's nine, almost ten.

"Too young."

"Seventeen is young," I offer.

"Are you trying to talk me out of doing this now?"

"No. I was just making a point that I don't think you have to die just because she did. There's like—"

He interrupts me, "She's dead because of me." His voice is a low growl and I scoot away from him.

"What do you mean?"

His shoulders tremble as he lets out a loud exhale. "I was babysitting her one night. But I wasn't really babysitting her, you know?"

I don't know, but I give him a slight nod, urging him to go on.

"My girlfriend was over and Madison, that was my little sister's name . . ." He takes a few shallow breaths and I'm terrified that he's about to start crying. I never know what to do when people cry. I haven't cried since I was ten. I think it's because the black slug sucks up any of my potential tears.

Roman continues, "Madison wanted to take a bath and I told her that was fine. But you see, Maddie used to have seizures. Like really bad seizures. So she wasn't really supposed to take baths alone."

"Uh-huh," I grunt, taking a move from Laura's playbook.

"But I wanted to, you know, with Kelly."

"Wait," I say. "Was Kelly our waitress at the root beer stand?"

He shakes his head. "No. That was Suzie."

"But Travis implied that you guys used to date."

"We used to date like forever ago."

"You've had multiple girlfriends?" I try not to gape at him.

"That's seriously your question right now?" He tosses his hands up in the air. "I'm telling you this story and that's your question?"

I shrug and go back to chewing on my thumbnail. I kick at the bottom leg of the picnic table. It shakes, and for a second, it looks like it might fall off. "Go on."

"Aren't you going to say sorry?"

"Doesn't it kind of not mean anything anymore? That word? Especially if you're asking me to say it?"

He draws his eyebrows together like he's actually contemplating whether or not "sorry" has any power anymore. For an instant, I feel a little bit bad and say, "You're right, I'm sorry."

"Yeah, okay." He goes back to his camp chair pose. "So anyway, I told Maddie she could take a bath because I was an idiot and all I could think was that her taking a bath would give Kelly and me fifteen minutes of uninterrupted time, so Kelly and I went to my room and I turned on my music really loud so Maddie wouldn't hear us, you know?"

I really don't know. I'm kind of amazed that FrozenRobot seems to think I've ever had a sex life.

"So Kelly and I . . ." He gives me an awkward look and dangles his hands at his sides. I fill in the nonverbal clues. "And then I come out of the bedroom to go check on Maddie and—" His voice cracks and I hear him choke back a sob. "I found my sister dead in the bathtub. She drowned while having a seizure. If she screamed for me, I didn't hear it because I was too busy fooling around with my stupid girlfriend."

His story makes me feel like someone stabbed me in the chest with a shovel. I suck in my breath as I try to process what he just confessed to me. I know I should say something sympathetic, something kind and comforting. But the black slug inside of me has eaten every possible kind or comforting or sympathetic thing I've thought of to say. So instead I blurt: "But what does that have to do with driving? I like thought you'd been in some terrible car accident or something."

He jerks his head up and I see that the rims of his eyes are red. He jumps off the table. "You know what, forget it. I thought I could do this with you, as weird and screwed up as you are, but I don't think so."

"Roman, please." I stand up on the table's bench, glancing down at him. "That's not fair. I don't know what you expect from me."

He runs his hand through his buzzed hair, refusing to look at me. He stares at the muddy ground. "I expect you not to make fun of me."

"Make fun of you? How am I making fun of you? You're the one who just called me screwed up."

"You don't think you're screwed up?"

"I know I'm screwed up."

He slow claps. "Thank you, ladies and gentlemen. There's at least one thing we agree on."

I jump down and stand beside him. I resist the urge to grab his arm. "Come on. We can still do this. I just didn't know what to say. I'm not a psychiatrist."

"Obviously," he says, and shakes his head at me. Slowly, a crooked smile appears on his lips.

"You wanted me to feel sorry for you?" I walk over to the swing set. I grip the smooth chain links and sit down on the paint-chipped metal seat. I start pumping my legs, straining for as much height as I can get. Maybe if I pump hard enough, I'll fly into the air and my kinetic energy will project me out of this universe. Unlikely, but a girl can dream.

He doesn't answer me, so I say, "I don't feel sorry for anyone."

"Why? Because no one's life could be worse than yours?" He takes a seat on the swing next to mine, but he doesn't make any effort to move. His swing drifts under his weight, but he doesn't pump his legs.

"No," I say. "I just figured the whole world feels sorry for you. You obviously aren't looking for someone to do what everyone else already does."

I'm getting higher and higher and I feel the swing set creak.

"Be careful," he says.

"Why?" I'm not thinking about being careful. I'm thinking about one last push, of letting go, of flying, and of falling.

"You aren't allowed to die without me," he whispers.

SATURDAY, MARCH 16

22 days left

Roman asks me to drive up to Crestville Pointe. Crestville Pointe is a park that sits on these huge hills above the Ohio River. The edge of the park is made up of rocky cliffs, and Roman has it in his head that it's the perfect place to die.

I'm not so convinced.

"What if the impact doesn't kill us?" I ask. "We could be alive for at least an hour in the water, whimpering and in agonizing, blinding pain. It could take a long time for us to actually die. I don't want a long, painful death. That's not what I signed up for."

"You are seriously twisted. Do you know that?" he says as

he walks along the trail. We're trying to find the easiest way to access the cliffs. The park rangers try to make it difficult. Mostly because they don't want teenagers to cliff dive for fun because they'll probably die. I just hope that the chance of death is more than probably.

"I've been thinking about this longer than eleven months," I tell him. "Sure, I'm twisted. But I also have more insight."

"Don't give me that eleven months crap. I want this just as much as you do. Besides, you have no idea what it's like to live with this kind of guilt." Roman's voice is cold and he doesn't stop charging up the hill. He's practically jogging and I'm struggling to keep up with him.

"You're right. I don't. But you don't know shit about me either." I barely spit out the sentence. I lean over and grab my side, panting heavily. I really should get out more. The cool grass tickles my ankles, sneaking into the open space of skin between where my jeans should meet my sneakers. My jeans are a little too short for me, but I'd rather swallow glass than go shopping with Mom and Georgia. I figure I can make it another few weeks without new pants.

"I don't know anything about you because you won't tell me anything," he says. He doesn't seem to be winded at all. Damn him.

I motion toward a grass clearing. "I bet if we cut through here, we'll get closer to the water."

He follows me through the grass. It's hard to see where we're going since it's now dark, and I wonder if in some ironic twist of fate, we'll soar over the cliff without even realizing it. Like the universe's final joke: you can't plan your death, even when you try.

The grass clearing slowly turns back into forest. Dark, thick tree trunks surround us, and our shoes crunch over leaves and twigs. I almost trip on a bumpy root and Roman steadies me. The thing about the Ohio River is it doesn't make a noticeable sound. No frothing or burbling. But I can still tell when we're getting closer—I can smell and practically taste the dank, musty water.

The ground turns from a muddy forest floor to gravelly stone. We've arrived at the edge. We both stare out at the river; the only sound around is a few warbling birds.

"I don't get why you won't tell me anything," he finally says.

"Why are you so curious? Does it even matter why I want to die?"

"Kind of," he says.

"Why?"

"Because if it's stupid, I'd try to talk you out of it."

I laugh. "No, you wouldn't."

"Yes, I would."

"You wouldn't because then you'd lose your ride, remember? You don't have the ability to get away from Mommy

Dearest. You never did explain that, by the way."

Even though the sun has set, he does that thing again where he cups his hands over his eyes as he looks out at the sky. We're standing close enough together that I can see the holes in the collar of his black T-shirt. His collarbone is sharp and visible beneath his skin; he's thinner than I realized.

He catches me staring at him and takes a few steps away from me, creating space between us. "After Maddie died, I was sent to therapy. Lots of therapy. The doctors suggested to my parents that I lose my driving privileges because they were worried about my ability to stay present in the moment. They also suggested that I never be left alone unsupervised. Apparently being completely alone tends to make people more depressed, but as far as I can tell, how I feel about Maddie's death doesn't change whether I'm alone or not."

Therapy. Right after my dad went away, my school made me visit with the counselor three times a week. But the meetings weren't productive. I just sat there, hummed a classical tune, and stared at her excessive collection of potted plants. Eventually she gave up on me.

"What?" he says. I must have made a face.

"Nothing. I once got sent to a counselor, so I found it funny that therapy didn't work for you either."

"Funny?"

"Not funny. Ironic."

"Not sure that's the right use of ironic, but you seem to be smarter than me so I'll trust you."

"You'll trust me?"

He doesn't answer. He sits down by the edge and leans his whole body back. He cradles his head with his hands and fans out his elbows. I sit beside him. I don't lie down, but I pull my knees to my chin.

"Do you want to die in the water because that's how she died?"

He closes his eyes and gives me a small nod. "It only seems fair."

"We can do it here, if you want. I'm just nervous about it." I unwrap my knees and reach out to feel the ground. The rocks are rough on the palm of my hand.

"I'm pretty sure it's a normal reaction to feel nervous."

I exhale loudly. "I'm not nervous about the act of it."

"Oh, you're such a hard-ass that the idea of jumping off this cliff doesn't make you the least bit nervous?" Roman props himself up on his side so he can look directly at me.

"Okay, maybe I'm a little scared. But I'm more scared about what comes next."

He goes back to lying flat on his back. "You mean like what happens to us when we're dead?"

I pick up some of the gravel and let it sift through my fingers. "Don't you ever think about that? What if this isn't the end and we just go on to a place even worse than this one?"

He sits up and grabs a stone. He tosses it over the cliff's

edge. It seems to disappear before it hits the water—too small to even make a splash. "Any place has to be better than this one."

"But do you think it's really possible to die?"

His face hardens, his jaw muscle tightens, and his eyes glow like they're burning. I wonder if FrozenRobot used to look different before Maddie died. With his chestnut-colored hair and clear skin and strong jaw, he's definitely classically good-looking. You know, good-looking in an obvious way. Like he's the type of boy who gets cast in back-to-school-shopping commercials. You could see him anywhere and you'd know from looking at his face that he was popular in high school. Yes, Roman is one of those people.

But the longer I look at him, the more I start to realize there's something different about him from the Tyler Bowens and Todd Robertsons of my world. I take back what I said when I first met him—FrozenRobot does have a frozen quality. All of his movements and facial expressions have a tension to them, like he was carved out of stone and locked in a chamber of ice and recently brought back to life. I don't know how to describe it, but the more I stare at him, the more I see his grief wrapped around him like shackles he can never take off. I try to imagine him without the grief, without the heaviness, without the frozenness, but it's hard to see him as anything other than desperately sad. Yes, he looks like someone who was designed to be popular and successful, but he also looks like someone who was made to wear grief.

He wears it well.

"How can you even ask that?" His voice brings me back to reality. "Obviously it's possible to die. Maddie died. She's dead. She's gone."

I shrug, rubbing my palms over the gravel. The stones' edges tear at my skin. "I've been thinking a lot about the energy of the universe. And if energy can't ever be created or destroyed, only transferred, what do you think happens to people's energy once they die?"

He shakes his head, stands up, and walks farther away from me, closer to the edge. I follow him. Looking down at the river, I try to imagine what it will feel like when I hit the water. The Ohio River moves so slowly, there's no churning or sputtering, only a lazy flow. Maybe the water will hug me tight, squeezing all the air from my lungs. Maybe it will feel like I'm being rocked to sleep, maybe I'll get pulled under and everything will turn black and it will be like dreaming. Maybe.

"You can definitely die," he repeats his argument from earlier. "Maddie's dead. I don't see her energy anywhere."

"Just because you can't see it doesn't mean her energy is gone."

His hands jump at his sides. He picks up another rock and throws it over the edge. "You have to stop talking to me about this. It freaks me out."

"It freaks me out, too," I say softly.

"I need to think that when we die, we're going to be dead. I can't think about anything else."

"Okay." I agree to stop talking about it, but that doesn't mean I can stop thinking about it.

We both go back to looking at the river in silence. We go back to imagining our watery deaths.

MONDAY, MARCH 18

20 days left

Monday morning in my house is probably my least favorite time of the week. I can't ever sneak in an extra fifteen minutes of sleep because Georgia always gets up extra early to root through her entire closet. God forbid she chooses the wrong outfit. Apparently the statement you make on Monday is really important—according to Georgia, what you wear on Monday determines how the rest of your week will be. Like, if you dress really nice and get tons of compliments, you'll pass your algebra quiz on Thursday. I don't really think polynomials have anything to do with wedges or skinny jeans, but Georgia is completely convinced. Good thing I wear a variation of the same thing every day—gray striped long-sleeved T-shirt, black jeans, gray sneakers—so there's no chance of things ever being different for me.

"Aysel," she hisses. "Aysel, wake up."

"Georgia," I groan, and roll over on my side. I press my face farther into the pillow in hopes of drowning her out. "I don't really care whether you wear your purple sweater dress or your red pencil skirt. I'm sure everyone will think you look beautiful either way."

I hear the end of my bed creak. She starts poking me in the sides and I squirm away from her, my limbs tangled in the sheets. "What the hell?"

"Wake up!" She bounces back up and paces around the room. "Look out the window."

I rub my temples. I was planning on sleeping for at least another fifteen minutes, twenty if I decided not to brush my hair. Sighing, I force myself out of bed. I stumble over to the small window that's positioned in the very middle of the back wall of our room. That window has been our dividing line for the last three years—left side for me, right side for Georgia. Her side is covered with pages she's ripped out of fashion magazines and pictures of her and friends and her collection of saltshakers. She has this strange obsession with unique saltshakers—shakers shaped like owls, trucks, wolves—she finds them at thrift stores. My wall is empty.

"Look," she presses, pointing at the window.

Outside, I see that the grass is blanketed with snow. I blink because the sun is out and it makes our whole yard glisten. The snow is piled against the trunks of the oak trees, and from what I can see, it looks like we must have gotten at least four inches.

"Isn't it amazing?" Georgia says, clapping behind me. "School is canceled!"

"It never snows in March," I say.

"It did once when we were little, remember?"

I remember. It was a good day. I couldn't have been older than nine, Georgia must have been seven then, and Mike was two. Dad drove me to spend the day over here because he still wanted to work at the store, hoping that he might get some extra foot traffic since all the kids would be out of school.

That morning Mom made us chocolate-chip pancakes and then we spent the rest of the day building snowmen in the yard and sledding down the hill on Vine Street. We felt like a real family that day—I didn't feel like an interloper who only came to visit on weekends.

That was a long time ago.

It's silent for a few moments. Me staring out the window at the fresh snow and Georgia watching me stare. Neither one of us knows how to talk to the other anymore.

"I think I'm going to go back to sleep," I say. That's what a snow day means now, not pancakes and snowmen, but extra hours in my bed. Alone.

I hear her make the verbal equivalent of a frown—a whiny snort. "Are you like still tired from Saturday night?"

"What?"

"You were out late," she says.

I flop back into my bed and pull the comforter over my face. I'm not going to talk about Roman with Georgia. Not in a million years.

She sits down at the end of my bed again. "Who were you with? Do you have a boyfriend now or something?"

I can't help but laugh. If I have a boyfriend, his name is Death. And I'm pretty sure Roman is in love with him, too. It's like a love triangle gone wrong. Or maybe it's a love triangle gone right: we both get the guy on April 7.

She huffs and I feel the bed move as she gets up. "Fine. Just laugh at me. I was only trying to talk to my big sister. Excuse me for making an effort."

Oh, now you want to talk to me? I feel the urge to laugh all over again. The irony of the whole thing. She's only interested in talking to me when a half foot of snow separates her from hanging out with her friends. "Half sister," I correct her, and for a second I feel a little guilty. Then the black slug comes to the rescue.

"You're impossible," she says, and sighs. If I didn't know her better, I'd say she was sad. She leans against the wall, her hand on the door handle. "So you know, Mom made pancakes."

I hear the door slam as she leaves. A few seconds later, it opens again. "Oh, and so you know, Steve . . ." She says "Steve" in the exact same way I always do, stretching it out like it's a loose rubber band. There's an awkward pause and then she continues, "Yeah, Steve, he's at work. Sparkle didn't close the factory."

"You mean your dad," I correct her again. "Your dad is at work."

"Yeah, my dad. The one you hate for no understandable reason. The one that gave you a home."

That's it. I throw the comforter off of me and sit up straight. "How generous of him. And I don't hate him, Georgia."

"Oh yeah? Well, you sure act like it. I'm tired of you spending every day feeling sorry for yourself just because of what your dad did. Newsflash: You aren't your dad. And you should stop blaming everyone else for what he did. Yourself included."

Tell that to everyone else, I think. I flash her a snarly frown, hoping she'll leave me in peace, but she stays. She stares at me for a while, her hands on her slender hips. I stare back at her, trying to figure out how we are even half sisters. With her fair skin, honey-colored hair, and tiny nose, she looks like the prototypical Kentucky beauty pageant contestant. She's like the sun and I'm like the bumpy, brooding moon. The only thing we have in common is our eyes. We both have

Mom's dark, almond-shaped eyes.

Right now, her hair is in a braid and she's wearing boy boxers and an oversized Kentucky Wildcats T-shirt. I wonder if she's given up on her Monday rule. I'm about to comment on it, but before I do, she says, "I just wish you weren't so sad all the time, Aysel."

Me too, Georgia. Me too.

I take a deep breath and get out of bed. "I'll meet you downstairs for pancakes. Just let me brush my teeth."

She smiles like I just told her she aced her algebra exam and skips out of our room. I don't think I've skipped since the last March snow day.

I walk down the hall to the bathroom and squeeze some toothpaste onto my toothbrush. I take the toothbrush back to our room and scrub my teeth as I look out the window. I overhear Mom and Georgia and Mike talking in the kitchen.

"She's coming down soon," Georgia says.

"Oh, good!" Mom says. "I'm so glad you convinced her to get out of bed."

The smell of maple syrup fills the entire house. I can hear Mike banging his fists on the kitchen table. "Make sure you add extra chocolate chips," he says. "Aysel loves chocolate chips."

My heart swells and I wait for the black slug to take the feeling away from me, but it doesn't. It lets me keep it. The swelling turns into a small, sharp ache—it's going to be

107

harder to leave them than I realized.

As I put on my slippers and pad down the stairs, I find myself wishing that every day were like this one. If every day were like this one, I don't think I'd be so eager to be gone.

The problem is, March snow days are miracles. You can't live for miracles.

Tyler Bowen is waiting for me at a table in our school's library. I'd figured he would blow the whole thing off, but it looks like sometimes I can be wrong about people.

Our school library is less like a library and more like a media center. It sits in the middle of our high school, a hollowed-out space that they filled with computers, tables, and flimsy plastic bookshelves. Recently, they've hung Brian Jackson banners on the back wall. They're the same ones that hang in TMC. I can't escape them.

"Hey, Georgia's sister," he says as I take a seat at the table.

"You do know I have a name of my own, right?" I unzip my backpack and pull out my physics notebook.

Tyler's pale face flushes, making his freckles more prominent.

"What?" I uncap my pen and tap it against the table.

"I don't know how to pronounce your name."

I laugh and his face turns a deeper shade of red.

"It's not funny," he says, looking down at his shoes. "You have a . . . strange name. Did your dad choose it?"

I blink, a bit stunned that he would actually willingly bring up my dad. "I think my mom picked it. But I'm not sure."

"So how do you say it?"

"Aysel," I say. "Rhymes with gazelle."

He squints with confusion and so I add, "Uh-zell."

"Got it, Aysel," he says, overpronouncing it, but it's a start.

"You seriously didn't know how to say my name?"

"I had an idea, but I wasn't sure. You know, it's hard to pronounce."

"Fair enough." I shrug as I realize I see myself in the same way Tyler Bowen does: as an unknown variable. "So should we get started?"

"Yeah, probably." He runs his hand through his auburn hair. I wonder if he thinks that makes him look suave.

"Any ideas for the project?" I nibble on the end of my

pen, ensuring that I look decidedly not suave.

Tyler doesn't answer me. He leans back in his chair and waves to one of his basketball buddies who just walked into the library. His friend shouts something at him but gets shushed by Ms. Silver, the school librarian.

"Hey, give me a minute?" Tyler asks.

"Sure." I watch him dash across the library to meet his friends. I can see them whispering to one another, motioning in my direction. Tyler shuffles his feet and shrugs. I imagine he's explaining that he was forced to work with me.

"See you later, man," I hear one of his friends say.

"Yeah, good luck," the other one adds.

Tyler eventually walks toward me, but his pace is slow, like he's doing his best to show that this is a punishment. Not a choice.

"Sorry about that."

I shrug. "No need to be sorry. Let's just get back to work."

"Sure thing, Aysel."

"You don't have to say my name every time." I reach into my backpack and pull out my physics textbook. I let it fall on the table with a slam. "So do you have any good ideas for the theme of our project?"

"Theme?"

Tyler Bowen evidently doesn't pay much attention during class. "Yeah, a theme. Mr. Scott said our project has to center around one."

"Oh, that theme." He stretches his long legs out. "Why not basketball?"

I give him a blank stare. "Seriously?"

"Yes, seriously!" Tyler leans over the table toward me. "Mr. Scott used it as one of the examples, so he clearly loves it as a theme."

"Or it's been done a hundred times before. We should be creative." Then again, I don't know why I care about this project. Meeting with Tyler is a waste of my time. It's not like my grade on this matters. I'll be gone before we even turn it in.

But I want to do a good job for Mr. Scott. Even if I'm not around to see his reaction to it, I want him to know I took his class seriously. I flip to a blank page in my notebook. I tap my pen against the paper, hoping to come up with an idea.

"What do you mean, creative?" Tyler says the word like it's as foreign to him as my name.

"Yeah, creative. Why don't we go to the zoo or something?" I jot down my idea.

He makes a face. "The zoo? That's like a place for little kids."

"Oh, c'mon. I bet you used to love it."

"When I was like eleven I did." He touches his hair again. To his credit, his hair is shiny and soft looking. And this fact obviously isn't lost on him.

"The zoo is perfect," I continue. "There are so many

photo opportunities. Like the bats hanging upside down have potential energy. And maybe we could even photograph a lion eating raw meat and label it as an energy transfer."

"But the zoo is a million hours away in Louisville. Can't we choose something easier?"

It's not like I can spell out the truth for Tyler: that I want to go to the zoo one last time before I die. That I'd love to see the lions bathing in the sun or the polar bears splashing around in their deepwater pool. FrozenRobot would probably tell me I'm a flake to be thinking like this, but I can't help it.

"Yeah. It's a long trip, but once we get there it will be easy. There are so many different things we could take photos of," I argue, mentally crossing my fingers.

"Fair enough, Aysel like gazelle. Put us down for the zoo theme." He takes my pen and grabs my notebook. He waves it in the air. I reach to snatch it back from him, but it's too late.

His eyes grow large as he stares at the page the notebook has fallen open to. "Whoa."

I reach for my notebook and glance down at the page. I take a shallow breath of relief. It's not as bad as it could've been. It's only a stick figure with a noose around its neck. I think I drew it a couple of weeks ago in class when Mr. Scott was rambling on and on about angles and velocity and I couldn't stop wondering about the destruction of energy.

"What's the deal with that . . . hangman thing?"

"I drew it when I was bored in class. Don't you get bored? Mr. Scott never stops talking about angles." My heart is racing, but I do my best to make my voice sound normal.

He frowns and scrunches all of his facial features together. "You sure I shouldn't be worried about you?"

"For playing hangman?"

"It doesn't look like any game of hangman I've ever played," he says softly.

I shrug again and force myself to smile. "I guess I just play a weird version of it."

"Okay . . ." He swallows and I can see him fumbling over his words. I've made Tyler Bowen speechless. I guess I can scratch that off my bucket list.

He returns my halfhearted attempt at a smile. "I once heard fish are the best animals to look at if you're depressed or whatever." He punches my shoulder lightly, like we're old friends. "And the zoo has a great aquarium."

I sneak a glance at the Brian Jackson banner. Words sit on the edge of my tongue and I'm half tempted to tell Tyler the truth, that the drawing isn't a joke or a game. I wait for the feeling to pass, but it doesn't. I'm like a grenade made of ceramic—solid and dense and cold—but still fragile. I could burst at any moment. I don't want to burst in front of Tyler.

In the steadiest voice I can manage, I say, "So when do you want to go to the zoo? We should probably go soon, get a jump start on this. I know you're going to think I'm a nerd, but I really want to do a good job."

"We could go on Saturday," he offers.

"During the day?" I think I'm technically scheduled to work on Saturday, but I can probably trade shifts with someone. Or I could just skip—my job seems more pointless now than it ever has.

He curls his lips up over his teeth, his blue eyes glossy with surprise. "Why? Do you have big plans on Saturday night or something?"

"No," I say, bracing myself for his teasing jab.

But it doesn't come. "How about I pick you up around ten?"

"Works for me." I don't have to tell him where I live; he's picked up my sister a few times. I bet she's going to have a heart attack when she sees Tyler Bowen in our driveway, waiting for me. The thought almost makes me smile.

"What?" he asks.

"Nothing," I say, and fold my hands in front of me on the table. "I'm just excited to go to the zoo."

THURSDAY, MARCH 21

17 days left

Today is Mike's tenth birthday. We're all gathered in
the back party room of Pirate Jack's Laserplex. Pirate
Jack's Laserplex is exactly what it sounds like—a run-down
pirate-themed laser tag facility. It's housed in a cement-
block building that has small dusty windows and stained
tiled floors.

Steve always has Thursdays off, and Mom used a vacation day. Georgia and I came straight from school to help
Mom decorate the room with black and red streamers, eye
patches, and fake gold coins. If you close your eyes, cover
your ears, and spin around a few times, you could almost

believe you were on a pirate ship, not stranded in Langston, Kentucky. Almost.

I'm currently seated in the back of the room, at a table by myself, balancing Mike's present on my lap and holding a plastic cup of orange soda in my left hand, trying to pretend like I don't feel ridiculous wearing a paper pirate hat. Steve sits in the front with his buddies, downing cans of cheap beer and applauding every time Mike opens a basketball or a baseball glove. Georgia, Mom, and some of Mom's friends sit at the table next to Steve's, gossiping about the cheer squad and lamenting how Christine Beth Thomas beat Sandra Dewitt in last month's beauty pageant.

Every once in a while, Mom glances back at me. Like I've said before, she, Georgia, and I all have the same eyes, but Mom has different eyelids. Hers are dusky and weathered looking. They have a sadness to them. She catches me staring at her and I look away.

Mike's ripped through his stack of presents like a tornado. Guess it's my turn. I reach out and carefully place my soda on the table. A sliver of sugary orange syrup sloshes over the edge of the cup and dribbles down my hand. I wipe my hand on my shirt and grip Mike's present. It's light in my hands when I want it to feel heavy, significant. I walk toward him.

Mike grabs the present from me. "Hey, Aysel," he says, his gray-green eyes lighting up. Mike looks eerily similar to Steve, a miniature version. They both have wavy blond hair, small and beady gray-green eyes, and sharp, pointed chins.

"Hey, Mikey," I say. "Happy birthday."

The rest of the room has gone silent. Watching us. I wrapped my gift in $E=MC^2$ paper. He doesn't seem to notice. He tears the paper away fast, and as he stares down at my gift, his small eyes stretch as wide as baseballs.

Mike squeals and waves the gift, a comic book, in the air. It's an edition of *The Amazing Spider-Man*, signed by Stan Lee. He clutches it to his chest and beams at me. "Spider-Man? This is awesome!" He stares at the cover and traces his finger over the signature like he's hypnotized by it. Then he carefully places the comic on the table next to him and stretches his arms out wide, pulling me into a tight hug.

My mouth feels dry and my stomach is heavy like a bowling ball. I weakly return his hug and run my fingers through his wavy hair. "You're welcome, buddy. I hope you enjoy reading it for years to come."

He squints at me like he knows that there's something wrong with what I just said. The problem is that I can't say what it is that I really want to say. I should tell him that I spent fifteen paychecks to buy him that comic book because I desperately want him to have something nice to remember me by. To think of me as kind, as cool, as caring. Not as the psycho offspring of a murderer who offed herself when he was ten.

I want to be more to him than that. I know that might

never happen, but I have this daydream where, a couple of years from now, when I'm gone and Mike misses me, he reaches for the comic book, and as he reads it, he feels better. He feels safe. He knows he can beat his demons in exactly the way I couldn't.

"Hey," I hear a gruff voice call out.

I let my arms drop from Mike's waist and turn around. It's one of Steve's buddies. He has stringy brown hair that falls to his shoulders and he's wearing a camouflage-print trucker hat.

"Hey," he repeats. "Those things are expensive." He gestures toward the comic book with the beer that's in his right hand. "I hope you obtained it legally." He grins, revealing his crooked yellowed teeth. His stare lets me know exactly what he's thinking about: my father.

"No worries," I say. "Obtained completely legally. I bought it with my own hard-earned cash."

The man turns his head to glance at my mother. "So she takes after you, Melda?"

My mom nods stiffly and walks to the front of the room. She places her hand on the small of Mike's back and turns to face me. "That was a very thoughtful present, Aysel. Thank you."

I swallow down the anger I feel thrashing around in my gut. *I love my little brother. Of course I got him a nice present. Why do you have to act so surprised, Mom?* I squeeze my jaw shut, afraid of what might come out if I open it.

Mike is the only one of them who has never acted like it was strange when I moved in. The first day I arrived at Steve's house, Mike was waiting for me on the front steps, his grin stretched so wide I thought his face might break. My heart swelled when I saw his gap-toothed smile, and remembering it now makes me ache. When I first moved in, I used to read to him before he went to sleep on nights when my mom worked late. And sometimes he would beg me to play with him in the backyard. We'd run around, kicking our mud-stained soccer ball back and forth. But recently, I don't have the energy for any of that.

My mom shuffles past me so she can stand behind the small table with the birthday cake. "Mike, come here and help me cut the cake."

Mike looks at her and then back at me. He gives me another tight hug and then bounds over to my mom. He's all energy and smiles and love. Mikey has always been that way.

My throat is dry as I walk back to my seat and watch my mom slice the chocolate cake. It has melted, droopy frosting. She encourages everyone to eat quickly since we are scheduled to play laser tag in twenty minutes.

While devouring the cake, Mike's friends take turns examining his presents. When one of them grabs for the comic book, his fingers coated with chocolate icing, Mike moves it away from his reach. "Don't get it dirty!"

He looks over at me and my heart seizes and I think that any second, it might explode. Sometimes I wonder if my heart is like a black hole—it's so dense that there's no room for light, but that doesn't mean it can't still suck me in. I'm going to miss Mike the most. I'm going to miss him so much, I almost can't stand it.

I stick my fork into my slice of cake and sigh. I stand up and head toward the door. Mom walks up behind me and places her hand on my shoulder.

"Where are you going?" Her heavy eyelids sag over her eyes, like any second they're going to snap shut so she won't have to see me anymore.

"Just to the bathroom."

"Okay, be back soon. You won't want to miss laser tag." Her words are simple. Benign. But I know what she really means is I'm not allowed to act like a mopey loser here. This is Mike's birthday party and I need to pull it together. And the thing is, she's right. It wouldn't be fair for me to go into the bathroom and sulk for hours.

I want to scream at her. She never bothers to ask what's wrong or what's going on with me. She doesn't want to know. Even though Mom never went through the Kentucky beauty pageant system, she's still learned how to put on a show. She's great at delivering a megawatt smile even when I know she wants to cry. Or speaking in a calm, measured voice even when I know she wants to scream. Sometimes I wish she would scream. Her always acting like everything's okay only makes me feel even crazier than I already am.

I wonder if her facade would finally crumble if I told her what I'm going to do. If she knew what FrozenRobot and I were planning. I shake that thought from my head. Telling her would do more harm than good. Nothing she has to say can save me. I need to remember that.

I walk down the hallway, staring at the specks of dirt that are sprinkled all over the tiled floor. I push open the door and head outside. I close my eyes as the cold wind smacks against my face.

I put my hands in the snow that hasn't completely melted. My fingertips freeze.

Seventeen days left.

FRIDAY, MARCH 22

16 days left

"I can't believe you're ditching me tomorrow," Roman says. He's sitting on the mattress, bouncing up and down. Despite his height, he can sometimes look like a little kid. I think his outfit is throwing me off, too. He's not in his standard hoodie and track pants. His mom must have made him put on the pressed dark slacks and a cream-colored button-up shirt for the occasion. He looks a bit uncomfortable in them, like he's playing dress-up.

"Ditching you?" I pace around his room. It's simple, kind of what I pictured, not that I spend a lot of time imagining Roman's room. With its beige walls, mandatory University of Kentucky Wildcats Basketball team poster, and maroon trim, it could just as easily be any other high school boy's room.

On his nightstand, I see a picture of a toothy little girl; her mouth is wide open in a smile and she's sticking her tongue out at whoever was taking the photograph. She has the same color hair as Roman, same deep-set hazel eyes. The girl must be Madison.

Roman's mom is downstairs cooking dinner, her attempt at Turkish cuisine. Should be interesting. His dad's still at work but supposedly is going to make it home in time for the Big Event. I'm kind of surprised Roman's mom is cool with us being in his bedroom alone. It seemed like she thought something was brewing between Roman and me, but maybe she's smarter than I give her credit for. Though she did tell him to leave the door open, so there's that.

"Hey." I spin around to face him. "Why did you let your mom go through with this?"

"This?"

I shrug. "This fake dinner thing. Don't you feel kind of bad that she's slaving away down there?"

He stops bouncing on the mattress and looks down at the ground. "Sort of, I guess. But it has to happen."

I scrunch my face together in confusion.

"I need her to really believe that we're getting close," he explains slowly. "So she'll let me be alone with you on April seventh. It's not like she's going to let me wander off with a complete stranger on the first anniversary of Maddie's death. She's too smart for that."

So I'm a pawn in your game. I guess I'd already figured that out. That's why he needs a Suicide Partner, after all. And really, he's a pawn to me, too. A means to an end. Or rather, the means to The End.

I go back to snooping around Roman's room. He has a signed baseball that's been strategically placed inside a Cincinnati Reds cap. "My dad got that for me," he says. "We went to a game when I was little."

I nod and keep fingering his things. I wonder if it bothers him. Me, searching for his secrets while he watches. I look over my shoulder at him and he's flopped out on the bed, his chin tilted toward the ceiling. If he does mind, it doesn't show. Maybe that's a side effect of knowing you're about to die: none of your secrets matter anymore. After you're gone, they'll all be discovered anyway. Pored over by other people.

I don't like the idea of other people poring over my secrets. I don't even know if I have any secrets. Besides FrozenRobot. And the secret I'm keeping from him: what my dad did.

"So you're going to the zoo tomorrow?"

"Yeah," I say, flipping through his copy of *Journey to the Center of the Earth*. It's almost cute that he seems to have a slight obsession with Jules Verne. I slide it back onto the shelf and pull out *Twenty Thousand Leagues Under the Sea*.

"I used to like those books when I was younger."

"Uh-huh." I turn the page, staring at the black-and-white illustrations. It's a nice copy of the book, like the kind you pay extra for. A collector's edition or something like that. A creepy-looking sea creature stares back at me with its grapefruit-sized eyes. I slam the book shut. When I do, loose pages flutter out of it. I grab for one of them. It's a pencil sketch of a small turtle. The picture is drawn so well, it looks three-dimensional. Even though it was sketched in charcoal pencil, you can still get a sense of the turtle's leathery neck and his smooth shell. But there's something different about it, too—it's almost like staring at a turtle through a blurry lens. There's a surrealist quality to the picture. The markings on the turtle's shell are overly emphasized and his front paws are elongated and thinned.

I flip through the other drawings; most of them are of the same turtle, but I find one that looks like it's a rendering of Madison. Her eyes are wide and expertly shaded, and the sketch has captured her toothy smile. But even though Madison is smiling, there's a sadness to the picture, like the artist knows her ultimate fate, even if she doesn't. I can't stop staring at the drawing. It's haunting.

FrozenRobot jerks up and scoots to the foot of the bed. "Those are stupid. Don't look at them."

I thumb back to the first sketch of the turtle and take a step toward the glass aquarium that houses the famous Captain

Nemo. Right now, the turtle is bobbing up and down in the shallow water, paddling with his leathery feet. "These aren't stupid. They're actually really good." I compare the sketch with the real-life Captain Nemo. It's almost dead-on, minus the fantastical quality of the sketch. The turtle Roman drew seems sad, almost like he's in mourning. His beady eyes are dark and his back feet look too heavy and swollen to be used for swimming. "You drew these?"

"Yeah." His voice is quiet and I can hear him shifting on the bed, the mattress sighing beneath him. "Can you put them away? They're embarrassing."

"Why are you embarrassed of them? I mean, you did make Captain Nemo seem a bit more emo than I think he is, but besides that, you nailed it." I hold the drawing up against the tank. "It's really pretty incredible."

Roman doesn't say anything, but I hear him let out a light sigh in protest. I turn to face him. He's pulled his knees to his chest and wrapped his arms around them.

"I didn't know you drew. I sketch sometimes, but I can only draw stick figures." I stare down at the drawing and run my fingers over the turtle's smooth-looking shell, almost expecting it to feel real. "These are impressive."

"Whatever. I'm not like an artist or anything." He shrugs. "It's just something to do when I'm alone in here. Kills time."

I nod and tuck the papers back inside the flap of the collector's edition of *Twenty Thousand Leagues Under the Sea.*

Roman's body visibly loosens once the drawings are put away. "So I'm guessing Captain Nemo was named after the Jules Verne character?"

"I told you before, I didn't name him." Roman's voice is suddenly cold.

I shake off his harshness. "Maddie did?"

"Yeah."

I drop the topic and stare at the real live turtle some more. I don't know much about turtles, but this one looks exceptionally well cared for. He has a bowl of fresh fruit, red Ping-Pong balls to play with, and a large, smooth slate rock to sunbathe on. I wonder how Roman can bear the thought of leaving Captain Nemo behind and if he knows what will happen to the poor guy once Roman isn't around to take care of him. I bite my lip—I'm not brave enough to ask. Or maybe I don't want to know the answer.

"So are you and that guy dating or something? The dude you're going to the zoo with?" Roman asks out of nowhere.

I try not to laugh and decide to ignore his stupid question. Roman obviously isn't too concerned about Captain Nemo's fate. Or if he is, he's not letting himself think about it. I lean over so I can inspect his shelf of trophies. I read the inscriptions, lots of standard Little League stuff, but there's a big silver plaque that stands out. Its inscription reads: WILLIS HIGH SCHOOL VARSITY BASKETBALL MVP. I pick it up to take a closer look at it. It's heavy in my hand.

"So your friends were right. You were really good at basketball. Why were you so modest about it?"

He shrugs. "Because."

"Because why?"

"It's not like I used to be good. I am good. And it's weird to brag about things you're still good at."

"But you don't play anymore?"

"Nope." He flops back on the bed. "I don't do anything anymore."

"Except hassle me about going to the zoo. It's not like you and I had plans, FrozenRobot."

"Don't call me that."

"Okay, okay."

He tosses a pillow at me and it hits me in the side of the face.

"Hey!" I say, rubbing my right cheek as if the pillow actually had the power to leave a mark.

"Sorry, I just wanted to get your attention because I had a thought."

"And what's that?"

He slides off the bed and sits at the foot of it. He pats the ground beside him. I take a seat next to him. I guess he's tired of me snooping out his secrets. I lean my head back against the edge of the mattress.

"I realized I'm going to die with you and I don't even know your favorite color."

I clap my hand over my mouth and shake my head. *Way to make everything weird again, FrozenRobot.* As I think about his question, I move my hand from my mouth and pick at the carpet. It's cleaner than the carpet in my and Georgia's room. There are no crushed potato chips or specks of lint hiding in the fibers.

"What?" he says.

"My favorite color isn't going to tell you anything about me."

He scoots closer to me so his shoulder rests against mine. "Fine. Then tell me something about you. I want to know something about you. It doesn't seem right that you're a complete stranger."

"Complete stranger? You know things about me. Hell, your mom is cooking me dinner right now." He gives me a blank stare, so I add, "Turkish food. She's cooking Turkish food for me. Because I'm—"

He waves his hand in the air and cuts me off. "You know what I mean. Not this fake stuff." His eyes widen and he kind of looks like a puppy. A sad puppy. "I want to know something real. Something that not everyone in the world knows about you." His puppy face deepens, his mouth sagging at the corners.

"I can't get to sleep when I have socks on, but my feet are always cold so it's kind of a problem."

I watch his face pull back up into a crooked smile. He

stares at my gray Converse sneakers. "Maddie hated to wear socks."

"Really?"

"Yeah. She always told me that wearing socks made it feel like her feet were suffocating."

"Smart girl."

"She was," he says. And then he rests his head on my shoulder and I'm not sure what I'm supposed to do. I think he's looking for comfort, but I don't have any to give. I awkwardly pin my hands at my sides and hum Mozart's Symphony no. 24.

He doesn't seem to mind, though. He doesn't move away and I can feel his shoulders rise and fall slowly with his breaths. Recently, I've become so much more aware of the things we do that keep us alive—our inhales, our exhales, our heartbeats.

"Can I ask you something without you getting mad?"

"Anything," he says.

"I know you blame yourself for Maddie's death, but do your parents?"

His whole body goes rigid, but he doesn't lift his head from my shoulder. If anything, he leans against me harder, like a slab of wood propped up against a wall. "They're in denial. But I still hear my mom cry every night. She tries to put on such a good face, but I know she's broken inside. And she's broken because of me. So I guess they don't blame me.

At least not actively. But only because I think they're terrified of losing me, too."

My heart constricts. I squeeze my eyes shut and try to forget what Roman just said, but images of his mom flash through my mind. I see her standing over his body—his clothes soaked with river water, his face blue and cold, his mouth open, his tongue swollen from lack of oxygen. Bile builds in the back of my throat and I slide away from him.

His body jerks in response and he sits up. He pulls his knees to his chest, his camping chair pose. People are funny. The longer you are around them, the more you start to realize that everyone makes the same motions over and over again. We all want to believe that every day is different, that every day we change, but really, it seems that certain things are coded into us from the very beginning.

I'm not sure if Roman was always a half-moon smiler and a camp chair sitter. Maybe that happened after Maddie's death. But one thing is for sure: His body is always on alert, like he's walking high above the ground on a trapeze wire. I think his potential energy is guarding him against the pain of his world, saying, *Smile, it will be over soon*, and *Wrap yourself up and you won't feel so much*. Maybe even in death, his energy will live on, and make those gestures. I wonder if those are the things his mom will remember about him, too. Or if she'll picture him on the basketball court, dribbling. Or maybe she'll remember him sprawled out on the couch, sketching pictures, or with his nose in a Jules Verne novel.

I wonder what my energy will do after I die. I wonder if our energy will really outlast us.

He reaches out to touch my arm. "Aysel?"

"Yeah?"

"You look like you drifted away."

"Sorry."

"Okay, well, I've been thinking . . . ," he says.

"Yeah?"

"I want to go to the zoo with you. You should bring me when you go with that other guy."

Before I can respond, Roman's mom calls up to us. "Guys, dinner is ready! Come on down."

He stands up slowly and offers me his hand. I take it and he pulls me up. I know he's waiting for me to tell him about the zoo, but I pretend like it never happened. He mock bows, signaling for me to go down the steps before him.

Roman's mom is waiting for us in the foyer. She grabs my face in her hands and pulls me close. "I'm just so glad you were able to make it. I really hope you enjoy the food."

I should probably tell her I'm not an expert on Turkish cuisine, that I know nothing about it, that she could have cooked me a cheeseburger and it would have passed as authentic. But I sort of like being the center of attention. I'm starting to understand why Georgia thrives on it so much. It's nice having people wait on your every move. I fold the feeling up and tuck it away. I'm glad I got to have it before April 7.

"Aysel," she says, pronouncing my name perfectly, "meet Mr. Franklin." Roman's dad is tall like him, almost bald, with a long, narrow face. He sticks his hand out and I shake it.

"Nice to meet you," he says, and I do my best to look friendly.

"Aysel and Roman met at the old playground," she tells Mr. Franklin, clutching on to his arm.

Mr. Franklin turns to face Roman. "You've been playing ball again?" There's a touch of surprise in his voice. My eyes dart from Mr. Franklin to Roman to Mrs. Franklin and back again. Mr. Franklin might be onto us.

"I'm starving," I say in hopes of avoiding any more questions about how Roman and I met.

"Me too," Mr. Franklin agrees. "Let's eat."

Once we're seated at the table, Roman's mom leads us in prayer. I don't close my eyes, but I notice that Roman does. The whole room smells like oregano and cumin, and my head fills with the image of my father's friend's wife, who cooked dinner for us one night when they'd come to visit. She'd held my face in her hands, much like how Mrs. Franklin did a moment ago, and she'd whispered to me in Turkish. I didn't understand any of it, so I'd pretended she was saying, "Everything will be okay, Aysel. It's all going to work out."

I know now that she probably wasn't saying that. And

even if she had been, she was wrong.

Mrs. Franklin passes a warm casserole dish to me. "This is kuzu güveç." She looks at me as if to ask if her pronunciation was correct. I have no idea, so I weakly nod. "It's sort of like a lamb stew."

The table is crowded with other dishes—stuffed grape leaves, lamb and chicken kebabs, a rice pilaf, and a yogurt sauce. There's also a small dish of jalapeños for Roman. It must have taken her hours and hours to prepare, and it all looks fantastic, but as I stick my fork into the lamb, ready to take a bite, I feel my appetite disappearing. I stare at Mrs. Franklin, her smiling, eager-to-please face, and know that Roman and I are about to break her heart.

This whole dinner, her effort to connect with me, is more than my own mother has ever done. Mrs. Franklin keeps smiling at me, wanting to know my opinion on everything. Her eyes are bright and I recognize the spark in them— hope. She thinks Roman is getting better, that he's made a new friend, that he's showing interest in a girl.

I slide my fork across my plate, pushing the lamb into the rice. I do my best to swallow my guilt.

"This is really good, sweetheart," Mr. Franklin says as he wipes his mouth with his napkin. "I have to admit I was nervous at first." He glances over at me. "Not that I didn't think it would be good, but I've just never had food like this before."

I nod at him to let him know I'm not offended. I don't know enough about Turkish cuisine to have any vested stake in whether Mr. Franklin likes it or not. I wonder what it would be like to actually know something about the place my parents came from.

Mrs. Franklin bobs her head up and down with excitement at Mr. Franklin's compliment. "And you like it too, Aysel?"

"It's delicious," I say like I'm some kind of expert.

"Oh, good." She squeezes her hands together and beams.

I really don't want to break her heart.

SATURDAY, MARCH 23

15 days left

Georgia and I are sitting at the kitchen table and she's peering out the window. I think she's hoping to catch a glimpse of Tyler before we take off.

"Who's the cutie?" She presses her face against the windowpane.

I take a sip of my black coffee. I keep trying to teach myself to like coffee, but no matter how hard I try, I can't get past the bitter taste. "I thought you knew Tyler?"

"Don't mess with me," she says. "That boy isn't Tyler. He's taller and his hair is shorter."

I look out the window and see Mrs. Franklin's red Jeep

pulling out of our driveway. The doorbell rings and I get up to answer the door, but Georgia beats me to it. She flings it open, puts her hands on her hips, and in her sweetest voice says, "Hello, nice to meet you."

"Uh, hi," Roman says as he walks into our house. I've never been embarrassed by anything at Steve's house, mostly because I spend all my time embarrassed about being me, but the second Roman enters, I start noticing everything that is wrong. Our carpet is stained and there's a pile of dirty dishes in the sink. It looks nothing like his immaculate, spotless house.

I know I shouldn't care what he thinks. It's not as if he's going to decide that he doesn't want to jump off the cliff at Crestville Pointe with me because my house is a disaster zone, but I don't like the idea of him feeling sorry for me. I wish the black slug would go ahead and eat my self-consciousness along with my happiness.

He sticks his hand out to greet Georgia like he's a statesman. Southern manners die hard, I guess.

"I'm Roman," he says. "I'm a friend of your sister's."

I'm surprised he was even able to deduce that Georgia was my sister, considering our lack of sibling resemblance. "Half sister," I blurt out before Georgia can say anything.

A flicker of annoyance washes over Georgia's face, but she ignores me and turns her attention back to Roman. She steps closer to him and tugs on the back of her shiny ponytail. "So how do you know Aysel?"

Roman looks down at the floor and shuffles his feet. "We met a few weeks ago at the basketball court out in Willis."

Georgia spins around to face me. "What were you doing in Willis?"

"Why do you care what I do?" I motion for Roman to come take a seat at the kitchen table. "Can I get you anything to drink?"

As I watch his eyes scan the room, I want to put my hands over them and lead him out of our house before he can see anything else. "My mom works," I say, trying to come up with any excuse for why the house is a mess.

"Yeah, she works down at Swift Mart," Georgia adds, skipping into the kitchen. "Six days a week, poor woman."

Poor woman? There are worse things in Mom's life than the fact that she works at Swift Mart. Try: Her first husband is a convicted murderer. Or: Her firstborn daughter is a depressed freak.

"Don't you have somewhere to be? Cheer practice or something?" I ask, opening the refrigerator. Roman didn't answer if he wanted something to drink, but I'm going to give him orange juice anyway. I pour it and put the glass down in front of him.

"Thanks," he says absently. His mind is elsewhere. I notice the glass is foggy with dust. Gross. Sometimes it takes watching someone else observe how you live to realize exactly how you live.

Georgia takes a seat next to him. "I don't have cheer practice today. I was thinking that I might tag along with you guys."

I try not to gape at her. *What?* "Um, but it's for a physics project."

She turns to Roman. "Are you working on the physics project?"

He gives me a slight smile before he says, "Nope. I just like the zoo. The sense of adventure, the animals."

She props her elbows up on the table and grins at me. "I like the zoo, too. And I'm all about adventures."

The doorbell rings again and I walk to the front hallway and open the door. Tyler Bowen is standing on the doorstep, his hands shoved in his pockets, wearing a white baseball cap that shades his blue eyes. "Hey, Aysel."

"Want to come in for a second?"

He shrugs. "Sure." He follows me into the kitchen.

"Tyler!" Georgia springs up from her seat. She darts over to him and gives him a hug.

He returns her hug, squeezing and lifting her off the ground. She giggles, and Roman and I exchange a what-the-hell look.

"What's up?" Tyler says, and I'm not sure if he's asking the entire group, but only Georgia answers.

"I just asked if I could go to the zoo with you guys." She gives Tyler a pleading look, like he can be the tiebreaker between my adamant no and Roman's indifference.

"I didn't know you two hung out," Tyler says to Georgia in a completely serious voice. Now I almost want to give Tyler a hug myself.

"I think Georgia should come," Roman volunteers. And now he's apparently switched his vote from indifferent to yes.

"I'm Tyler, by the way," Tyler says, sticking his hand out to greet Roman. "And you are?"

"Roman." He grips Tyler's hand. Firm. *Way to go, Frozen-Robot.* "I'm a friend of Aysel's."

Tyler tries to hide his shock, but it's obvious to everyone what he's thinking. It's the same thing any of my classmates would think if they saw Roman and me out of context—a good-looking basketball player and the dark girl from school with the murderous father. I guess everyone sees us out of context, though.

"They met at a playground in Willis," Georgia interjects, beaming at Roman.

"I see," Tyler says. "Well, should we get going, since the animals are sleepy later in the day? We need photographs of them moving, right?"

"Are you driving?" Georgia asks.

"Yeah," Tyler says, dangling his keys in the air. "We can all fit in my car."

"I call the front seat!" Georgia says, jumping to her feet.

I run upstairs to our bedroom and dig through my

backpack to find the camera I borrowed from the school library. I find it and put it into a smaller purse I borrow from Georgia's closet. It's baby blue, shaped like a seashell, and made of fake leather. It's not something I would buy in a million years, but it fits the camera perfectly, and who cares about the stupid color. Fashion is the least of my concerns right now.

I sit on the bedroom floor and take a couple of deep breaths, humming Mozart's requiem, mentally preparing myself for what's about to happen. Just as I'm about to head back downstairs, I hear a shuffling behind me.

"Today is going to be interesting," Roman says. *Way to follow me upstairs without an invitation, FrozenRobot.*

"You're telling me. I don't get why you wanted to come in the first place," I say.

He holds out his hand and helps pull me up from the floor. "Don't lie, you're now real glad I decided to come or else you'd have to suffer through the Tyler-Georgia show all by yourself."

"You're the one who told her she could come," I mumble as we walk down the stairs.

"It's better this way." He opens the front door for me.

I grab my jacket off the coat hook and pull the house keys out of the pocket and lock the door. "I doubt it."

"It is," he says. "Trust me."

The air outside is crisp and the sky is clear and you can

smell spring's moist, floral scent in the air. It's a perfect day for the zoo. As we walk toward the car, I look up at Roman. I don't know if it's trust I feel for him. I guess I have to trust that he's going to jump when I do, not that it really matters as long as I go. I know that's an awful thing to think, but that's one thing where the trolls on the internet are maybe right: It's a selfish act. It's all about you, which is what makes the Suicide Partner thing so weird.

You only need your partner. Until you don't.

SATURDAY, MARCH 23

15 days left

We arrive at the zoo after about two hours of driving. The drive wasn't as bad as I thought it was going to be—everyone was pretty quiet, we spent most of the time listening to Georgia hum along with the radio. Occasionally, Tyler would ask her a question and she'd answer him in her animated-Georgia way.

She interrogated Roman and he handled it pretty well. She all but asked him if we were dating and he managed to keep her guessing. Having met his mom, I'd bet he's had a lot of practice at answering rapid-fire questions.

Tyler parks the car and the four of us make our way to

the entrance. We wait in line to buy tickets. There's an awkward moment when I can tell Tyler is considering buying Georgia's ticket for her, but then he'd feel obligated to buy mine, and let's face it: Tyler Bowen doesn't want to waste his money on me.

Roman shoulders past me and hands the woman working at the counter a wad of cash. "Four student tickets, please."

"Roman," Georgia says in fake outrage. "You don't have to do that."

"Seriously, dude," Tyler says. "I can pay for my own ticket. It's no problem."

"Don't worry about it." Roman flashes me a smile. The woman at the counter counts out his change and hands it back to him. I notice that her hands look much older than her face. I look down at my own and don't know if I feel happy or sad that I'll never see them wrinkled.

Once we're inside the zoo, I whisper to Roman, "What was that?"

He shrugs. "You can't take your money with you."

Tyler raises his eyebrows when he sees me leaning in to Roman's ear. "I didn't know you were turning our science project into your personal date."

Georgia loops her arm through Tyler's. "That's why I came along, Ty. Now, you won't feel so left out."

He pets Georgia's arm as he turns his attention to me. "The zoo was your idea, Aysel. Where should we go?"

"Why don't we go to the nocturnal house? We can photograph the bats. They hang upside down. Potential energy."

"Right. Bats are like living hangmen," Tyler says, an edge to his voice. Roman and Georgia give Tyler questioning looks, and I do my best to also act confused. Which turns out to be pretty easy since bats are nothing like living hangmen, but now doesn't seem like the appropriate time to push the subject with Tyler.

"It's this way," I say, and dart ahead of the group. I basically have the Louisville Zoo memorized. When I was younger, Mom used to take me here on the weekends a lot. She thought it was good for me to have alone time with her. She gave up on that when I was about eight since Georgia was getting older and Mike was a handful of a toddler. She'd never admit it, but she was busy building her new family and happy to leave me to my father. It took him finally snapping for her to really notice me again. And no one wants to be noticed because of something like that; it's like being an invasive species that no one pays any attention to until you've strangled and ruined all the beautiful native plants.

The inside of the nocturnal house is how I remember it. It's dark and smells like rotting fruits and vegetables. I hear Georgia giggling behind me, which must mean the group managed to keep up with my quick pace. I rush past the cages of opossums and raccoons and find the vampire bats. When I reach the exhibit, I see the bats hanging from the ceiling, their black, leathery wings wrapped around their bodies.

Roman comes up behind me and puts his hand on my shoulder. I jump.

"It's just me," he says.

"I know." *And that's exactly why I'm skittish.* I pull the camera out of the purse.

"Thanks for asking if you could borrow my purse," Georgia says.

"You should really keep your voice down," I say. "You don't want to scare the animals."

Georgia glares at me and she curls her upper lip, her white teeth glinting in the dark room. "That's funny. You telling someone else not to be scary."

"Georgia," Tyler hisses at her.

"What?" she says as she tosses her head back. Her barb lingers in the air like smoke from a bonfire.

"Uh," Roman says, shifting his weight from his right foot to his left. "How about we just let Aysel take the photo?"

"Fine," Georgia says. "Let's leave her to it. Wanna go see the armadillos? They're so cute!"

"Sure. Whatever you want," Roman says, and they head down the hall.

I turn the camera on and look through the viewfinder. I snap a few photos and then scroll through the images. "Here," I say, holding the camera out to Tyler. "I think this is a good one."

"Yeah, I think Mr. Scott will like it," Tyler answers.

Too bad I won't be around to see his reaction. I shove the camera back into my purse. "So should we go meet them by the armadillos?"

"She just wants to be your friend, you know," Tyler says.

I close the purse with so much force that I almost break the zipper. "Um. I don't think so."

"Yes, she does. That's why she came today."

"Right."

"It's pretty obvious." I give him a blank stare and he continues, "She's always trying to get your attention, trying to make you laugh. She's not so bad, you know?"

As we walk down the dark hallway in search of the armadillos, I consider what Tyler said about Georgia wanting to be my friend. I'm pretty sure it's complete bullshit. Georgia came to try to cozy up to Tyler. Dating Tyler Bowen would skyrocket her social standing: freshman cheerleader dates junior basketball player. It's like an awful teen movie. "I think you're wrong about the reason she came today," I say. "It's not me. It's you."

As we approach the armadillos, I see Roman and Georgia standing right next to each other, pressed up against the glass. They're peering at the animals and laughing like they're old friends.

"I'm not so sure I'm the one she's interested in." Tyler gives my shoulder a nudge.

I roll my eyes at him. "She can have Roman." I don't say, *But good luck with that because he'll be dead in a few weeks.*

Roman grins when he sees us. "Where to next?"

"The lions?" I suggest. "I think they feed them around noon. If we hurry, I can get a shot of them eating."

"I'm really thirsty," Georgia says. She turns to Roman. "Want to go with me to get a lemonade?"

Roman looks at me and I shrug. "You can meet us by the lions."

"I'm actually thirsty," Tyler says. "I'll go with you."

Georgia slightly frowns. "Oh, okay."

"Then I'll go with Aysel," says Roman, and he walks over to stand beside me. "We'll catch up with you guys soon."

Once Georgia and Tyler are gone, I say, "Aw, you missed your chance to make out with Georgia by the concession stand!"

"I thought you promised you were going to stop making stupid jokes."

I give him my you-caught-me face. We leave the nocturnal house and head toward the lions. When we get outside, I notice that the sky has darkened and the sun is hiding behind some scary-looking rain clouds. I tuck my hands into the pockets of my jacket and run my fingers over the fleece lining. "That wasn't a joke. I'm pretty sure she wants to eat your face."

"The two of you are nothing alike. What's up with that?"

I stare straight ahead, not making eye contact with him. "We don't have the same dad."

"Yeah, you said she was your half sister, but still. She's like a lion and you're like . . . an armadillo."

"An armadillo?"

He touches my shoulder. "You know what I'm trying to say."

"My dad." I give him a hard look, hoping he'll drop the subject. "I don't expect you to understand, but he makes all the difference."

We reach the lions. Only three of them are visible, and it doesn't look like they're eating. Damn. We must have missed feeding time. The male lion is lounging on a large rock and the two females are huddled together in the opposite corner of the fenced enclosure. The male lion opens his mouth to yawn and a little kid near us jumps up and down with excitement. Another kid, who's apparently not as brave, tucks himself into his mom. I reach for my camera and wish I'd had it out in time to capture the moment.

"Where's your dad now?" Roman asks.

The answer to Roman's question is state prison. As far as I know, my dad's locked up in some podunk town, miles and miles away from me.

"Away. Gone," I say, and snap a few photos of the lions. Maybe one of them will be usable. "Just drop it, okay?"

Roman reaches his hand out and presses it against the

back of my wrist. "I don't understand how someone who's not in your life anymore can make all the difference."

I walk away from his touch, away from the lion enclosure, and take a seat on a bench. Roman follows me. "Look, I'm sorry. I'll let it go."

I drop my elbows to my knees and hunch over. "I know it's hard to understand, but it's true. My dad . . ." I take a breath. "My dad ruined my whole life."

I don't tell Roman that my dad not only ruined my life because of what he did, but also because he made me scared of what I am, what I'm made of.

As I think about this, something inside me shifts. I don't know if it's the black slug sliding around in the base of my stomach or something new, something I didn't even know was there, but I feel it crackle and burst, like a tiny sparkler inside of me.

"I should go visit him," I blurt out before I remember that I shouldn't keep talking about my dad with Roman. That Roman knows Brian Jackson. That Roman would hate me if he knew the truth.

Roman clears his throat. "What?"

I bounce up from the bench. "I've decided I want to see my dad one last time before I die."

Roman doesn't get up. When I bring myself to look at him, he's frowning. "You aren't dying from cancer, Aysel," he says, raising his voice. "You aren't terminally ill."

"What is that supposed to mean?"

"We aren't making wish lists. This isn't about doing things we want to do before we die. This is and has always been about dying. Only about dying." He shuffles his feet and wrings his hands. "Are you bailing on me?"

Blood rushes to my face. "I'm not bailing on you. I just need to see him one last time. I want to look him in the eye and . . ."

Roman gets up from the bench. He puts his arm around me, and this time I don't jump at his touch. I lean into his body. "And what? What are you hoping to find? It sounds to me like you are looking for reasons to live."

My throat is tight and all these words line up ready to spill out, but the black slug devours them one by one. "That's not it," I manage to squeak out.

"Then what is it?"

"I just need to see him, Roman. I think if I see him, I'll be able to jump from that cliff. Nothing will be holding me back."

He tilts his head toward the sky. "And right now something is?"

I don't know how to tell him that I'm not sure I can truly destroy my potential energy until I understand the root of it all. And as of a couple of minutes ago, I'm convinced the only way to do that is to see my dad one last time.

Roman lowers his chin to look at me again. "We can go

see your father. If this is what you need, I'll help you with it."

Part of me wants to toss my arms around his neck and pull him close, press my face against his chest and thank him, but I know for sure that isn't what he or I signed up for. I wish someone would give my heart a polygraph; it keeps lying and flipping and changing its mind. I can't decide what matters more to me—Roman being there with me to face my father or Roman not discovering the truth.

As I watch him watching me, his hazel eyes wide and wanting, a slight shiver ripples across my chest. Maybe I'm naive, but I'm starting to think that Roman would understand. That he wouldn't hold me accountable for what my dad did. Maybe I need to give him the chance to prove he really is different from everyone else.

I scan his face, searching for any sign that he already knows. My name isn't mentioned in the internet articles about my dad (believe me, I've checked), but I'm pretty sure a basic Google search would've given him an inkling. There aren't that many Turkish people in Langston, let alone in Kentucky. But as I stare up at his deep-set eyes, his full lips, his cheeks that are slightly flushed from the sun, I don't find any clues that he knows. All I see is someone who seems to care, and that makes me almost as uneasy as the fact that he could discover everything about my dad at any moment.

Maybe it would be better if I told him, if he heard it from me instead of from someone else. The words form in the base of my throat and I'm about to tell him everything when he stretches his hand out and grabs mine. He squeezes it, massaging my fingers with his. "It's seriously okay, Aysel. I'm sorry I yelled before. We'll go see your dad together, okay?"

"Okay," is the only word I manage to utter. I press my tongue up against the roof of my mouth and make a small promise that I will tell him the truth about my dad. Not today, but sometime soon.

He squeezes my hand again. "So what's next?"

"Wanna go see the polar bears? I should take some pictures of them swimming."

"Sure." He flashes me his half-moon smile. "It'll be nice to see the polar bears one last time. The polar bears were always Maddie's favorite."

That's when I wonder if maybe FrozenRobot has a list of things he wants to do before he dies, too, and he just doesn't know it yet.

I want to know it.

TUESDAY, MARCH 26

12 days left

I get off work early and drive as fast as I can. My plan is to beat everyone home before dinner so I will have a few moments alone to poke around in the study. If my mom's saved anything about my dad, I'll find it in there.

I open the front door and stand in the hallway for a moment, holding my breath, hoping I'm the only one here.

"Hello?" I hear Mike call out.

"Mike, it's just me," I say softly, not wanting to make my presence known if someone else is home with him.

"What are we having for dinner?" His loud voice practically shakes the whole house. Mike inherited Steve's vocal cords. If I didn't love him so much, I might be irritated.

"I don't know, Mikey. Mom will be home soon. You can ask her, okay?"

"Okay," he answers. "Do you wanna come up and play FIFA with me?"

My lips twitch and I fight the urge to smile. "Maybe later. I have lots of homework."

"Okay." I can hear the disappointment in his voice.

I do my best to shrug it off and focus on the task at hand: snooping through Mom's stuff. I walk down the narrow hallway and turn the corner into the study. It's cramped and cluttered, hardly bigger than a closet. I hop over a few boxes so I can get behind the flimsy plastic desk.

I crane my neck to examine the boxes on the upper shelves of the bookcase. If I know my mother at all, which admittedly is questionable, she'd store our family's dirty laundry in the most inaccessible place.

Standing on the computer chair, I reach for one of the cardboard boxes filled with manila folders. The chair swivels under my feet. As I stretch my fingers out, grasping for the box, I lose my balance and manage to knock two of the boxes and some books to the floor.

I fall off the chair with a thud and press my palms into the worn carpet to break my fall. My wrists burn and I see papers scattered all over the carpet. *Fuck*.

"Aysel?"

I look up and see Mike standing in front of me. *Double fuck.*

He's clutching his video game controller to his chest and his mouth gapes open. "Are you okay?"

"Yeah, sorry about the noise." I wave my hands in the direction of the scattered papers. "I lost my balance."

He narrows his eyes. "What are you looking for?"

I crawl on my knees and start picking up the papers and shoving them randomly back into the boxes. *So much for Mom's organized study.* One of the papers catches my eye. It's an old report card of mine from fourth grade. I pick it up and run my fingers over the thin paper. I'm surprised she saved it.

"Aysel," Mike says, his voice escalating in volume. "Why are you going through Mom's things?"

I hold up my old report card. "Oh, sorry. I, uh, was looking for some old stuff of mine from school. You know, for college applications."

"Why do you keep saying sorry?" He passes the video game controller to his left hand and runs his right hand through his blond wavy hair. He always touches his hair when he's nervous or uncomfortable.

I do my best to brighten my face. "Because I scared you."

He gives me a toothy grin. "You didn't scare me."

I force myself to smile. "Hey, you wanna go back upstairs?"

He frowns. "I can't help you look?"

"I think Mom would be mad if I let you play around in here."

He juts out his lower lip. "I wouldn't be playing, I'd be helping you."

"I know, but she doesn't want you in here."

He sighs. "Fine."

As he walks away, I say, "Hey, Mikey?"

"Yeah?"

"Can you do me a favor?"

"Depends. What is it?"

"Don't tell Mom I was in here."

"So it's like a secret?" he asks excitedly.

"Yeah, our secret."

"Cool. Come up and play later?"

I bob my head enthusiastically. It hurts my neck. I'm not used to moving it so fast. "For sure."

Once he's gone, I go back to picking up the papers. I find all sorts of things. Old birthday cards, bills, credit reports. I would say there's no rhyme or reason to the way things are ordered, but I probably destroyed the organizational system when I accidentally dumped out the boxes.

I'm about to give up hope when I come across an envelope. It's empty, but the return address catches my eye: McGreavy Correctional Facility. That must have been about my dad. *McGreavy Correctional Facility, that's where he is.* I'm crawling around, searching for the corresponding letter, when I hear the door open.

"Hello?" Mike bellows.

"It's me, sweetie," I hear Mom answer.

I quickly finish shoving all the loose papers back into the boxes. I'm about to try to put them on the upper shelf when I hear footsteps behind me.

"Aysel, what are you doing in here?"

I turn and face my mom. She's dressed in her work uniform—a red polo and pressed khaki pants. Or the khaki pants are supposed to be pressed. Hers are a bit wrinkled and beginning to fray. I notice that her shoes are old and scuffed. Maybe once I'm gone and there's one less kid to worry about, she'll be able to cut back on her hours. Or at least afford to buy herself some new shoes.

"Looking for something for my college applications."

The look on my mom's face shreds my insides. It's warm and full of hopeful surprise. "Really?"

"Yeah, I needed to check to see if I got an A or B in freshman bio." Her mouth pulls into a thin line like she isn't quite convinced, so I continue, "You know, because that, my grades, they'll determine what schools I apply to."

She looks hard at me and brings her fingers to her lips. "Isn't there someone at your school who can help you with that?"

"Yeah, but I was too curious to wait." The lie makes my

tongue feel thick as I watch Mom's face brighten all over again.

"Well, did you find what you were looking for?" She eyes the boxes like she knows their contents are all mixed up.

"Yup." I step in front of them to try to block her view. "Sorry for getting them down. I'll put the boxes back on the shelf."

She shakes her head. "No. You could hurt yourself. I'll have Steve put them back when he gets home."

She hovers in the doorway and I can tell she's waiting for me to walk out with her. I move to join her in the hallway and she flicks off the light in the study. We walk in silence to the kitchen and then I excuse myself to go upstairs.

Once I'm in my room, I flop on the bed and try to erase the image of my mom's bright, hopeful face from my mind. Pulling the comforter over my head, I sink down into the mattress. I place my hands on my stomach and urge the black slug to remind me that Mom will be better off when I'm gone. Safer. That what'll happen on April 7 is the best thing for her in the end.

How it's the best thing for everyone. Especially me.

WEDNESDAY, MARCH 27

Today at work we're conducting a phone marathon for the town of Langston. Every year at the end of March, Langston throws a carnival in the backyard of the middle school to raise money. (Mostly for the basketball program, but the Langston Public School District puts on a good face and claims they are using the money to beef up our science and math programs.) They always cart in a few low-grade rides—a Ferris wheel and spinning teacups—set up concession stands that sell sticky cotton candy and extra-sugary sodas, and have the cheer team perform a few risqué dance routines. The creepy middle-aged men of Langston really love the Spring Carnival.

I pick up the phone's receiver and dial the next number on my call log: John Gordon, who lives at 415 Mound Street. Maybe John is the demographic that will already be at the Spring Carnival, and so he won't even need reminding. It rings twice before John picks up. No such luck.

"Hello?" His accent is spot-on Kentucky.

"Hello, Mr. Gordon," I say. "My name is Aysel, and I'm calling from Tucker's Marketing Concepts on behalf of the city of Langston."

"Yes?" He sounds a little impatient, but he's less irate than the usual voice I find on the other end of the phone.

"As you may know, the city is hosting its annual Spring Carnival." I deliver my spiel about how the proceeds raised by the carnival provide invaluable funds for Langston's schools. I gush about the cheerleaders' upcoming performances and how fun and safe (yeah, right) the Ferris wheel is. I end with the mandated final line, "It's a great time for people of all ages. A real family-friendly event." I obviously don't mention that the cheerleaders normally wear leopard-print bikini tops and dance around outside, even though it's barely over fifty degrees.

There's silence on the other end of the phone.

"Mr. Gordon?"

"Yeah, I know the Spring Carnival," he says. "My family's planning to go tomorrow afternoon."

"Great. Thank you, Mr. Gordon." The one thing that

can be said for the people of Langston is that they tend to show up for Langston.

Today at work, I'm more focused than usual. I want to get through my call log. Really, I just want my shift to be over. I've recently noticed that if I actually work at work, the time goes by faster. After I've called about six people in a row, I look over at Laura. Her brow is furrowed and she keeps blinking.

"What?" I ask, and reach for the phone receiver to dial my next number.

"You're just weird today." She gets up and heads to the coffee maker. "It's almost like you're happy. Did you finally meet someone?"

I laugh and it comes out as a dry rattle. *Happy?* The sad thing is, she's not that far off base. I did meet someone. But not in the way she thinks. "It's weird that I'm working?"

She nods. "Very weird."

"Just trying to make you proud, Laura." I give her a fake salute and she shakes her head.

Two minutes before my shift ends, I open up the internet browser. I haven't goofed around all day, so I feel like I've totally earned this free time. I search the web for McGreavy Correctional Facility's phone number. It takes me a minute, but eventually I find the number I'm looking for. I scribble it down on the legal notepad next to my desk and then rip the paper off the pad and fold it up and slide it into my pocket.

I get up out of my seat and fling my backpack over my

shoulders. On my way out, I wave to Mr. Palmer. He looks like he might have a heart attack.

"Bye, Aysel," he says weakly.

Like Laura pointed out, I know I seem to be in a better mood, but I'm not sure if I'm really in a better mood or if it's a trick my mind is playing on me. Like I know it's all going to be over soon so there's no need to be anxious about things anymore. I have everything planned out. I know exactly how I want to spend my last days, and that sense of purpose is comforting.

I used to feel so devastated thinking about the length of days, about how time seems to stretch on forever, unforgiving and unchanging. And like John Berryman said, so boring. I wonder if this is how marathon runners feel once they reach the last mile; they know they can make it through the final stretch, so there's no use in getting fatigued at this point.

I toss my backpack into the passenger seat and then climb into the front seat. I unzip the front pocket of my backpack and grab my cell phone. I pull the folded notepad sheet out of my pocket. I take a deep breath and then dial the number.

I call unknown numbers all the time at work so this shouldn't make me nervous, but I feel my heart racing and so I turn on the classical radio station ever so slightly. Bach's Mass in B Minor pours out of the speakers, and as I listen to the music, it feels like someone wrapped a blanket around my shoulders. I adjust the volume so it's not too loud in case someone at McGreavy Correctional Facility eventually decides to answer the phone.

Kicking my legs up on the dashboard, I fold the driver's seat back so I can lie flat. I'm humming along with the music, tapping my fingers against the torn fabric seat, when I'm startled by a voice on the other end.

"This is Tom. How can I help you?"

I lurch forward in my seat. "Is this McGreavy Correctional Facility?"

"Yes," he says with an aggravated sigh.

"I'm calling because I'm looking for information on how I can visit my father."

"Huh?"

"My father. He's an . . ." I search for the word. "Inmate there."

"Ah," Tom says. I guess Tom is a man of one-syllable answers. "Lemme transfer you over to Visiting."

Before I can say anything, the phone line goes blank and the cheesy elevator holding music comes back on. I turn the volume up on my car radio.

After not too long, a new voice greets me. "This is Bob." McGreavy Correctional Facility employees aren't only into one-syllable answers, they're also into one-syllable names.

"Hi, Bob," I say, trying to seem friendly so he'll help me. "I was calling to get some information on how I can visit my dad."

"Your dad's locked up here?"

"Yeah," I say, trying to sound like it's no big deal, like I'm down with the prison system or something.

"And you're on the list?"

"What?"

"His visiting list. If you're his daughter, you should be on the list."

I gulp. "I don't know if I'm on the list." Mom's never let me visit Dad. Not even once.

"Well, if you aren't on the list, there's nothing I can do to help you. But my guess would be that you're on it. When people get locked up, they tend to put their immediate family on the list as a default. In case any of them ever want to visit."

"Okay," I say slowly. "So I just show up?"

He makes a sound that's somewhere between a laugh and a snort. "Yeah. You just show up during visiting hours. It's a first-come, first-serve basis. If all the visiting booths are filled when you get here, you'll have to get on the waiting list. And I can't make any guarantees about the waiting list."

So many lists. "When are visiting hours?"

"Girl," Bob says, and I can practically hear him shaking his head. "All this info is on our web page. But because I like you, I'll tell you."

Looks like the friendliness paid off. "Thank you so much, Bob."

"So Tuesday through Saturday we have visiting hours.

We have a morning session that runs ten a.m. to twelve p.m. And an afternoon session that runs one p.m. to four p.m. And want a tip?"

"I'd love one, Bob."

"Try to get here as early as you can. You'll have better luck that way. System can get jammed toward the end of the day."

"I really appreciate it. I'll see you Saturday."

"Yeah, okay." Bob hangs up first.

I adjust my car seat so I can sit straight up, but I don't drive away from TMC. My head feels crowded and over-whelmed with competing thoughts. I cradle it in my hands and take deep breaths. After a few minutes, I pick up my phone again and call FrozenRobot. I know it's stupid, but I can't help myself. I want to share my thoughts with someone, and he's the only person I could possibly talk to. I guess this is another reason why people have Suicide Partners. They come in handy.

"Hey," Roman says.

"Hey, what are you up to?"

No answer.

"Just hanging out in your room?" I prompt.

"What else would I be doing?"

"I don't know. Playing basketball."

I imagine him glaring at me. Him, flopped on his back on the cotton comforter, his golden-green eyes narrowed, a pencil in his hand, balancing a sketch pad against his knees. I picture Captain Nemo telling him to chill out and that only making him angrier. I guess I laugh because Roman says, "Please cut it out."

"Okay, I'll stop. I promise," I say quickly.

"You keep saying that and you don't stop. It's starting to get really annoying."

I dig my fingernails into the car's seat. I don't want to be annoying to FrozenRobot. I know I shouldn't care what I am to him. But a small part of me kind of does.

"Sorry," Roman says in a low voice. "I shouldn't have said that."

"No, it's okay. I deserved it."

"No you didn't."

I pause for a moment. The line is silent and all I can hear is his shallow breath. I want to ask if he's drawing, but I don't. "Can I come pick you up?"

"Why would you do that?"

I inhale sharply and try to come up with an excuse to see him. My mind swirls and I remember all my phone calls from today. "I was thinking we could go to the Langston Spring Carnival."

"Have you gone completely insane?"

"Is that a yes?" I tease, and then quickly correct my tone. "I mean, you are the one who said that it was going to be easier for you to sneak away on the seventh if your mom really believed we were close friends."

"True, but I still don't get why you want to go to the carnival."

"I'll be there in fifteen minutes," I say, and hang up.

And he's right. By all standards, by my own standards, I should want to avoid the carnival. But the closer we get to April 7, the more reckless I feel.

The truth is, the Spring Carnival is one of the last places I can remember being truly happy. I don't know how old I was when I first realized that the black slug inside of me would inevitably eat any and every positive thought of mine. But I do know that the last time I was at the carnival, my little hand interlocked with my dad's, my happiness didn't disappear.

It stayed.

11 days left

I text him when I'm in front of his house and within seconds FrozenRobot is walking toward my car. The hood of his blue sweatshirt is pulled over his ears and he's hunched over, like he's trying to hide from some invisible enemy.

Once he's inside the car and I've turned to pull away from his street, he says, "So why are we are going to the carnival?"

"I thought I was doing you a favor. Your mom will be really excited that you're out doing normal social things."

He bangs his head back against the headrest. "Yeah, you said that on the phone. I'm asking why *you* want to go to the carnival."

I glance over at him. His jaw is clenched and his eyes are downcast. He doesn't look like he's in the mood for any nonsense. *No need to be so angry, FrozenRobot.* "Okay, fine. I'll level with you. I called McGreavy Correctional Facility." I pause. "That's where my dad is, by the way. He's locked away there. And anyway, I wanted to tell you what I found out about the possibility of visiting him."

He lifts his chin and stares straight ahead out the windshield. He doesn't seem to have any reaction to my confession that my dad is locked away in prison. It's like I just told him my dad flips pancakes at the local diner or something. "Did you hear me? My dad's an inmate at McGreavy Correctional Facility."

Roman doesn't look over at me. He keeps staring out the windshield. "Couldn't you have just told me that on the phone?"

I shrug even though I know he's not watching me. It's funny the things we do even though no one is watching. "Well, yeah. But I thought it might be fun to go to the carnival and then I could tell you in person."

"Fun?" He spits the word out in the same way he spit "friends" out on the first day I met him. He finally turns to look at me. "Who are you?"

I press my foot against the gas pedal and stare straight ahead, doing my best not to show how hurt I am by his tone. I don't answer his question because I'm not sure I even know the answer anymore. We drive the rest of the way in silence.

Once we get to the carnival, I park my car in the muddy lot across from Langston Middle School. We walk side by side to the entrance and I buy tickets for the both of us. It's the least I can do considering I made him come with me and he paid for me at the zoo.

On the gates leading into the main ground, someone's hung five large banners, all of which feature Brian Jackson. I sneak a glance at Roman and see him studying the photographs. The inside of my mouth is dry, but I force myself to speak. "When's the last time you two talked?"

He shrugs. "A while ago. I don't really know the guy anymore." I may be paranoid, actually I know I'm paranoid, but it sounds like there's something lurking just beneath the surface of Roman's voice. Like he knows something that he doesn't want me to know he knows.

"Were you really as fast as him?" I think back to the first time I met Roman, when his friends Lance and Travis boasted about his athletic skills.

Roman lets out a cold laugh. "No. Bri was always way faster." He turns from the banner to me, a sly grin on his face. "But I could dribble circles around him."

A shallow wave of relief washes over me. Maybe what I sensed in Roman's voice wasn't judgment about my dad. Maybe he still really doesn't know. Maybe it was just jealousy, a reminder of how much his life has changed since

Maddie died. I'm about to ask more questions, but Roman nods his head in the direction of the carnival. "So are we going to go in or what?"

I hand him his ticket. "Yeah. Let's go."

The carnival is already crowded. Younger kids dart by us, chasing after one another, their hands sticky with cotton candy and their lips dyed blue from drinking one too many slushies. My heart drops into my stomach. I miss being that age. Before I completely realized that there was something seriously wrong with my dad, that there was something seriously wrong with me.

Roman places his hand on the small of my back. I can't quite figure FrozenRobot out. For someone who can be so cold, he's awfully handsy. "You okay?"

"Just memories," I say. The ground is soft beneath my feet and my sneakers sink into the mud. The whole place smells like popcorn and fried food and dirt.

He nods and takes his hand off my back. "Maddie loved this carnival."

I don't know what to say, so I make a lame suggestion. "Want to ride the Ferris wheel?"

He shrugs. "Sure. Why not?"

We wait in line. I see a few other kids from my class. I wonder if they're here to watch my sister's performance. I should probably go to that. Even though my presence would likely hurt more than it would help. It always does.

I see Stacy Jenkins lean into Nate Connors and whisper to him. I imagine she's saying something about me. I bite down on the side of my cheek and do my best to ignore them.

Roman glances at me and seems to sense me tensing up. "What's wrong? Do you have a problem with—"

I cut him off. "Don't worry about it."

He turns around and gives Stacy and Nate a dirty look. If they weren't already whispering about me, this really makes them take notice. I hate the feeling of their eyes on the back of my neck like I'm a target they can't wait to hit. I wrap my arms around myself and try to tune it all out. I hum Mozart's requiem, slowly rocking back and forth on the balls of my feet. I don't want Roman to engage my classmates in a conversation about me. If they start talking, he'll definitely figure out who my dad is. I can't think of a worse way for him to find out.

We reach the front of the line and a man who maybe has half his teeth left motions for us to get into the next car. We hop in and slowly start to leave the ground.

"You really think visiting your dad is going to help you?" Roman asks. He's looking at me instead of at the ground below, missing the entire point of riding the Ferris wheel.

"I don't know if it'll help. But I need to know some things."

I gaze out at the concession stands and game booths that

are becoming tinier and tinier. I wonder if dying is like that. Everything in your mind becomes tinier and tinier until it all disappears.

"What things?" Roman presses. "You said that seeing him again won't change your mind about . . . you know." His hands jump on his lap. I think about telling him that he should be comfortable enough with the topic of death now to just say it, but I let it go. The last thing I need is to pick another fight with him.

"Look," I say, my voice rising in volume. "My dad was an awful guy, right? He did an unimaginable, horrific thing. I just want to know why he did it."

"But why? If it doesn't matter anyway, why do you need to know?" His voice is soft and calm. No pressure. No judgment.

I'm overwhelmed with the urge to hug FrozenRobot. I love that his question isn't what my dad did. He isn't interested in the gory details. I stare at his broad shoulders and imagine my face pressed up against his chest. I can't let myself think like that, so I shift my eyes to the ground, zeroing in on the soft-pretzel stand. My dad loved soft pretzels. He used to joke that they were one of the best things about life in America. He'd buy a cinnamon-sugar one for me and a cheddar-cheese-and-onion one for him. We'd stroll around the festival, pretzels in hand, pointing at the different rides and debating which ones we should check out. And in those rare moments, I felt at home.

"Hey, wake up." Roman taps my shoulder and waves his hand in front of my face.

"Sorry. I guess I spaced out. I like looking at the ground below. I like watching everything get smaller."

"Right, but you still haven't answered my question. I want to understand, Aysel. I really do. But I don't. If you're going to jump with me on April seventh, why does it matter why your dad did what he did?"

I bite my thumbnail and force myself to think about the weeks leading up to my father's crime. He'd been on edge, even more than usual. He was convinced he was losing money because kids were shoplifting, pocketing candy bars and magazines when he wasn't looking. I remember one day I bounded into the store after school and found him sitting behind the counter, maniacally leafing through papers. He looked up at me with bloodshot eyes. "I try and I try, Zellie. But I just don't know if it's going to be enough." Part of me wanted to run far away from those eyes, but I swallowed my fear and joined him behind the counter. I put my arms around him and pressed my nose into the fabric of his shirt, which always smelled like garlic. After a few moments, he started to hum a piece from Bach's Brandenburg Concerto no. 1.

I squeeze my eyes shut. Sometimes I can still hear my dad's low voice in my ear. "I don't know, Roman." I sigh and open my eyes. "But he raised me, you know? I just need some closure."

Our car comes to a stop at the bottom and we jump out of it. Roman drapes his arm around my shoulder and pulls me close to him. "As long as you aren't flaking out."

"I told you, I'm not a flake."

"That's my girl."

My heart jumps a little when he says that and I remind myself to get a grip. Anyway, Roman's wrong: I'm not flaking out or looking for reasons to live. I'm looking to validate my reasons for dying. But when I glance up at his face and see the dark shadows under his eyes, I'm not sure if it's him or me I'm trying to convince of that. *I'm not a flake*, I repeat mentally to myself. *I'm not a flake. This is what I want.*

"What's going on with you?" Roman frowns.

"Nothing," I say, and I wish that were the case. "So can you go with me this Saturday?"

"To visit your dad?"

"Yeah."

"Sure, I guess," he says. "I'll have to come up with something to tell my mom so I can get away."

"Okay. I'll pick you up Saturday morning. Probably pretty early. Does that work?"

He shrugs. "Just text me."

"Okay."

We stand in silence for a few awkward moments. "Well,

you dragged me here. We might as well try to have some fun." He says the word "fun" like it's a foreign word, a joke.

He steers me toward the mini basketball game stand. He hands the worker some rumpled bills and she gives him a basketball. I don't recognize the woman, but she's probably one of my classmates' moms. She gives me a look like she knows who I am and who my dad is, but she doesn't say anything.

He holds the basketball in his hands and eyes the hoop. I write the physics practice question in my head, trying to calculate the potential energy of the ball. Roman puts the ball down on the edge of the booth and looks at me. "You're doing it again, aren't you?"

"What?" I cross my arms over my chest. The woman working at the booth raises her eyebrows at me. I can tell she's one of those moms that gets off on teenage drama. Great.

"Your science nerd thing. You're always thinking about physics."

My cheeks burn. "How did you know?"

His face lights up with his familiar crooked smile. "You had the same face you made when you were taking photos at the zoo. Like you're really concentrating on something." He turns back to the basketball hoop and takes the shot. Swoosh. It goes through the net effortlessly. FrozenRobot has game.

The woman running the booth holds up one thin finger

to indicate he scored a point. *Thanks for that. We can count to one. We're suicidal, not innumerate.* I nod at her to let her know we understand.

Roman turns the ball over in his hands. "I like that thinking look, though. It's cute."

I can't help but laugh. I don't think anyone in the entire history of my life has ever referred to me as cute. Even when I was little, I was always "unique"—code for not looking like everyone else in Langston—or "sweet"—code for being quiet and unassuming—but never cute.

"What?" He crouches down slightly and thrusts the ball into the air again. It bounces against the rim, but ends up falling through the net. I hold two fingers up at the woman and she gives me a weak smile.

"Yup," she says. Her southern accent is heavy and thick. "He's made two and he has two more left."

Roman studies the different stuffed animals. There are rows and rows of pink pandas and fluorescent-orange tigers. I even spot a few blue elephants. "What can I win?" he asks.

She bounces up, straightening her posture, and does her best game show host impression as she stretches her arm out in front of her, making a sweeping motion in the direction of the stuffed elephants and pandas and tigers. "If you make all four shots, you can pick whatever one you want."

"Even that huge lion?" Roman asks, craning his neck so he can get a better look at the giant lion that sits at the very top. Its mane looks like it'd be really itchy if you pressed your face to it, but it's impressive looking nonetheless.

She smiles wide at me. "Including the lion. Is that the one you want?"

"Me?" I blink at her.

"Yeah. He's winning the prize for you, sweetheart. Isn't he?" She makes a clucking sound. I've never understood why women from Langston love to do that. I guess they feel some kind of strange affinity with the chicken population.

"I don't think so." I slip my hands into the pockets of my black jeans and shift my weight from my right foot to my left.

Roman pretends like he didn't hear her comment. He prepares to make his next shot. As I watch Roman—his face pulled in concentration, his deep-set eyes wide and eager, his ropy arm muscles tensed—I wonder if he sees something similar to that when he watches me think about physics. Sure, he still looks pretty miserable, pretty FrozenRobot-ish. But yet, there's something there, like the shadows that sometimes sneak their way into the frame of a picture. Part of me wants to reach out and grab it, bring it into focus.

All of a sudden, I realize what that shadowy something is. It's joy. FrozenRobot loves basketball. He loves playing it. No matter how hard he tries to push that joy away, it's there. I wonder if joy has potential energy. Or if there is potential energy that leads to joy, like a happiness serum that lingers in people's stomachs and slowly bubbles up to create the sensation we know as happiness.

If that's true, my black slug eats all of mine. Scratch that. Most of mine. Watching FrozenRobot play basketball has almost made me smile. Key word: almost.

He nails the third shot and the fourth shot. I've hardly been paying attention to the actual shots. I like his process of preparing for them more than the actual moment. The moment goes by too fast; it's almost impossible to catch.

"So what will it be?" the woman asks. I notice she has mulberry-colored lipstick smudged on her front tooth.

"Whatever the lady wants," Roman says, and I'm completely caught off guard.

The woman with the lipstick-stained tooth turns to me. "The lion, then?"

Any words I had are all jumbled in my throat. FrozenRobot should not be winning me prizes at the carnival. The last thing I need is more stuff to leave behind. The last thing I need is to feel more confused. I shake my head at the lady. "I don't want anything."

She frowns, and Roman nudges his shoulder up against mine. "C'mon, Aysel. You have to choose one. I won."

"I know," I sputter. "It's just I want something else."

The woman's frown deepens. "These are the only prizes we have available, hon."

I shake my head again, harder this time. "No, no. I don't

want a different prize, I just want you to give the prize he won to someone else."

The woman raises her eyebrows in confusion.

I try my best to explain. "Like if another kid comes to play but doesn't make any shots. Can you let them have a prize anyway?" I bite my bottom lip.

The woman puts her hands on her hips. "But how will I know what kid to give it to?"

I shrug. "Give it to the one who looks like they need it the most, whoever looks like the loneliest."

Her nose twitches as she considers this, and then she gives me a small smile. "Okay, darling. Whatever you want. You're going to make some little kid's day."

"That giant lion is going to make someone's day," I say, and then whisper to myself, "At least I hope so."

As we walk away from the game booth, Roman holds out his hand. I grab it and he laces his fingers with mine. I don't say anything. I know it's not like that. It's a different kind of hand-holding. It's the way we'll probably hold hands on April 7.

But as much as my mind knows that, a warmth still spreads over my skin. I hope he doesn't notice. Maybe he'll just think I have naturally sweaty palms.

"That was really cool," he says, swinging our hands up in the air and then back down. I let him move my hand like we're one entity. "Were you a lonely kid?"

I contemplate this for a moment. "Not always."

He tilts his chin down so he can look me in the eye. He doesn't say anything, but he doesn't have to. I know he's asking for me to explain.

"After what happened with my dad, I lost all my friends. Some of them distanced themselves immediately, but some of them I pushed away. It was too scary to let anyone be close to me." I sigh. "I don't know how to explain it."

Roman nods. In the outside light, his eyes are a golden green, like grass that's been stained by summer sunshine. "No, I understand. It's like your sadness is so deep and overwhelming that you're worried it will drown everyone else in your life if you let them too close to it."

He gets it. "Exactly."

He reaches out with his other hand and brushes a strand of hair away from my face. "I did the same thing, you know? I pushed my friends away. But it's what you have to do, I think. It's the only way."

He's still holding my hand, his fingers entangled with my mine, and I wonder how quickly he'd drop my hand if he knew what my dad did to Timothy Jackson. "Tell me more about it, your sadness," he presses.

"Why?"

"I want to understand. I like understanding you. It's been a long time since I related to someone else, but I think I get you."

My black hole of a heart stalls, sucking all the air out of my lungs. It can't be like this. It will only make April 7 harder. A crowd of middle school boys rushes by us and makes "oooh" and "ahhh" noises. Roman's cheeks flush red, but he still doesn't let go of my hand. I feel myself blushing, too.

We stand still for a few moments, and then he lightly tugs on my hand to encourage me to keep walking and we wander the fairground in silence, our sneakers crunching the straw they've laid on the ground to soak up the mud.

As we approach the twirling teacups ride, Roman starts talking again. "Sometimes, for me, it feels like my grief is eating me alive. I always thought that the hardest moments would be when I remember things about her, but that's not true. The hardest moments are when I miss her in the future. Sure, holidays are hard, but I'm talking about small things, like when we're at the grocery store and I pass by the frozen section and imagine Madison begging Mom to buy a large pack of Popsicles." He stops talking for a moment and lets out a low choke of a laugh. "Yeah, for six months, my mom never let me out of her sight. So she forced me to go to the grocery store with her." He hangs his head, staring at his mud-stained shoes. "The worst part is that I know I'm the reason she's not there to beg for Popsicles. What I wouldn't give to see her one more time, to switch places with her."

I tighten my grip on his hand like I'm scared that he's

going to disappear, that his grief will devour him right here on the spot.

"That's why I draw," he confesses. "Before Madison died, I used to sketch, but I hid it from everyone. It wasn't something I did seriously. And let's be real, my basketball buddies would've given me so much shit about it. But now I draw because sometimes it feels impossible to talk. It's like I'm trapped in this deep hole that I can't get out of. I draw to try to escape it, even though I know I'll never be able to."

I swallow the heavy lump in my throat and process everything he just confessed; I'm not sure I've ever heard FrozenRobot say so many words in a row before. My body aches for him and I wish there was something I could do, but I know enough to know there isn't. There's no saving him from his deep hole. There's no saving me from my black slug.

"But at least you have a right to miss Madison," I say softly.

He must understand what I'm trying to say because he asks, "Do you miss him? Your dad?"

"Yeah," I say without hesitation. "Yeah, I do. And that's how I know I'm crazy."

He stops moving and turns to face me, closing the distance between our bodies. We stand chest to chest, or rather, my chin to his chest. He keeps holding my one hand and puts his other on the back of my neck. His palm is warm and clammy. Maybe, just maybe, he's a little nervous and confused, too.

"I don't think you're crazy," he whispers. "But I understand why it's confusing. I wish it wasn't like that for you. That none of it had happened."

"Me too," I breathe, my voice barely audible.

He pushes on my shoulders with his right hand to make the space between us a little wider so he can look at me. "Can I ask you something?"

"Sure."

"As a science nerd, do you believe in other universes? Do you think there's another dimension where we're happy? Where you still have your dad and I still have Maddie? Where we're just a normal boy and a normal girl at the carnival?"

I drop his hand and shrug away from him. "I can't think about that."

He scrunches his face up and rubs the back of his neck. "How come?"

"It's confusing."

"And all your shit about potential energy isn't?"

My face burns. "I don't know. That feels different. Less hypothetical, I guess."

I'm trying to come up with something smart to say. Something to make him understand why my jabbering about potential energy is more hard science and less science fiction, but before I can come up with anything, he says, "You know what's confusing?"

I nod to let him know to go on.

"Watching you be so happy when you think about science. It makes me kind of . . . happy." He slouches his shoulders and shuffles his feet. "And that's confusing."

I feel pressure build in the back of my throat and I know I should say something about what I saw when he was shooting hoops, but I don't. I think of my black slug, slithering around, slurping up my potential energy for joy. I press my hand to my stomach and desperately wish that it didn't exist, that there was a way to fix me, to fix him. I dig my nails into the flesh of my stomach and wince.

Roman reaches out and puts his hand on top of mine. "But the most confusing thing is that me being confused about seeing you happy doesn't change anything." He lowers his voice so only I can hear him. "I still want to die on April seventh. And I still need you to do it with me."

All of a sudden, the carnival seems too loud. I hear the clunking of the metal Ferris wheel and the swirling of the teacups and the screams of delighted kids. I move to touch my hand to my head, but he grabs it, interlocking his fingers with mine and pulling it down to his side.

"I get it," I say in a strained whisper. "I won't flake on you."

He squeezes my hand so tight, I can't feel it anymore. I wish someone would do that to my heart.

FRIDAY, MARCH 29

9 days left

I slide into my seat just as the bell rings and toss my backpack down under my desk. Tyler nods at me. He's been doing that recently, like he thinks that ever since we went to the zoo we're close friends or something. I imagine the whispers this will ignite among my classmates.

Mr. Scott has written "Einstein" in sloppy blue letters on the whiteboard. He's tapping the cap of the dry-erase marker against the board, waiting for everyone to quiet down. "Good morning, good morning."

Some people mumble a response back to him. I stay quiet.

"Today, I want to take a break from all the math and

equations and take some time to talk about theory. We'll call it a fun Friday." The class groans and Mr. Scott turns to the board and scribbles: "The Special Theory of Relativity."

"Raise your hand if you've heard of this theory before." He taps the board again as some people in the class raise their hands.

I've obviously heard of it before. Everyone knows Einstein. I bet even Mike could pick Einstein out of a lineup. And I'm sort of familiar with the theory, but it's not like I'm going to volunteer; I hate speaking in class.

He points at Melanie Taylor. I don't think she even raised her hand. "Want to explain it to everyone?"

Her round cheeks flush pink. "Um, I don't know, like, that much about it." She fiddles with one of the gaudy brass buttons on her cardigan. "But I've heard of Einstein. Hasn't everyone? He's that genius guy with crazy hair."

See? Everyone knows Einstein. Even Melanie Taylor.

"Okay," Mr. Scott says slowly. "Anyone else?" He surveys the room and then points at me. I'm not raising my hand. I don't know what he's trying to pull.

"Aysel," he says. "Do you know anything about the theory?"

I shrug and shake my head. It's a combination of moves that make me vaguely look like I'm doing some kind of dance—the dance of I-don't-know and Please-please-please-don't-force-me-to-answer.

"Come on now. I'm sure you know something. Given your last test score, physics seems to be an area of natural interest for you."

Some people in the class whistle and make stupid howling noises.

I never understand why teachers think shouting out that someone got a good score on a test will help their social standing. Besides, my score on the last test only proves I was able to learn what Mr. Scott taught me, not that I know anything beyond that. "Come on, Aysel," he prompts. "Take a stab at it."

I want to take a stab at you, I think bitterly, and tap my fingers on the top of my desk. It's a good thing I didn't say that aloud. Stacy Jenkins and her posse would have gone nuts. The thought even scares me a bit and I wish I could take it back, erase it.

"Aysel," he urges, and there's a desperation in his voice. I almost feel sorry for Mr. Scott. His life must be pretty terrible if I'm the student he's depending on. I wish I could tell him he needs to place his bets elsewhere, that I'm a losing ticket. I wonder what the physics term for that is. Sure, there are dead stars. But at least before they died, they were stars.

And their death was a supernova—their death demanded attention. I'm pretty sure my death won't qualify as a supernova. No one is going to be around to see my energy go out. Except maybe Roman, but I doubt he'll be paying much attention.

"Aysel," he repeats. It's as if he thinks it's some magic word that is suddenly going to jump-start my brain and turn me into the type of girl who would know the answer.

Mr. Scott and I engage in a staring contest. He doesn't blink.

Finally I give up and I say, "Doesn't it have to do with how our perception of things can't always be trusted? Like our human mind is too slow to be able to fully comprehend things that are fast."

"Things that are fast?" He rolls his wrist in the air, urging me to go on.

"Like the speed of light. Doesn't it have to do with the speed of light? I think the special theory of relativity has to do with light and then there's the other theory he came up with."

"The general theory of relativity," Mr. Scott adds.

"Yeah. And that one mixes gravity in the equation."

"Perfect." Mr. Scott gives me the cheesiest thumbs-up and I want to fade into the ether. In these moments, it always feels like my skin is too thin, like everyone can see right inside me, can see my empty and dark insides.

"You're exactly right, Aysel. Bravo." He grins like he has no idea how uncomfortable this situation is.

I pull at the sleeve of my striped shirt and stare straight ahead at the board. Mr. Scott goes on to explain that Einstein transformed the whole field of physics with this theory. He gives us the most basic explanation of the special theory of relativity. He explains that nothing travels faster than light and that light is always measured at the same speed, no matter how fast you move or in what direction you move. Basically, the speed of light is constant. We can't ever travel faster than light and we have no way of slowing it down.

And time isn't constant. At least not our human concept of time. Einstein theorized that the faster we move, the slower we perceive time to move. The clocks will still tick away at the same rate regardless—but it's all about the perception of the observer.

I guess pretty much everything in life is about the perception of the observer.

Mr. Scott says, "And you know Einstein has a pretty famous quote about relativity. Does anyone know what it is?"

The class is completely silent.

Mr. Scott picks up the dry-erase marker and starts writing on the board. Once he's finished, he reads aloud what he scribbled down. "Put your hand on a hot stove for a minute, and it seems like an hour. Sit with a pretty girl for an hour, and it seems like a minute. That's relativity."

I press my pencil into the notebook paper, making little graphite smudges all over the page. I wonder if there really is something to Einstein's theory. Ever since I met Roman and made the Crestville Pointe jump plan, time has flown by. I want to believe that the change has nothing to do with Roman. That maybe time just moves the quickest at the end. I guess that would make sense. I know everything is close to being gone forever, so my desire to rush it is a little less.

I do everything slower recently, like chewing my granola bars so I can really savor the chocolate chips. And I slosh the orange juice around in the back of my throat a couple of times before swallowing to make sure I really taste the sour-and-sweet citrus. Maybe Einstein was right. Maybe because I'm moving slower now, time is moving faster. Maybe that's just the way the universe works and it has nothing, nothing at all, to do with Roman and how getting to know him has shifted my perspective.

But honestly I don't know. I just don't know.

The bell rings as Mr. Scott is saying he isn't assigning any homework over the weekend. The class erupts with applause and I try to mask my disappointment. I enjoy doing the practice problems. They give me something to do when it's 2:00 a.m. and the house is silent and dark and Georgia is conked out, snoring slightly. The practice problems make me feel less alone. It's funny how figuring out the gravitational pull of a random object can make you feel more grounded.

I get up from my desk and shove my physics notebook into my backpack. I'm about to dart out of the classroom when I see Mr. Scott walking toward me. "Aysel," he says. "Wait up."

I sit back down in my seat and look up at him.

He places a glossy brochure in front of me. "The University of Kentucky sponsors a two-week summer program for students interested in the sciences." He grabs a chair from the desk in front of mine and pulls it up so he can sit across from me. He opens the brochure and points at the text on the third page. "There's even a special physics program. I think you'd really enjoy it."

I take a deep breath. I can't exactly tell Mr. Scott that I won't be able to attend that summer program because I won't be alive. "I have to work during the summer."

His lips twist into a sympathetic smile. I've never noticed how dark and soft his eyes are; they remind me of a horse. Maybe I was wrong about Mr. Scott. Maybe he did always want to be a teacher. Maybe he's one of those people who were built for caring. "You don't have to worry about the money if you get in. They give you a scholarship for the tuition and room and board for the two weeks." He pushes the brochure closer to me. "I think it'd be a really great experience for you, Aysel."

I take the brochure and slide it down into the depths of my backpack. I tell him I'll consider applying and thank him for thinking of me. Later, in math class, I pull the brochure back out and run my fingers over the shiny photographs. I wonder about all the so-called great experiences I'm going to miss; I wonder about the relativity of greatness.

I arrive at Roman's house a little after 7:30 a.m. I'm about to text him to come out when the door opens. Mrs. Franklin steps onto the front porch in her cream-colored bathrobe and fuzzy pink slippers. She waves at me and I make myself wave back.

She walks toward me and I step out of the car. "Good morning."

"Good morning, Aysel!" She reaches out to hug me and I jump—I'm not used to people actually wanting to touch me; most people try to stay as far away as possible, as if by touching me, they could somehow catch my dad's madness.

But Mrs. Franklin doesn't know about my dad and so she pulls me as close as humanly possible. I can smell her mint toothpaste and hear her rapid heartbeat. She releases me from her tight embrace but keeps her hands on my shoulders. "So are you excited to go camping?"

Camping? I guess Roman must've told her we were taking a camping trip to explain why we're going to be away for so long. I forgot his mom actually cares where he goes and what he does with his time. I'd told my mom I was working late this weekend so she shouldn't wait up for me, and Georgia usually spends Saturday nights at a friend's house. Though I'm pretty sure I could take a weeklong trip to Antarctica before anyone in my household would be at all concerned about my absence.

"Oh, yeah. I haven't been camping in forever," I say to Mrs. Franklin, and she lets go of my shoulders and circles my car, peering into the backseat. In this case, forever is a code word for never.

She must pick up on my lack of camping knowledge because she asks, "Did you bring a sleeping bag?"

"Yup, it's in the trunk," I lie. Roman and I had planned on spending the night somewhere up near McGreavy Correctional Facility so that I wouldn't have to make the drive twice in one day. Plus, who knows how long I'll have to wait to see my dad. The original plan had been to crash in some dingy motel room; he could sleep in the bed and I could sleep on the floor. But I guess he's arranged a camping trip. Or at least made his mom go through the motions of planning one.

"Good, good. You'll want a sleeping bag for this weather," she says. "Anyhow, Roman is running a bit late. He's not so good at waking up early. I practically had to drag him out of bed. He's in the shower right now, but he should be out soon. Want to come in and have some breakfast?"

"I already ate," I lie again, and curse Roman in my head for not being ready. This is exactly what I was trying to avoid. I don't want to get to know his mom any better than I already do.

"Oh, well, at least come in and have a coffee." I make a face and it must be obvious that I'm not a fan of coffee. "Or hot chocolate? Don't wait out here." She heads back toward the house and waves at me, commanding me to follow her.

I let out a slight groan and follow behind her, keeping my eyes on the manicured stone path. Once we're inside, she has me take a seat at the kitchen table. She fills the teakettle up with water and puts it on the front burner. "The water will be ready in a minute."

I nod at her like there's nothing I want more in the world than a cup of hot chocolate. I glance around the Franklins' kitchen. The walls are painted a canary yellow and the cabinets are made of cherrywood. On the ivory-colored countertop, there's a framed picture of Roman and Madison. Madison has her arms around Roman's neck, and Roman's eyes are crinkled like he was midlaugh. I drop my eyes to the tiled floor; I can't look at that picture.

I don't know how Mr. and Mrs. Franklin can stand to look at it every day.

Mrs. Franklin sets a mug in front of me and takes a seat at the table. "So tell me where you guys are going. I love camping. We used to go camping a lot as a family. I keep trying to get Jim and Roman to agree to plan a trip for this summer. You know, Roman used to be quite the outdoorsman. Loved any kind of adventure."

I take a sip of the hot chocolate. It burns the tip of my tongue and I wince.

"Oh! Be careful. It's hot."

"I don't know where we're going," I say. "Roman's the one who suggested camping."

Mrs. Franklin's face clouds over. "Ah, yes. Like I said, he always loved the outdoors. It'll be good for him." She looks me in the eye. "I'm so glad he met you, Aysel." She looks over her shoulder in the direction of the stairs and then scoots toward me. In a quiet voice, she adds, "This is new for me. Letting him go off alone, unsupervised. But I couldn't say no to him. He just seems so happy when he talks about you. This will be good for him, right?"

Her eyes glaze over like she's sorting through past memories. "You'll make sure he's okay, right? That he stays safe?"

I can't ignore the pinching feeling in the base of my

stomach, and I imagine my guilt as a noose, slowly tightening around my neck. My palms feel clammy and I press them against the sides of the mug. The steam from the hot chocolate rises up and tickles my face.

"Hey," I hear Roman say, and he walks into the kitchen. His brown hair is damp and he has a backpack slung over his shoulder. "Sorry. I didn't hear my alarm."

I shrug at him even though I'm planning on tearing into him the second we're alone in the car. I'm pretty sure there isn't an etiquette book for Suicide Partners, but there should be. If I weren't going to be gone in eight days, I'd write one. Rule number one would be: Never wake up late on the day you have plans with your partner. Rule number two: Never make your partner have breakfast with your mom, because they will end up eating a gigantic plate of guilt and regret.

"I'm going to get the tent from the garage," he says. "Can you give me your keys? I'll put it in the trunk."

"Oh, Roman?" Mrs. Franklin says.

"Yeah, Mom?"

"I put some drinks in the cooler and took it out to the garage for you. I was thinking you could take that. I also tossed some hot dogs in there. They should be easy to grill. And I packed a basket with snacks and put it next to the cooler. Though, you might want to stop at the grocery store on your way there so you can pick up some buns for the hot dogs. I'm afraid I don't have any here." She flips her palms up and flashes me an apologetic smile. "I didn't have any in the cupboard. Roman didn't let me know until last night that you guys were planning on going camping. Or I would've been more prepared." She brushes her hands against the soft surface of her robe.

"Sounds good, Mom. No worries. We'll stop at the grocery store and get whatever else we need."

"You should definitely get some stuff to make s'mores." She places her hands over her heart and sighs. "S'mores are the best part of camping."

"Right, Mom. I'll handle it. Don't worry."

"Yeah," I chime in. "Thanks for everything, though." I toss Roman my keys and he heads outside to the detached garage.

Mrs. Franklin stands up from the table and opens the pantry. "I'm going to make him a peanut-butter-and-jelly sandwich to have on the road so he doesn't delay you guys any longer."

"Oh," I say. "He can eat breakfast here, if he wants."

She spins around to face me, a wide grin on her face. This is the first time I've seen Mrs. Franklin without makeup. Even though she's smiling, the large dark circles under her eyes give her away. Maybe what FrozenRobot said was true. Maybe she does spend every night sobbing. That must be strange for her—silent crier in the night and cheery homemaker in the day. I don't think I'd ever be able to do it. Chop my life in two. But maybe that's what you do for people you love.

I frown as I think about how much she must love Roman. She notices me frowning and says, "Oh, sweetie. I won't delay you guys any longer."

"No, no . . ." I stumble over my words. "I'm not worried about that."

She swings a dish towel in the air and slaps it against the kitchen counter. "Well, don't look so unhappy. You guys are going to have such a fun trip."

If only she knew this trip isn't about having fun or camping. It isn't about s'mores and hot dogs and sleeping bags. It's about facing my past so I can validate what I almost know for certain about my (nonexistent) future. And there's nothing fun about that.

"Anyway, y'all need to get a move on. Roman can eat on the road." She goes back to fixing his sandwich and I stare at my hot chocolate. I can't see my reflection in it, but I pretend I do. I don't like the girl I see. The girl who would do this to Mrs. Franklin, who wouldn't warn her.

I wonder if there is more than one way to kill someone. Maybe my father didn't only kill Timothy Jackson—he also killed Timothy's mom because he broke her heart. Wrecked his whole family. I guess that's why Brian Jackson is so motivated to make it to the Olympics—he needs to repair the damage my dad did.

Regardless, I don't want to do that to Mrs. Franklin, wreck her like that. I spin the mug around in my hands. It makes my palms sweaty. Finally, I take a sip. Then a gulp. I drink my chocolaty reflection away. I make that girl disappear.

Once Roman comes back, she hands him the sandwich and gives him a tight hug. "Did you find everything?"

"Yeah, Mom. I packed it all. Thanks again."

She beams at him and pulls him even closer to her. "Oh, and Mom?"

"Yeah?"

"Can you make sure to feed Captain Nemo?"

Mrs. Franklin puts her hands on Roman's shoulders and leans in to his face so she can look him in the eye. "Of course, sweetie. I'll check on him all the time. And call you with updates."

Roman rolls away from her grasp, shrugging her off. His face reddens, and the patch of freckles on his nose glows with his embarrassment. "Just make sure you feed him, okay?"

Mrs. Franklin doesn't seem put off by his attitude. She reaches out to hug him one last time. "Whatever you say, darling." She looks over his shoulder, making eye contact with me. "But you kids should definitely get on the road. Be safe, and call me once you've reached your campsite."

My skin itches and I know that I can't watch them hug anymore. I can't listen to her go on and on about him staying safe. I give her a little wave and run out the door. "It was nice to see you, Mrs. Franklin."

"Have fun!" she calls after me. "And Roman, make sure you call!"

I climb into the front seat of my car and bang my hands against the steering wheel, waiting for Roman. I gaze out the windshield. It looks like the frost hit Mrs. Franklin's flower bed pretty hard. The soil is watery from where the snow melted. One of the bushes is brown, its limbs still bare. I don't know if the late frost means it will take longer for the flowers to bloom. I hope the flowers bloom soon for her. She'll need them.

Finally, Roman comes out and ambles down the pathway. His hair is still wet, making it look darker, which in turn makes him look paler. More frozen. He's standing straighter, though. And there's a lightness to his step, instead of the usual reluctance. Maybe Mrs. Franklin was right—he really does love camping.

He comes around to the driver's side and knocks on my window. I roll it down. "What?"

"I forgot my cell phone in the garage. I'll be back in a second."

"Hurry up," I groan, and watch him jog toward the garage that sits behind his house. It looks more like a shed than a garage with its rusted shingle roof and peeling blueberry-colored paint. He returns quickly, waving his cell phone in the air so I can see he retrieved it.

"What the hell," I say once he gets into the car. The whole car fills with the smell of his pine-scented body spray. I clasp my hand over my mouth and almost cough.

"What?"

"You've committed two crimes." I pull out of the driveway.

"Huh?" He rubs his eyes. FrozenRobot, apparently, doesn't function very well in the early morning. I'm not sure what time we're planning on going to Crestville Pointe on the seventh, but it better not be early.

"Crime one, you're wearing way too much body spray."

He sinks down into his seat, knocking his head against the headrest. He puts his backpack down at his feet and rests them on it. "I don't wear body spray."

"Okay, well, whatever it is, you smell like a Christmas tree."

He sniffs his shoulder, pulling on the fabric of his black T-shirt. "And so what's the second crime?"

I tighten my grip on the steering wheel. "The second one. That's the big offense."

"Is that why we're on our way to the prison? How many years are on my sentence? I hate to break it to you, but I'm not sure I'm going to be around to serve the entirety of it."

I ignore his jab. "You made me have an intimate meeting with your mother. Scratch that. Another intimate meeting. You most definitely should serve time for that."

"Intimate?" Roman pivots so he can face me. I'm not used to having passengers in my car. I forget how small it is, how small it can feel when someone leans over toward the driver's side. If I tilted my head, my cheek would be against his. I scoot away from him and crane my neck to the opposite side.

"Yeah, intimate." I resist the urge to point out the similarities between the words "intimate" and "inmate." I move my posture back to neutral. It's not like I can drive all the way to McGreavy quirking my head to the left. "And don't pretend like you don't know what I mean. It breaks my heart to be around her. She's so nice."

He snorts and shakes his head. "You don't really know my mom."

"Oh, really?"

"Yes, really." He pulls his sandwich out of the plastic bag. He tears off the crusts and then takes a bite of it. "But can we please stop talking about my mom? What goes on with her isn't any of your business."

"Fine. Then don't make it any of my business." I steer the car away from his neighborhood and head down the winding hill toward the highway. The hills begin to give way to the flat, muddy river basin. I avoid looking at the Ohio River. It's uncomfortable to stare at it now; it's like it knows secrets about me. Sometimes it feels as if the river's judging me, that it's disappointed in me. I know it's all in my head, but some feelings are harder to shake than others.

I turn my attention back to Roman. I've let the issue of his mom drop for all of five seconds. "I still can't believe she let us take this trip alone. That doesn't seem like her."

Roman's lips pull into a sly grin. It's calculated, straight. Not like the crooked one I'm used to. "Before what happened with Maddie, she never would have allowed this. But considering I've spent the past year locked away in my bedroom, she's thrilled I have any interest in doing something outside."

Before I can comment on that, he unzips his backpack and pulls out a wrinkled map. "Here, I figured out the easiest way to get to McGreavy." He gives me directions as I merge onto the highway. I turn the radio to the classical music station and he makes a noise in protest.

"What?"

"Why do you like this boring music?"

"You've asked me this before."

"I know. But you never gave me a good answer."

I shrug. "Like I already told you, it helps me think." *And someone once told me that I could find answers in it if I listened hard enough.*

"It has no personality."

"Not true. It has a personality that isn't as flashy. It's deeper. It demands more from the listener. That's why I like it. It isn't easy."

"Right. Whatever you say." He rests his head against the

window. "So are you ready for this?"

I tap my fingers against the wheel, humming along with the radio. I don't know if I'm ready for it. I don't know if I'm ready for any of it. Last night, I had trouble falling asleep. I was up all night playing out imaginary scenarios in my head, but every time I envisioned myself sitting in front of the glass window, the orange phone in my hand, I couldn't make out who was on the other side of the window. It was all blurred out, and no matter how long I stared, I couldn't see my dad.

And when I finally fell asleep, I had a nightmare where I was standing at Crestville Pointe, waiting for Roman, but he never came. I waited and waited and waited, my knees bloody from having fallen in the gravel. And then finally Roman showed up, but he was with Brian Jackson. They laughed at me, and their cold, haunting laughs circled me like a wolf pack. Roman and Brian shouted, telling me to jump, and I got closer and closer to the edge, but then I couldn't move.

"Aysel?" he presses.

I can't tell him about the dream. I can't tell him that I'm not ready for this trip at all—that I'm scared this trip is going to ruin everything Roman and I have. That this trip is going to show him that I haven't been telling him the whole truth, the real truth.

He turns the radio off. "Aysel, look at me."

"I thought you told me not to take my eyes off the road."

"Yeah, yeah, but whatever."

I glance over at him. "What?"

"Are you ready for this?"

"Yeah, I'm ready," I lie. "I mean, I guess I'm ready."

"You have to be more sure than a guess."

And the problem is I'm not more sure. About any of it, anymore.

He reaches into his backpack and pulls out a sketch pad. "Do you mind if I draw?"

I glance over at him and he's staring at me intently. "Draw me?"

He shrugs. "Yeah. If you don't want me to . . ."

"No. It's fine," I say quietly, and turn the radio back on. I force myself to stare straight ahead at the open road and forget that he's inches away, studying me.

"Relax. If you tense up, it's harder for me to draw you."

"Right," I say more to me than to him. After a few minutes, I glance over at him. He's propped against the side door, his neck dipped forward, charcoal pencil in hand, intently staring at the sheet of paper. He looks more relaxed, more comfortable, than I've ever seen him.

He catches me looking at him. "Stop," he says.

"What?"

"If you think about me drawing you, I won't get a natural picture. I want to draw you how I see you, not how you're trying to make me see you."

I wrinkle my nose. "That doesn't make any sense."

"Just trust me."

"Whatever you say." I don't bother to ask him why he cares so much. There's a slight fluttering in my stomach, a lightness I haven't felt in a long time, if ever, and I'm scared of what it means. And I'm terrified his answer would ruin all of it, so I clamp my jaw shut.

Raising the radio volume, I focus my attention back on the road. I pretend I don't hear Roman's pencil scratching against the paper or his heavy, slow breaths. Instead, I start to count the miles to McGreavy Correctional Facility, the miles until I see my dad again.

SATURDAY, MARCH 30

8 days left

We get to McGreavy Correctional Facility in the midafternoon. The sun's hot on my face as we walk toward the entrance. The place looks less threatening than I'd envisioned. It's a large, one-story brick building. Sure, it's surrounded by two less-than-appealing outdoor spaces that are framed by high-wire fences, but if it weren't for the barbed-wire curls at the tops of the fences, I wouldn't have even known it was a prison yard.

Roman grabs my hand. "You sure you want to do this?"

I grip his hand and then drop it, trying to signal that I'm okay. But my mouth is dry and the honest answer is I don't know if I want to do this, if I can do this. I've become so attached to this thought—the idea that I needed to see my dad one last time before I offed myself—but now, I'm not sure what I was thinking. I don't know what I was hoping to find here at McGreavy, but the longer I stare at the building in front of me, the less I think that whatever it is I'm looking for is here. If I'm even looking for anything at all. Maybe Roman was right. Maybe I am just trying to find excuses to live.

McGreavy Correctional Facility is not somewhere I'm going to find an excuse to live.

My knees buckle and I have a sinking feeling that the man I'm about to face won't match up with the father I remember. The father who taught me to love Mozart and who shared candy bars with me on lazy afternoons. But I guess that father never really existed, because that man never would've killed someone in cold blood.

So maybe that's the point of all this. For me to finally face that fact, face him, the real him. Maybe.

Roman holds the door open for me and we walk in. A metal detector and four security guards greet us. We make it through the first security check with no problem. I walk up to the front desk.

"You don't look like you should be here," the man at the desk says. He's dressed in an officer uniform but has added some panache to his style by sporting a Kentucky

Wildcats baseball cap. The name tag on his uniform reads JACOB WILSON.

Jacob Wilson is awfully presumptuous. "I'm looking for my father," I say, and fumble around in my purse for my wallet. I pull my driver's license out of my wallet, place it on the counter, and slide it to him. "His name is Omer Seran. I called a few days ago and was told you have visiting hours on Saturday until four p.m. I think I should be on his approved list of visitors. I'm his daughter."

I don't have any idea about the list, but it seems like the right thing to say. I glance at my phone to check the time: 2:17. Visiting hours aren't over yet.

Jacob Wilson types something into the computer. The computer is large and bulky, like the ones we use at TMC. Jacob pushes a few more buttons and frowns. He clicks the mouse and then lets out a sighing whistle.

I brace myself for the fact that I'm not on the mythical list of approved visitors. Great. My dad's not even going to give me the chance to confront him, to demand answers about what made him snap. Before I can say anything, Roman interjects, "What's wrong?"

"Your dad's no longer here," Jacob says to me.

"Huh?" I'm not processing what he's saying.

"He was transferred."

I blink a few more times but tuck my hands at my side. *Show some restraint.* The goal of this trip was not to get locked up. "How is that possible?"

He holds his hands out, flips his palms up, and shrugs. "I don't have the details, sweetheart. I only know what's in the computer. And the computer says he's been transferred."

Roman steps up closer to the desk. He slaps his hands down and leans in toward Jacob. "Don't you have to inform the family before you transfer someone?"

"Easy there," Jacob says with a chuckle. "Dial it down a notch, will you?"

"Sorry." Roman backs up.

"But you're right, son. We do inform the family." He squints at the computer screen, scooting forward in his chair. Then he looks back at me. "Says here that a phone call was placed to Mrs. Melda Underwood. A letter was sent, too." He frowns and stares at the screen again. "Underwood?"

"That's my mom."

The guard raises an eyebrow at me, so I add, "Remarried."

He raises the right side of his upper lip over his teeth, making a semi-grimace. "It happens a lot when guys get locked up. Tough break."

I wouldn't describe anything in my dad's life as a "tough break." From my perspective, his life was more of a "tough break" for other people than it was for him. "So where is he now?"

"According to the computer he's at Saint Anne's Behavioral Health Hospital."

Behavioral Health Hospital. "Where is that?"

"Not sure," Jacob says. "My guess is it's in-state since I don't see them transferring him out of Kentucky, but you never know."

"Do you have any idea how she could get in touch with him?" Roman interjects again.

I don't know why Roman thinks it's his place to take over this conversation, but I'm oddly grateful. Usually, I'd be annoyed, but right now, I can hardly see straight. All I can think is: *My dad's locked away in a mental institution.*

Jacob gives us a sad smile. "Like I already told you, he's at Saint Anne's Behavioral Health Hospital. If you want, I can place a call there for you and see if someone there can get you some information on how you could contact your father."

"Okay," I say weakly. "Can you please do that?"

He glances over his shoulder like he's looking for his supervisor or something. "I can't do it right now, but I can do it later. You could probably call the facility, too, but it might take you longer to find out the information you need. Red tape and all that." He gives me a small wink. "I'm really not supposed to do stuff like this, kid, but I want to help you out."

He rips off a sheet of paper from a legal notepad and pushes it toward me. He hands me a pen. "Here. Write down your number. I'll see whether I can find someone who knows how to get in touch with your dad. I'll give you a ring if I do."

I scribble my number down quickly. The paper is bright gold. It seems like the wrong color for this type of occasion. Whoever orders the prison's office supplies should really think about these kinds of things.

I hand him my number. "Thank you so much."

"Sorry I couldn't help more. I know how frustrating it can be when your parents keep things from you." He adjusts his baseball cap. "You should really talk to your mother about that."

I nod. *I would if I talked to her about anything.* "Yeah, I probably should. Thanks for all your help."

"No problem. I hope you end up finding what you're looking for." The way he looks at me makes me think that maybe he understands my situation more than he's letting on. I stare at him for a moment and then tug on Roman's shirt and drag the sorry pair of us out of McGreavy Correctional Facility.

Once we're outside, Roman shades his eyes with his hands and looks off into the distance like he's staring out over the Grand Canyon or something other than an empty prison yard. "I thought you called."

"I did. I asked about visiting hours."

"You didn't think to ask if your dad was still here?"

I chew on the inside of my cheek. "I had no reason to

think he wouldn't be." I pause and look at him. He doesn't turn to look at me—he keeps staring off into the distance. "Wait, are you accusing me of something?"

He drags his sneaker along the cement. The sun glints off his hair, making it look less brown and more blond. The air feels thicker than it did before, like the steam after a hot shower. It doesn't feel like March air. Maybe spring is here. Maybe Mrs. Franklin's flowers will bloom soon. "I don't know, Aysel." He scratches the back of his neck. "It just seems like you're searching for reasons to delay it."

"Delay what?"

"Never mind."

I cross my arms over my chest. "No. Say it."

He turns to look straight at me, his eyes wide but empty. "If you don't talk to your dad before April seventh, you're still going to jump with me, right?"

I say yes, but I don't look him in the eye. I can't.

SATURDAY, MARCH 30

8 days left

I park in front of the campground. If you can even call it a campground. It looks more like a muddy lot to me. I'm no expert in campgrounds, but I'd have to think this is about as basic as you can get. The only amenities it seems to offer are a fire pit—complete with half-burnt logs and ashes—a large oak tree, and a rusted trash can.

Roman steps out of the car and walks around to the trunk to grab the tent. Far off in the distance, I can see a rocky shoreline, the river lapping up against the pebbles. Maybe this won't be so bad. Maybe this will give us some time to talk. Maybe I'll finally find the words to explain what's going on with me.

I pull my backpack out of the backseat and follow Roman toward our campsite. When he unzips the tent bag, I notice he's hidden two bottles of wine inside it.

"Classy," I say.

"You can drink red wine warm. Warm beer is gross. I made an executive decision."

"You could've put the beer in the cooler." I ignore the fact that he's talking to me like a loser who's never drunk alcohol before. Even though, to be fair, I am a loser who's never drunk alcohol before. Unless you count a few sips of Steve's beer he gave me when I was like eleven and he and Mom were hosting a backyard barbecue for some of their friends.

"Yeah, but my mom packed the cooler. She would have noticed."

"You could have put them in later."

"Jesus, do you really want beer that much? I can run into town."

I shove my hands into the pockets of my black jeans and walk farther toward the river. "No. It's fine. I was just giving you a hard time."

He pulls the tent out of the bag and fumbles around with it. A couple of times I think about offering him help, but I know nothing about tents. I hear him cursing under his breath and I decide to take a walk by the water.

"I'll be back soon," I call out, and he doesn't answer.

I walk down the other side of the hill. My sneakers sink into the damp grass. As I move closer to the river, I see an empty dock. There's no one around. Broken fishing lines float in the water, and I try to imagine the place full of people, laughing families and eager fishermen. It doesn't seem like a place that would ever be crowded. It seems like a place that was meant to be lonely. I hear a few birds chirping to one another and the roar of a boat's motor off in the distance, but all I can focus on is the ringing in my head. I cup my hands over my ears and hum to myself. Bach's Mass in B Minor fills my mind.

I lean against the splintered wooden railing and a gust of wind slides off the water and touches my face. Sometimes it feels like the wind has hands, has fingers. Sometimes I wonder if I could reach out and grab it. If it would grab me back, squeeze the space between my fingers, take me away. I wonder if Roman ever thinks about these things, if anyone else ever thinks about these things.

I look behind me and I can't even make out our campsite. I go back to staring at the water. The rocky bottom of the riverbank is covered with slimy algae and rusted fishing hooks. I know that if I jumped, I'd only end up wet and dirty. I wouldn't end up dead.

It's not Crestville Pointe. That jump will kill me, will kill Roman.

I head back to the campsite. My steps are heavy and

sluggish. I'm not in any rush to get back to Roman and his beerless cooler and his questions about whether I'm going to flake out on him. I see him before he sees me. I guess he managed to set up the tent—a flappy blue structure sways in the wind. His back is turned to me and he's hunched over the fire pit, lighting a match.

As I step up behind him, I watch the two old logs burst into flames. The fire crackles and I take a seat on the ground next to him.

"Did you find what you were looking for?"

"Huh?"

"I thought you wandered off to find something."

"Nope." I cross my legs to sit Indian style on the grass. "Everything's still the same."

"Glad to hear it." He rubs his hands together before he stands up. "Are you hungry?"

I shrug, which he interprets as yes. He walks over to the cooler and pulls out the hot dogs his mom packed for us. They're shoved together in a plastic bag, looking sad and slimy. He hands me the bag and then grabs some steel skewers from his backpack.

I slide one of the hot dogs onto the skewer and watch the metal point poke through the hot dog's casing. I hover my skewer over the flames and Roman does the same. I turn it over every so often, but to be honest, I have absolutely no idea what I'm doing. My family doesn't camp.

"I think it's done," Roman says, nodding at my hot dog.

"Oh." I pull it away from the flame.

"I forgot to pick up the buns. My mom would be horrified." He gives me a sheepish grin as he plops back down on the ground. He folds his legs up to his chest and pulls the hot dog off the skewer, repeatedly blowing on it.

I do my best to imitate him, except I'm pretty sure I look like a five-year-old that can't manage to successfully blow out her birthday candles. I tear off a piece of my hot dog and it burns my fingertips. I shove it in my mouth and chew. There's a charred taste on the outside, but it's cold on the inside. I manage to swallow it.

He puts his hot dog down on a piece of newspaper and gets up and grabs two plastic cups. He unscrews the cap off one of the bottles of wine. The bottle sways in his hand as he says, "You're right. We are being classy. Hot dogs and wine."

I know he's teasing, but it's my first time drinking wine and I can't help but be a little bit excited. A month ago, I would've told you there was nothing in the world left to be excited about. Who knew something as silly as wine would do the trick? I try to maintain a neutral facial expression so I don't give myself away. He pours us each a glass and then hands me mine.

"Thanks." I put the glass down beside me and barely manage to balance my half-cooked hot dog. I guess the only thing worse than a half-cooked hot dog would be a half-cooked hot dog complete with a dusting of dirt.

"We probably should have gotten napkins," he says in between chews.

"Probably."

He finishes his hot dog quickly. Maybe his was under-cooked too. I force myself to gulp the rest of mine down and then take a swig of wine. It's sour and I cringe.

He laughs. "Not much of a drinker?"

"Guess not."

He holds his plastic cup out toward mine. "To Aysel, my Suicide Partner."

I clink my cup against his. "To not being a flake."

That really makes him smile and he chugs down the rest of his wine and then goes to pour himself another glass.

The sun is starting to set in the sky and I have no concept of what time it is. I think about pulling my cell phone out of my pocket and checking, but then I realize it doesn't matter. All that matters is this day feels so much shorter than most. The days with Roman always feel the shortest.

I flip over onto my stomach and stretch out. Roman lies down beside me on his back, his eyes glued to the sky. "I'm sorry we weren't able to find your dad."

I slide my tongue over my teeth, tasting the wine's tart aftertaste. "Maybe that guy, Jacob, will call."

"Maybe." Roman puts his hand on my lower back. "But maybe he won't. You'll be okay with that, right?"

I don't know the answer to his question. I guess I'll try to call the facility myself if Jacob doesn't call with information. But like I said, I just don't know. A few birds squawk at one another and take flight from a nearby tree. The fluttering of their wings startles me for a moment and I sit up. I would've thought the closer I got to death, the less on edge I'd be, the less afraid I'd be. It's turning out to be the opposite.

"I'm sorry," he says, taking his hand off my back and tucking it in the pocket of his pants.

"No," I say. "It wasn't you."

He raises his eyebrow. "The birds scared you?"

I want to tell him that everything scares me now. But I stay silent and let him ramble on about how birds are harmless. He is drinking more and more wine and I am trying to keep up, but my head is dizzy and my eyelids are starting to feel heavy.

I roll over on my side to face him. The fire is still going strong and the tendrils of smoke cast shadows over his thin cheeks. He's been chugging the wine in silence and I know I should say something that will make him understand how I feel, but I'm already on rocky ground and I don't want to make it even worse.

"I'm scared too, you know," he finally says. I can smell the wine on his breath as he lifts his face, moving it closer to mine. "But also excited."

I squeeze my eyes shut. My brain feels like it's swimming.

"Have you ever heard of Einstein's theory of relativity?"

He takes another long sip. "There you go again with science. You're a real nerd, aren't you?"

"I think to be a nerd you have to be smart."

He draws his eyebrows together. "You seem pretty smart."

I wink at him. "I put on a good act." I sit up and pour myself a little more wine.

"So tell me about it."

"The theory?" The wine has started to taste less sour. I don't know if that's a sign I'm getting used to it or a sign that my taste buds are drunk. I don't even know if taste buds can get drunk.

"Yeah, Einstein's theory. Your nerdy theory." His words are sloppy and blurred together. It'd be kind of cute if it wasn't also kind of scary.

"You know he had two theories, right? The special theory of relativity and the general theory of relativity."

Roman shakes his head. "I don't know shit about Einstein. And honestly, if it weren't for you, I wouldn't really care about the guy."

"I make you care about Einstein?" I bite on the rim of my plastic cup.

He gives me his half-moon smile, all crooked and sweet. "I can't help but care about the things you care about. I feel like we're kind of connected in that way now."

I find myself smiling. My cheek muscles feel different—

they're like a room that hasn't seen light in years that suddenly had all the blinds pulled open and the sun is beaming in at full volume. And I can't help myself, my smile keeps stretching, wider and wider. That's the nicest thing Roman has ever said to me. Hell, that's the nicest thing I can remember anyone ever saying to me in the last three years.

"I made you happy," he says. His words come out heavy and slow.

"Yeah, you made me happy."

He shakes his head and closes his eyes. He's swaying back and forth like one of those hula dancers that people put on their dashboards.

"What?" I say, and reach over to tap his shoulder.

"I can't make you happy. We can't let each other make each other happy."

I pause, decoding his sloppy, slurred sentence. I lean in toward him. "Would that be so bad?"

He snaps his eyes open. They're bright and glossy, and at the same time, light and watery. "That would ruin everything."

It takes me a second to find my grounding again. I pick up a twig and start dragging it across the grass. "But you told me at the carnival that when I talked about science, it made you happy and maybe . . ."

He raises his hand in the air, signaling for me to stop talking. "It doesn't matter." He points at me and then back at him. "This can't matter. This is temporary." His eyes widen and I can see that red semicircles are forming around the bottom of them. Too much wine for FrozenRobot.

"Look, Aysel." He reaches out and squeezes both my hands in his. "I know this is confusing. We're in a strange and fucked-up position and we can't let ourselves get fooled by the situation."

I try to jerk my hands away from his, but he doesn't let go of them. His fingers dig into my knuckles. "The situation?"

"The fact that we're Suicide Partners. We have this intimacy and, yeah, sure, we have chemistry."

"Chemistry?" I can't help but laugh.

"Okay. I'll leave the science to you."

He leans in close to me, his nose bumps against mine, and I can feel his eyelashes fluttering on my skin. I lift my chin and our lips meet. It's clumsy, but it's perfect. I can't stop thinking: *We're kissing, I am kissing FrozenRobot, we're kissing.* It rings in my ears like a cheesy mantra.

I keep kissing him back and I try not to think about whether I am doing it right or wrong. My heart is pounding, which I think means I like it, and I hope his heart is pounding too. I know humans have been kissing since the history of time, but right now, in this very moment, it feels like kissing is a secret that only Roman and I know about.

After what feels like only a second and also a hundred years, he pulls away slowly and brushes a strand of hair from my face. "We do have chemistry," he says.

I give him another smile. That's two. I can't develop a smiling habit. I wouldn't even recognize myself if I became someone who smiles voluntarily. "I guess we do." I take a breath and notice that the air has changed flavor from campfire smoke to sweet vanilla and there's a soft sound in my head that I don't quite recognize but reminds me of pennies being tossed into a fountain. The pitter-patter of wishes, desperate wishes.

He nuzzles his head into my neck and I try to relax my body and pretend like that's perfectly normal. Then he wraps his arms around my waist and pulls me down to the ground with him. We lie there in the darkness, in silence, a few feet from the tent, my spine against his stomach, his hands on my sides. I've never been so aware that I am made up of bones and skin, and I can practically feel my bones inching closer to the surface of my skin, aching to get even closer to his.

Out of nowhere, he whispers, "But this can't change anything."

I squirm so I can press myself even closer to him. I can feel his beating heart—it is wildly alive. There's a burning in the pit of my stomach and it feels nothing like the black slug chomping away at my happiness. There's a light fizziness where there used to be unbearable heaviness, and I wonder if my potential energy is changing. I imagine graphing the whole process like a scientist would chart her lab experiment.

My whole life is starting to seem like an experiment.

"Aysel," he says as he holds me tight, his lips brushing against my hair. "You know this can't change anything, right? This type of happiness is fake, it's fleeting. We need to remember why we want to die. I need to remember Maddie. And you need to remember your reasons."

My reasons. That sounds so vague. But I guess I haven't really told him my reasons, since I'm terrified of how he'd react if he figured out who my dad is. And maybe that's why I haven't told him. Not because I'm scared that he won't want to die with me anymore, but because I'm terrified that he'll still want me to die. That he'll agree that I should die.

I guess he's right: I am a flake. But maybe meeting Roman has helped me to understand myself better. Yes, I'm broken. And yes, he's broken. But the more we talk about it, the more we share our sadness, the more I start to believe that there could be a chance to fix us, a chance that we could save each other.

Everything used to seem so final, inevitable, predestined. But now I'm starting to believe that life may have more surprises in store than I ever realized. Maybe it's all relative, not just light and time like Einstein theorized, but everything. Like life can seem awful and unfixable until the universe shifts a little and the observation point is altered, and then suddenly, everything seems more bearable.

"You know?" he presses. "Us doing whatever we're doing,

becoming whatever we're becoming, it doesn't change any-thing. It can't." His actions don't match his words, though, because as he's talking, he's pulling me closer.

"I know," I whisper.

But deep down, what I know is this: Everything has changed.

SUNDAY, MARCH 31

7 days left

'm woken up by the glare of the morning sun. Roman's arms are still wrapped around me and I roll away from his grasp. We fell asleep a few feet from the tent, and my shirt and jeans are streaked with muddy grass marks.

I pull my phone out of my pocket and see I have a missed call and voice mail from an unknown number. I start to walk away from where Roman is sleeping, but I stop when I hear him sleepily groan in my direction.

"Where are you going?" He sits up and rubs his eyes. "What time is it?"

"Almost eight a.m."

"Ugh." He flops back down on his back and squeezes his eyes shut. "It's too early and too bright."

"Someone had too much wine," I say in as normal a voice as I can. I know he said that last night didn't change anything, but I don't know how to act like things haven't changed. He's no longer FrozenRobot, my Suicide Partner from the internet. He's Roman, the boy who kissed me by the river and held me all night. To me, there's a difference. A big difference.

He's no longer the person I want to die with; he's the person I want to be alive with.

"I'll be right back," I say, and head off toward the river. I walk down the same path I did yesterday. I look at my phone's screen again. I missed the call around 7:00 p.m. last night. Maybe I'd already drunk too much wine to notice my phone vibrating.

I press my ear to the phone and listen to the message. It's Jacob, the guard from the prison, calling with information about my dad. My breath shortens as I replay the message. Jacob located someone who works at Saint Anne's Behavioral Health Hospital who knows something about him. Jacob gives me the name of the person, Tara Woodfin, and her number. I replay the message again and then glance down at my phone. It's probably too early to give Tara a ring, especially on a Sunday. I'll have to wait a bit.

Once I get back to the campsite, I find Roman in the

same position I left him. He's lying on his back, his eyes squeezed shut and his face frozen in a painful frown. I kneel down beside him and shake his shoulders. "Come on, we should go. Let's take down the tent."

"Why do we have to leave so early?" His speech is still slurred and he rolls over on his side.

I walk over to the tent and try to figure out how to collapse the thing without breaking it. I fumble around with the poles until I figure out that they can be removed from the tent's flaps, and once they're out, you can bend them in half. I'm sure there's an easier and prettier way to take it down, but Roman's too zoned out to judge me, and if he has his way, he's never going to need to use this tent again anyway.

The thought is almost unbearable, and I push away the sinking feeling, swallowing the lump in my throat. *Stay busy. Don't go there.* Once the tent is collapsed, I shove all the parts into the bag Roman packed it in. There's no order to it, but I'm sure Mrs. Franklin will fix it once we get back.

As I head toward the cooler to grab a bottled water for Roman, I notice his backpack slumped next to it. I peek at him to make sure he's still sleeping and unzip it. I pull out his sketch pad. I know it's wrong, but I can't help it.

I sit down cross-legged on the ground and flip through his sketch pad. My breath catches when I reach the last page, the drawing of me. The girl I'm staring at is not me, but she is me. Her large eyes are focused away from the viewer, but there's something in them I don't immediately recognize: hope. Her posture looks straighter than mine, like she's stronger, more resilient.

"Thank you, FrozenRobot," I whisper to myself. I tear the drawing out of the sketch pad. I don't care about how angry he'll be when he realizes I took it. I need it. I need it to remind myself that I can be this girl, that this girl is inside of me. This hopeful, strong person. I fold the drawing into a tiny square and slide it into my pocket and then carefully put his sketch pad back inside his bag.

As I pull a water bottle out of the cooler, I think about what I have to do. I have to do for Roman what he has done for me: I have to show him the person still inside of him, the person he thinks is gone and defeated. A boy full of adventure and talent, with a sloppy smile and an infectious laugh. A boy with eyes like summer grass and sunshine that see things most people don't, and hands that create incredible sketches. I close my eyes and remember holding his hand at the carnival, how solid and tight his grip was.

I have to help him save himself. I have to.

Taking a deep breath, I muster the courage to walk over to Roman. I crouch down beside him and press the cool bottle to his forehead. "Wake up."

"Hey!" he yelps out in surprise.

"I figured that would feel good."

"It does, thanks. It just startled me a little." He takes the water bottle from me and rolls onto his side so he can gulp down a few sips before pressing it against his forehead again.

"I'm going to put everything in the car and then we can take off. Okay?"

I'm about to get up, but he reaches for my hand and pulls me back down to the ground beside him. "I wasn't so drunk that I don't remember last night, Aysel."

I stare at him blankly. I can't say what I want to say, and I figure silence is better than all the words he doesn't want to hear. And besides, I don't want to speak until I have the right words. The magic words. The words that will convince him to live.

He shakes his head and takes another gulp of water. "Don't pretend like you don't know what I'm talking about."

I stay silent and run my tongue over my teeth, searching for the right words.

"Aysel," he says as he reaches for my hand again.

I grip his hand and stare down at it. The hand that drew that picture. "Jacob called," I say.

His fingers softly massage mine. "And?"

"He gave me the name of someone I can call to get some information on my dad."

Roman drops his gaze to the ground but keeps my hand in his. "We might not have time to visit him before . . ."

"I know, but . . ." I pause and inhale, letting the cold spring air fill my lungs. "About last night. I know you told me not to let it change anything, and maybe last night in particular didn't change anything, but I'm starting to think that maybe we should stop and really consider . . . everything." I stare down at our hands.

He drops my hand and scoots away from me. I take a sharp breath. "Look, I knew it was a bad idea. It's just you're, you're, you're . . ." He sputters like a stalling car's engine.

"I'm what?"

"You're you. You get it. You get all of it. And you're sad like me, and as screwed up as that is, it's pretty beautiful." He reaches over and brushes his hand across my face, touching my hair. "You're like a gray sky. You're beautiful, even though you don't want to be."

But he's wrong. It's not that I don't want to be. But I never wanted to be beautiful because I was sad. FrozenRobot of all people should know that there is nothing beautiful or endearing or glamorous about sadness. Sadness is only ugly, and anyone who thinks otherwise doesn't get it. I think what he means to say is that he and I are ugly in the same way and there's something familiar, comfortable, about that. Comfortable is different from beautiful.

I think about his drawing of me. The girl that he drew, she was beautiful. That girl wasn't a gray sky. She had hope. Hope is beautiful.

And so I don't want us to be ugly in the same way anymore. I don't want to be a gray sky. I want us to find hope.

Together. I look away from him to hide the fact that my eyes are welling up. After a few moments of silence, I stand up and dust myself off. "We should probably get going."

"Aysel," he says, and there's an urgency to his voice. "We should talk about this."

"I know, but I don't know what to say."

He squeezes my hand and all I can do is squeeze back because I'm too scared of letting go. Of losing him.

SUNDAY, MARCH 31

7 days left

We've been driving for about an hour when I pull off the highway to stop at a tiny diner that was advertised on a billboard near the exit. Roman's been sleeping the whole ride and he slowly wakes up as I park the car.

He rubs his eyes. "Where are we?"

"I thought it'd be good if you ate something before I dropped you off at home."

He gives me his half-moon smile and my heart feels like it's being strangled. I can't look at that smile anymore. I glance out the windshield. Rain pours down from the sky, and off in the distance, I hear thunder rumble.

"I like your thinking. You're right, my mom would totally flip if you brought me home in this condition," he says as he steps out of the car. "You'd lose your Saint Aysel status."

I'm pretty sure I'm going to lose that if I let you jump to your death from Crestville Pointe. I bite down on my bottom lip. Roman doesn't react to the rain. It falls on our hair, our faces, our clothes.

We walk slowly into the diner and get seated at a booth in the back. He looks at the menu and I find myself staring at him. He catches me and I drop my eyes, reading the omelet choices over and over again. I pretend to be really interested in the difference between the southwestern and the Florentine choices.

When I'm sure he's not looking at me, I sneak another glance. His T-shirt is damp with rainwater, his hair is soaked, and beads of water pool on his forehead. The rain—the water—makes him look younger, more alive. It's made his cheeks redder, his skin brighter. I try to picture it on a grander scale, how he'll look after diving from Crestville Pointe, how he'll look after the water has drowned him. His lips turning from a pale pink to a cold blue, his skin changing from dewy to impossibly pale. I wonder if we feel those transformations, if we can sense our kinetic energy fizzling away into nothingness. I wonder if we can hear it, if it sounds like the symphony or if it sounds like screaming. I don't know the answers to any of my questions. And I don't want to know them anymore; I don't want Roman to know them, either.

I go back to silently staring at my menu. I can't think about any of that right now. Our waitress comes over to the table and takes our order—two eggs, bacon, hash browns, and a side of jalapeño peppers for him and the Florentine omelet for me. She's probably around my mom's age, but her hands are much more wrinkled and her face has a lot more meat. Her hair has clearly been dyed blond and the roots are dark and greasy.

"Good choices," she says with a smile as she scribbles our order. She looks out over her notepad at us, her smile widening. "Y'all are a cute couple, you know that? I bet you get that all the time. Anyway, I'll be back soon with your food."

Before we can correct her, she walks away. I pick at the booth seat's cushion, which is splitting down the middle and oozing fabric stuffing.

"You can smile, Aysel," Roman says. "She thinks we're a cute couple."

"Right. A cute couple." I look directly at him and he drops his eyes to the table.

Our waitress returns quicker than I expect, which always makes me nervous about the food. Then again, we're eating breakfast in the middle-of-nowhere Kentucky at a run-down diner, so I guess the quality of the food is pretty much already established.

I don't have an appetite, so I push my omelet around on

my plate, my fork making little scratches on the dull white surface. Roman, on the other hand, shovels his bacon into his mouth, chewing loudly. It's funny how once you like someone, even the unattractive things they do somehow become endearing.

I hate it. Also, I'm not sure how he can have an appetite at a time like this. Did he completely forget about our fight by the campsite? Did he forget that April 7 is only a week away?

"Can I ask you something?" Roman says in between chews. He's moved on to the eggs. He's covered them with the jalapeño peppers. He pops the peppers into his mouth, sucking down the seeds.

"Sure." I take a gulp of the tap water the waitress brought us.

"When are you going to tell me exactly what your dad did to get himself locked up? All you've said is he's in prison. . . ." He trails off.

I pause and study Roman's face for a second. His deep-set hazel eyes have brightened since eating and he looks genuinely curious. I tilt my head down so I can stare at the metallic tabletop instead of his face. I'm torn between using his curiosity to my advantage and actually having to tell him the truth. As terrified as I am, I like to imagine he'll understand. The boy that drew that picture I found seems like the type of boy who would understand.

"So does this mean you're not going to tell me?"

I don't look at him. I can't. I close my eyes for a second and hum a familiar song under my breath. As I hear the music starting to build in my head, the part where the notes gain momentum and begin to sound like they're reaching for something, I get an idea. I lift my chin and meet his eyes. "I'll tell you exactly what my dad did if I can ask you something, too. Fair deal?"

"Depends on what it is."

"Okay. Here's the question: If you weren't going to die in seven days, what would you want to do with your life?"

He sets his fork down and glares at me. His eyes go from bright to stormy in all of three seconds. "What kind of question is that?"

"A curious one. But I guess all questions are curious."

His lips wrinkle like he's fighting a smile. "Why are you talking like the Mad Hatter?"

"You know me, always making bad jokes."

He picks up his fork again and takes another bite of his eggs. "That wasn't exactly a joke."

"So do we have a deal or not?"

He gives me a mock salute. "The terms are acceptable to me."

I press my elbows down on the table and lean toward him. "So what's your answer?"

He points his fork at his chest. "I have to go first? How is that fair?"

"Of all people, you're really going to talk about fair?"

He shakes his head; his signature smile has worked its way across his face again. I look away.

"Fine, fine. I'll go first. It's stupid, though," he says.

"My question?"

"No. My answer."

"Let's hear it." I hold my breath. I want to hear so many things, but I don't know exactly what I want to hear. Maybe he'll tell me something dumb like he's always imagined owning a sporting goods store so he'd have a lifetime supply of basketballs, or maybe he'll tell me something heartwarming like he's always wanted to be a pediatrician so he could help sick children.

But in the end, it doesn't matter what Roman wants to do. I'm beginning to learn that this is the exhilarating and puzzling and, frankly, the frustrating thing about love. Things that matter to the other person start to seem intriguing, even if they are actually quite trite when you really think about them.

I once read in my physics book that the universe begs to be observed, that energy travels and transfers when people pay attention. Maybe that's what love really boils down to—having someone who cares enough to pay attention so that you're encouraged to travel and transfer, to make your potential energy spark into kinetic energy. Maybe all anyone ever needs is for someone to notice them, to observe them.

And I notice Roman. So honestly, all I want is for him to have an answer to my question. I just need to know something about him that will make me believe that there's even a sliver of a chance that his particles have a longing to go in a certain direction and only need a nudge.

"I'd want to go to college," he says.

I can't help it—my heart leaps with a surge of hope. *That's a start.* I make a gesture for him to continue.

"And I'd want to play basketball there."

I nod. "Even though you don't play anymore?"

He gives me a sly smile. "Well, this all takes place in a hypothetical universe, right? I can be whoever I want to be."

The surge of hope I felt a moment ago is gone. My insides collapse and I sink into the booth's torn cushion. *It doesn't have to be hypothetical.* I force myself not to give away my disappointment and say, "Fair enough. Go on."

"What else is there?"

"I don't know. What would you want to study?"

His face flushes and he shifts in the booth. "Ah, that's the stupid part."

I tap my fingers against the table. "Then it's the good part."

"You would say that." I give him a look and he holds his hands up above his head. "Fine, fine. I'd want to study marine biology. I know it's dumb, but I'd love to explore the ocean."

I grin and I'm sure I look like an idiot, but I don't care. "Like *Twenty Thousand Leagues Under the Sea*. Like Captain Nemo."

His smile returns. "Exactly. I've always been fascinated by the idea of an underwater adventure. But it's stupid since I've never even been to the ocean." He stops talking and his eyes go hazy, distant. "And I guess I'll never go."

I bite my tongue. *Maybe not, FrozenRobot. Maybe not.* I briefly imagine us on a road trip to the coast. Maybe we'd head out to somewhere in North Carolina—that's not too far from here. I see him walking along the beach in his UK hoodie, the waves lapping at his ankles. He'd inspect the water and I'd stay back, sitting in the sand, reading a book on the philosophy of physics or something. We could be happy. And it doesn't have to be in an alternate or hypothetical universe.

I need to figure out how to show him that. Maybe I should buy him a book on marine biology. But that seems too heavy-handed. He'd flip out. Maybe I could propose a last-minute road trip to the beach.

I wonder if anyone on Smooth Passages would have any advice for me, but that thought makes me bite down hard on the inside of my cheek. I know everyone on that website would totally go nuts if they knew I was changing my mind. And worse, trying to convince my partner to change his mind. That's precisely what's not supposed to happen.

And this is exactly why Roman didn't want a flake. But

he ended up with a flake. A grade-A flake. Though, it's his fault. He's the one who turned me into one.

I just need to turn him into a flake, too. Maybe flakiness is contagious.

While I've been spaced out, he's gone back to devouring his food. When I come back to reality and glance at him, he's staring right back at me. "Oh, hey. You're back. Did you come up with some pressing physics problem you had to work out or something?"

I shrug at him. Now seems like the wrong time to pitch my ocean road trip plan. "Something like that."

"Well, it's your turn."

"Huh?"

"To tell me about your dad," he says.

I bring my hand to my face and chew on the skin around my thumb's fingernail. "It's kind of a long story and I don't really know all the details . . ."

Roman's face hardens. "Don't play games with me. I answered your question. Now you have to answer my question. Straight up." He lowers his voice so he's practically whispering. "Suicide Partners keep their word to one another."

And I know he's right, but I wish keeping my word didn't mean drowning my heart. Literally.

SUNDAY, MARCH 31

7 days left

I convince Roman to let me wait to tell him the story of why my dad was locked up until we get to the playground. I didn't really feel like airing my family's dirty history under the fluorescent lights of the shabby diner. Then again, I was probably just trying to buy time. It seems like all I'm trying to do now is buy time.

He's on the phone with his mom when I pull into the playground's parking lot. She's called him approximately fifty-seven times since our trip began.

"Everything's good." He pauses, nodding like he's in agreement with whatever his mom is saying. "Yeah, it was a fun trip." She must say something funny because he smirks. "Aysel's great. But hey, Mom, I was calling because I'm going to be a little later than I thought." He starts nodding again. "Aysel and I thought we'd swing by the playground and play a pickup game." He laughs. "Yes, I'll take it easy on her. I promise. See you soon."

He hangs up and turns to me. "You're really doing your job, by the way."

I blink at him. "What are you talking about?"

"My mom thinks I'm completely normal again. Before, she would've never let me come home later than I was supposed to." When he smiles, it's different from his half-moon one. It's a calculated one. It makes my stomach flip in a bad way. "And did I tell you she hasn't even come check on me in the middle of the night for the past week? Thanks to you, I don't think she's that worried about me anymore."

I open the car door and step outside. The knot in my chest grows and I shuffle my gray Converses in the muddy dirt of the playground. It's stopped raining, but the air is still damp and cold. I wrap my arms around myself and walk over to the picnic table I sat on the last time I was here. I climb on top of it and press my palms against the wet wood and lean back, staring up at the sky. Roman hops up on the table and sits beside me. I look over at him and he's shading his eyes with his hand.

"You always do that," I say.

"Huh?"

"Shade your eyes with your hand. I've noticed you always do that. Even if it isn't sunny."

His half-moon smile returns. "You're so observant. In another universe, you'd make a really great scientist."

"Maybe in this universe, too," I whisper.

His posture stiffens. Before I can say anything, he's jumped off the picnic table and is standing with his arms crossed, glaring at me. "Take me home." His voice is flat. It'd almost be better if he was angry. At least then I'd know he felt something.

"Come on, Roman," I say, trying to downplay it. I mentally slap myself for saying something so stupid. I should know better than to try to surprise him like that. I need a more subtle approach. He's going to have to come to the conclusion himself—I can't push him there.

I attempt to backpedal. "I was just saying that to say that. I'm not a complete idiot."

He raises his eyebrows, pulling his lips into a straight line.

"I mean, I was trying to say that if things were different, I could be a great scientist." I pause for emphasis. "In this world."

"Yeah. If things were different. But what things are you talking about?" He doesn't uncross his arms. The sun has poked out from beneath the clouds, and the sunlight is making his eyes look especially golden. They almost look like they're on fire.

"My dad," I blurt without thinking. After three years of trying to run from the shadow of my dad, now I'm dangling his dark history like some kind of bizarre bait. It's pathetic, really. I've spent so much time trying to conceal the truth from Roman out of fear of his reaction, but now, I can't worry about that; all I know is I need him to stay here. Stay with me. And I'll do anything, say anything, that will make him stay just a moment longer.

"Your dad." Roman shakes his head, staring down at the ground. "I don't get you, Aysel. Your dad's the reason you want to die. Yet you're desperate to see him one last time, despite the fact that you supposedly hate him. And you won't even tell me what he did. Do you really not trust me at all?"

I clench my teeth and resist the urge to tell him that I don't want to die anymore. That everything has changed. But I don't think this is exactly the moment to make that big proclamation, not when he's so angry with me. I pat the table beside me, urging him to sit back down. "I promise I'll stop messing around. I'll tell you what really happened with my dad. What I know, anyway."

Roman pinches his lips together and I can tell he's contemplating what he should do. In the end, his curiosity wins out. He jumps up and takes a seat next to me. This gives me a perverse sense of hope. After all, being curious by definition means you want to see what comes next. It's a feeling of some kind. I can maybe work with that.

I look at him out of the corner of my eye. His head is tipped down and he's staring at his hands. "Roman?"

"What?"

"Do you promise not to judge me if I tell you the truth about my dad?"

He touches my wrist gently, wrapping his fingers around it. "Why would I judge you?"

I look away. My throat feels strained, loose, like a tire swing hanging from a frayed rope. It's like any moment it's going to collapse and crash, sink down into my gut, and leave me voiceless.

He touches my shoulder. "What do you mean?"

"Timothy Jackson." Those are the only two words I manage to push out.

Roman drops his hand, tucking it behind his back. He spins so he can directly face me. I force myself to look into his wide eyes. It's in those eyes I found perspective and light again—they pushed their way into my black hole. I let out a choking heavy breath, a gasp for air. I'm so scared of watching those eyes turn from summer to winter, from warm to frozen.

He runs his hand along the small of my back. "Aysel, it's okay. I know."

Another choking breath. "No, you don't. You have no idea."

His fingers trail along the base of my spine. "Yes, I do. I know about your dad."

I jerk away from him, moving to the very edge of the picnic table. I pull my knees to my chest and rock back and forth. I try to hum Mozart's requiem, but I can't hear anything except my own beating heart. It won't slow down.

He moves to be next to me and drapes his arm around my shoulders. "Shh, it's okay."

My eyes blur and a wet ball forms and hardens in my throat. I haven't truly cried in years. I'm not going to cry now. My shoulders shake and I bite down hard on my bottom lip. My mouth fills with the taste of blood. "Why?"

"Why what?"

"Why didn't you tell me you knew?"

He grabs my chin and gently pulls on it so I'm forced to look at him. His golden eyes are still warm. "Because I didn't know how to bring it up. And I wasn't completely sure." He drops my chin and pulls his hands away from me. He places them on his knees and takes a deep breath. "It was just a hunch I had based on your name and what you'd said about your family. It's kind of hard to avoid the story . . . it's everywhere. And I thought that was probably your dad, but couldn't know for sure. Not until I heard it from you."

"You don't have to tell me about the story being everywhere." I press the heels of my hands into my eyes. I suck in a sob, refusing to let the tears stream down. My whole body stings with shame. It's not even my dad—that's bad enough—but I can't believe I was so stupid to think that I could hide the whole thing from Roman.

I sniffle and a briny taste crawls up my throat. "If you knew, why did you want me to tell you? Why did you keep asking about my dad?"

He grabs my hand again and squeezes it. "Because I wanted to know that you trusted me. That you felt comfortable enough with me to know that I wouldn't judge you for it. And I wanted to hear the whole story from you." He tugs on my hand, begging me to look at him. I tilt my head so I can gaze at the side of his face, but I refuse to meet his eyes. "I thought it would be good for you to talk about it. Hell, I still think it would be good."

"Why?"

He shrugs. "Sometimes it helps to talk. It helped me to tell you about Maddie."

My insides jolt with hope. "It did?"

"You gave me something no one else has given me."

"What?"

"You looked at me the same way before and after the story. I want to do that for you."

"Fine."

"Fine what?"

"I'll tell you what I know."

He lets go of my hand and moves to put his arm around me. I rest my head on his shoulder. "Don't be mad at me," he whispers.

"I'm not."

"You promise?"

"Promise."

His shoulder is broad but bony, and I can feel his muscles tensing under the weight of my head. "Do you really not hate me? Even now that you know for sure that my dad is the crazy guy that was all over the news? I just thought you'd be really upset because . . ." I focus my eyes on a faded soda can that's been tossed under the picnic table. "Well, because you used to be really close to Brian Jackson."

He strokes the back of my head, running his fingers through my tangled curly hair. "I promise I don't hate you, Aysel. I could never hate you. And I definitely wouldn't hate you because of this. *You* didn't do anything to Brian's brother. *You* didn't kill him."

His sentence replays in my head: You *didn't do anything to Brian's brother.* You *didn't kill him.* As I digest his words, my eyes become blurrier and blurrier. A tear rolls down my cheek and then the flood happens. My body trembles and I heave. I don't understand why I'm sobbing now, why now of all times, why now when I finally don't want to die.

He wraps me in his arms and I press my face into the soft cotton of his T-shirt. It smells like a mixture of fabric softener and campfire smoke. He continues stroking my hair and I focus on his kinetic energy. I don't want him to stop. I want him to stay in motion.

He presses his lips to my ear and whispers, "Tell me, Aysel."

I suck in the damp air and it fills my lungs. My heart feels like it might burst, and I untangle myself from him. I wipe my eyes and clear my throat. "I'm sorry."

He smiles slightly. "You don't have to be sorry. Stop saying that. Crazy girl."

I frown. "See? You do think I'm crazy. Because of my dad."

He shakes his head, his smile becoming wider and more crooked. "No. I think you're crazy in a completely different way. In a beautiful way."

My heart stalls. I want to ask him how he can say things like that—seven days before we're supposed to die. It's not fair. He can't make me love him when he's going to leave me. When he wants to leave me. When he knows this is the end.

The tears keep streaming down my face and he nudges me with his shoulder. "Tell me the story."

I wipe the snot from my nose. I stare at his T-shirt, now stained with my tears. "I ruined your shirt."

"I don't care about my shirt. I care about you."

Something inside me clicks. It's like I've spent my whole life fiddling with a complicated combination only to discover I was toying with the wrong lock. And now, the vault inside of me that contains all my secrets is swinging open and I feel this rush of blood swell in my chest. "Okay, I'll tell you what I know."

I don't look at him, but I swear I can feel him nod. And I can definitely feel his eyes on my face, soft and gentle, like the first snow of the year. We're silent for a while, sitting side by side, shoulder to shoulder. I press my gray sneaker against his dirty white one, and I wish we could stay like this forever. But deep down, I know that we can't, and so finally I tell him the story, the complete story, the whole story.

"My dad and mom moved from Turkey to the US before I was born. At first, they lived somewhere in Michigan, but some relative of my dad's or maybe it was my mom's . . ." I stop talking for a second and catch my breath. Roman is right—I've never told this story, not since my dad got locked away. It's been whispered behind my back or talked about in hushed voices by my mom and Steve late at night when they think Georgia, Mike, and I are all sound asleep. It's been twisted and manipulated and changed. I've never owned it.

"Anyway," I continue, "this relative ran a convenience store here in Langston and when he passed away, my parents moved here to take over the store."

Roman snorts.

"I know, Langston of all places. But, yup, they moved here and a couple months later, Mom got pregnant with me. After I was born, I guess they started to grow apart. When I was less than a year old, they separated. Apparently my dad had really violent mood swings. One morning, he'd wake up at dawn and make her scrambled eggs and toast. But other days, she'd wake up to find he'd smashed a hole in the wall from anger and had locked himself in their small basement study and refused to come out. He was like that when I lived with him, too. But I was too scared to ever say anything to Mom about it."

I work up the nerve to look at Roman. He places his hand over mine, interlacing our fingers. "Go on," he says.

"Dad stayed in Langston and took over the store because he wanted to keep me in his life. I was everything to him—" My voice cracks as I say that. "And then Mom met Steve and they got married and had Georgia and Mike and I'd visit with them on the weekends, but I lived with my dad. And he hated losing me on those weekends."

I stare off into the distance at the swing set. In the wind, the swing is swaying back and forth, making it look like a ghost is pushing it. I wonder if Roman and Maddie used to come to this playground and swing. I swallow down the salt of my tears. I can tell that Roman is waiting for me to say something else, but this is the part I'm scared of, the part I've never been able to make sense of in my own head.

After a long, heavy silence, I say, "One day, I went over to Mom's after school. Usually after school, I'd meet up with Dad at the store, but this day was special because it was Mike's first Little League game and I promised him I'd be there. I remember the look on Dad's face when I told him I wouldn't be home until late. Things were going badly at the store and Dad counted on me to keep him company and help out. That month, Dad was convinced we had a shoplifting problem. He was completely obsessed with it." I pause and bite the inside of my left cheek. I don't let go of Roman's hand. I squeeze it as hard as I can over and over again, each squeeze a little wish.

"So I wasn't there when it happened. When Timothy and his friends walked into the store, I was watching Mike run from first to second base." I shake my head and stare at the ground. "Timothy and his friends came into the store and started goofing around. They were running through the aisles and one of them knocked over a display and my dad, my dad, he—" I choke over my words. "My dad got angry. Really angry. He started shouting at them and Timothy and his friends thought this was really funny for some reason so they knocked over another display and one of his friends grabbed a few candy bars and threw them in the air, daring my dad to do something about it.

"So my dad grabbed the baseball bat from behind the counter and went after them. I guess Timothy stepped out in front and tried to reason with my dad, but he just snapped. Nobody could stop him. By the time the police came, Timothy was unconscious and my dad was just sitting next to him, still holding the baseball bat like a madman. Timothy never regained consciousness and he died at the hospital three days later." I take a few shaky breaths. "I don't think my dad even knew who Timothy Jackson was."

I can't look at Roman's face, so I press my head against his chest. "My mom never let me see my dad again. I didn't even get to go to the trial. I never got to say good-bye."

He strokes the back of my head, running his fingers through my curls. "She probably thought that was the best thing for you. He was . . ." His voice trails off. "Well, you know."

I pull away from him so I can face him. I take his hand in mine. "You know you were wrong before when you said my dad was the reason I wanted to die. He's not. The reason is that I'm terrified whatever madness was inside of him lives inside of me, too. That I'm capable of doing something just as awful."

There's a long silence and Roman doesn't say anything. He lets go of my hand and my heart plummets. *He hates me. He's scared of me.* I look away and am about to jump off the picnic table when he tugs at my arm. "Aysel, look at me."

I keep staring at the swing set. The chain links are rusted. Someone should change them. Someone should really clean up this place.

"Aysel," he urges. "Please."

When I turn to look at him, I see his face is inches from mine. His jaw is clenched and his eyes are somber. I hold my breath as I wait for him to say something. Say anything.

He pushes a stray hair away from my face and then bends his head down so he can kiss my forehead. My whole body tingles. "I want you to know you're nothing like your dad. Do you hear me? I know you, Aysel. You'd never do something like that." He puts his hands on the sides of my face, cradling my head in his hands.

"But then why do I miss him so much?" My nose is inches from Roman's and I want to look away from his eyes, but I can't.

He pulls me closer to him, wrapping his arms around me. "Because you're human. No one person is all bad or all good. I'm sure you had good times with your dad. It makes sense that you miss him."

"That's why I wanted to see him one last time, you know? Not only to try and figure out if I'm like him, but also to let him know I miss him. That I'm sorry for leaving him alone. As messed up as it is, I want his forgiveness."

Roman rubs his hand along my spine, working his way up to the base of my shoulders. "I'm sure he doesn't blame you, Aysel. And I'm sure he still loves you. He always will."

Hearing him say that makes my tears turn into sobs. He holds me tighter and I bawl into his T-shirt. We sit there, me crying, him rubbing my back, for what seems like hours. Once I've composed myself, I scoot away from him and wipe my eyes. "Sorry."

He reaches out and grabs my hands. "Don't ever be sorry."

I swallow a couple of times and look up at the sky. It's turned a gloomy indigo and the sun is starting to set. I don't want this day to fade, for any more time to pass. I shut my eyes and stay as still as I can for a moment. When I open my eyes, I see Roman staring at the ground.

"Thank you," I say.

"For what?"

"For understanding."

He gives me a small shrug like it was nothing, but it definitely wasn't nothing.

"I found your drawing of me," I say slowly.

His eyes lighten with surprise. "It's not finished."

I take it out of my pocket and unfold it. "It looks pretty finished."

He shifts his weight from his left foot to his right. "You can keep it."

I know that should make my heart lift, but it doesn't. The way he says it sounds so final. "I wish I could draw."

He looks off in the distance and rubs the back of his neck. "I'm sure you can."

"Not like this," I whisper. "I wish I could draw you how I see you." I'd draw a boy with the most magnetic smile and the kindest hands and eyes that are gloomy but can sometimes be bright. I'd draw a boy who deserves to see the ocean.

But it's like he has a sixth sense for my flakiness and he cricks his neck in the direction of the car. "We should get going."

A breeze cuts across my face, which is still damp with tears, and as I stare at him, standing there, his hand on the back of his neck, the wind making his loose T-shirt flap, his face frozen in a pained expression, I know he's thinking about Maddie. I know he's thinking about diving headfirst into the Ohio River. I know he's thinking about dying.

I want to cry all over again.

On the ride home, I make him agree to meet with me sometime next week. It's pretty twisted, but he agrees that we both need to plan what we want to do about suicide notes. I can hardly talk about it and I'm pretty sure that he knows that I'm lying now, but neither of us says anything.

After we've made a halfhearted plan to meet up, the rest of the drive is silent. I don't bother to turn on the radio. Not even Mozart's requiem is going to comfort me right now. As I'm pulling into his driveway, Roman says, "Last night you slept with your socks on."

"What?" I turn off the engine and park the car so I can look at him. He's staring out the passenger window, crunched up close to the door, like he needs to create as much physical space between us as possible.

"You said you can't sleep with socks on. Remember, you told me that? You told me how it's a problem for you. But last night you slept with socks on."

I can't tell if he's serious or not. "Um. And what's your point?"

He slowly turns to face me. His eyes are wide and watery. "My point is you can change. You're resilient. Remember that, Aysel, you're resilient."

"It's just socks," I say quietly.

He shrugs. "It's still a change."

I'm about to tell him that he can be resilient too. That I know he can. But I bite down hard on my tongue. I step out of the car to help him unload the trunk. I'm not really one for praying, but I do my best attempt and will Mrs. Franklin to stay in the house. Hopefully some riveting romantic drama is on TV and it will have more appeal than the one being enacted outside on her doorstep. "What are you trying to say, Roman?"

His lips form into his crooked smile. "Nothing. I was just making an observation." His eyes don't look so sad anymore. They don't look like anything—they're empty—and that almost makes my heart ache more. He spreads his arms wide and pulls me into a hug. "See you."

"Wait, did we decide on Thursday or Friday? Which one works better for you again?"

He doesn't answer. He just drops his arms, letting me go, and then turns and walks up the pathway to his house, carrying his backpack, the tent, the cooler, and the picnic basket. I wonder if I should help, he's fumbling to manage everything, but I don't think he wants my help. I wish he would want my help.

"I'll let you know if I hear anything else about my dad," I call out. At this point, I don't even care if his mom hears. For the first time in my life, my dad is the least of my worries. I watch Roman drop the camping supplies on the doorstep. He gives me a small backward wave, but he doesn't turn around.

I need to figure out some way to turn him around. To turn him all the way around.

MONDAY, APRIL 1

6 days left

When school gets out, I call the number Jacob left for me on the voice mail. I called it once on Sunday after I dropped off Roman, but no one picked up and I couldn't muster the courage to leave a message.

I curl up in the front seat of my car and press the phone to my ear. It rings a couple of times and then a glassy voice answers. "Saint Anne's Behavioral Health Hospital, this is Tara. How may I help you?"

I swallow. "Uh, hi, Tara. My name is Aysel Seran. I'm Omer Seran's daughter. I was told he was transferred from McGreavy Correctional Facility to Saint Anne's and . . ."

The words are tumbling out of my mouth quicker than I mean them to, but I'm scared that if I don't spit out everything, she's going to hang up and I'll lose my chance of ever finding my dad.

"I see." Her voice is clipped. "Are you a minor?"

"What?"

"Are you under eighteen years old?"

I contemplate lying. "Why does it matter?"

"I'm not authorized to give any information regarding patients to minors. I'm also not authorized to give out any sensitive information over the phone."

"But . . ." I bite down on my lower lip. "What am I supposed to do? I really want to see my dad."

I hear her sigh. "If your father is a patient here, which I'm legally not allowed to confirm, you would need to have your guardian call us to set up a visit. Depending on the state of the patient, a visit may or may not be possible."

"You can't give me any more information than that? Not even a hint that my dad's there?"

"I think it would be a good idea to talk with your mother about arranging a visit here." Another sigh. "This is the number she should call."

A small smile creeps across my face. "Thank you."

"You're welcome. Have a good day." The phone clicks off.

I shove my phone back into my pocket and push my car

seat down so I can lie flat on my back. The sun is peeking out from behind the clouds and it splashes against my face. *I need to talk to Mom about Dad.*

I imagine visiting him. I wonder if he'll be in white scrubs. Or worse, in chains. I squint and try to picture his face, but all I can see is the man I remember. The man who would never have beaten a boy to death with a baseball bat. Maybe we all have darkness inside of us and some of us are better at dealing with it than others.

What my dad did was wrong, awful, inexcusable, but maybe there's still hope for him. Maybe if he can get the help he needs, they'll be able to resurrect the man who taught me about Bach's toccata and slept in the chair in my room when I was afraid of the dark.

And if there's still hope for my dad, there has to still be hope for me. Maybe it's true that he and I have the same black slug inside of us, but it's up to me to conquer it. I owe that to my dad. I owe that to myself.

I adjust the car seat back to its normal position and put the key in the ignition. *I need to talk to Mom.* As I pull out of the school parking lot, I make a promise to myself: *I will be stronger than my sadness.*

I will do my best to become the girl from Roman's drawing. The girl with the bright eyes. The girl with hope.

MONDAY, APRIL 1

6 days left

When I get home, Mom is at the sink peeling potatoes. I make my way to the cupboard and sort through the junk, trying to find a chocolate-chip granola bar.

"Aysel," she says, giving me a tiny wave.

I turn to face her, holding the empty box of granola bars. "Mike always takes the last one and he never throws the box away. It's annoying."

Mom smiles weakly. Her light brown hair is pulled back into a loose braid. When her hair is like that, exposing her wide forehead and angled cheekbones, she looks more like Georgia than normal. She puts down the potato peeler and dries her hands. "Can we talk?"

Looks like she's not going to answer me about the granola bars. I set the box down on the kitchen table. "Sure."

"TMC called today. Mr. Palmer was wondering where you were. You missed a shift on Saturday and you were supposed to work today, too?" She sounds so uncertain, like she's afraid to reprimand me.

She's right, though. I have been blowing off work. I guess I figured that if I was going to die, it wasn't so important to hold on to my job. Money is worthless to a dead person. But the thing is, even if I don't jump from Crestville Pointe, I'm pretty sure I never want to work at TMC again.

"I'm quitting my job," I say.

"What?" she says in a calm and measured voice.

"You can yell at me," I say. "I'm not him, you know? I may be like him, but I don't have to turn out the same way." I feel a heaviness building behind my eyes. I do my best to blink away the tears.

My mom recoils like I've just slapped her. She brings her hand to her cheek. "Oh, Aysel. Oh, sweetie." She reaches out for me.

I let her hug me, but I don't hug back. I collapse against her and feel her stiffen as she holds my body's weight.

She takes my hand and leads me to her bedroom. I haven't been in this room since I moved in. It's the master bedroom of the house, but that isn't saying much. It's not that much bigger than the room Georgia and I share. I notice a few of Steve's dirty shirts on the floor in the corner, but besides that, it looks like Mom works hard to keep this space clean. It's her one sanctuary away from the messy storm that is the rest of the house.

We take a seat on her bed. My palms press against the floral comforter. I stare down at it. The threads are fraying, making the roses look like they're fuzzy and bleeding. I pick at one of the loose strands.

She pulls away from me so she can look me in the eye. "Aysel," she says, "you're nothing like him."

I can feel my heart pounding and it feels so heavy and big and I wonder if it's the only thing the black slug has left me. Like the rest of my insides are empty, and all that's left is my lonely, beating heart. "But I am like him."

She touches my hand lightly. "What do you mean?"

My breathing is shaky and I take a few gulps to try to steady myself. "I'm sad, Mom. I'm sad all the time. And I think he was, too."

"Oh, sweetie," she says in a heavy voice. I finally look up at her and see that her eyes are misty and bloodshot. "You should have told me. Why didn't you come to me sooner?"

I hang my head, pressing my chin to my chest. "I was scared—" My voice breaks and I taste the salty tears building in my throat. "I was terrified you'd send me away. Or worse, that I'd cause more problems for you. You don't deserve more problems."

Mom pulls me close to her again. We rock back and forth in silence. She lets go of me and wipes her face. "I don't know how to explain this, Aysel, but I think I've never tried to talk with you about all of this because I was terrified of saying the wrong thing." She pauses for a moment and her lips twitch like she's about to say something, but she doesn't.

"Mom?"

She sighs. "I guess I still don't know what I want to say. Or what I should say. You know, when you were younger, I used to see you standing by yourself under the tree in the front yard of the elementary school wearing that blue wind-breaker jacket your dad had bought you. The one with little yellow ducks all over it. Remember?"

I do remember. She continues, "I would be there to pick up Georgia and I knew that your father was coming to get you, but I could never shake the feeling that there was some-thing I should do for you. You looked so lonely, even then. I wanted to get out of the car and hug you, talk to you, but I never did. And then when everything with your father hap-pened, I let my fear overwhelm me even more. I'm sorry. I'm so sorry. I should've been stronger for you."

She reaches for my hands, but I move away from her grasp. Tears dribble down my cheek and I blot them with the sleeve of my shirt. I clear my throat. "I want to visit Dad."

She doesn't say anything. She stares at the floor.

"Mom, I really want to see him. I think it would help me."

"He's not in prison anymore," she says slowly, reaching for my hand. This time I let her grab it. She gives it a squeeze. "They moved him to a psychiatric hospital."

"I know."

She jerks her head up. "What?"

"I tried to visit him at McGreavy and they told me he'd been moved. And I need you to go with me to be allowed to visit him at Saint Anne's."

She brings her hand to her lips and makes a fist, lightly biting on her knuckles.

"So will you take me?" I press.

She takes a deep breath and slowly reaches over and runs her hand through the back of my hair, the way I've seen her do to Georgia and thought she'd never do to me again. "I'm not sure that's the best idea, but I'll look into it and see what we can arrange."

"Promise?"

She grabs my hands. "Promise. But I'm also going to need you to do something for me."

"What?"

Our hands are locked together in a tight grip and she gives them a squeeze. "Talk to me about your sadness, Aysel. Do you need to see someone?"

I look away from her. "I don't know."

For as long as I can remember, I've been terrified of

telling anyone about my sadness because I thought for sure they'd see it as proof that I had inherited my father's insanity. But now, I realize that I'll never be able to change what my dad did or the fact I wasn't there that afternoon to try to stop him. Every day, I will wake up and he'll still be responsible for the death of Timothy Jackson.

And maybe the black slug will always live inside of me. Maybe I'll always have bad days where the heaviness seems unbearable. But as cheesy as it sounds, maybe the good days will make it worth getting through the bad ones.

For too long, I've made my past my future, afraid to imagine anything else. And I acted like that—static—afraid of my own kinetic energy. Maybe it's time to start imagining, maybe it's time to be in motion. Maybe it's time for me to fight back against the sadness inside of me.

I wonder if it's possible to make Roman understand that. Make him see that my change of heart isn't about flaking out; it's about fighting back. I'm going to have to find the courage to finally be honest with him.

"Can I think about it?" I finally say.

"Sure," she says. "But even if you don't talk to a professional right away, you have to promise to keep talking to me. You can't keep all of this hidden inside of you, Aysel. Not anymore."

"I know," I say, and lean into her again. I breathe in her floral perfume and it reminds me of when I was younger, before the heaviness inside me became so overwhelming, so unbearable. I wonder if that's how darkness wins, by convincing us to trap it inside ourselves, instead of emptying it out.

I don't want it to win.

WEDNESDAY, APRIL 3

4 days left

In English, we've moved on from talking about depressed American poets to our unit on *Paradise Lost*. I guess we're just hopping across the pond, shifting our focus from depressed American poets to depressed English ones.

Mrs. Marks is in love with John Milton. She keeps clutching the book to her chest, like it's a baby and one of us is going to rip it from her hands and run away with it. Apparently she had to fight for years to be allowed to teach it, and she still acts like any second the superintendent is going to come in and shut the whole thing down.

She's pacing around the classroom. That's her thing. She

has us sit in a horseshoe and she spends the whole class doing laps around us. "As you know by now, I'm a sucker for a great quote. A clever turn of phrase."

A few people in the class snicker at her use of "sucker." I rub my eyes, trying my best to stay awake. The classroom is hot and stuffy, and I can hardly ever pay attention to Mrs. Marks even when the classroom is a normal temperature. I check the clock. Thirteen more minutes until the bell rings and I get to go to physics.

"And, as much as I love me some John Berryman and Sylvia Plath and Allen Ginsberg, I'm partial to English poetry," she says to the sound of more groans. The American poetry unit wasn't that popular. Surprise, surprise. "And John Milton might have the distinct honor of having penned my favorite quote of all time."

She stops doing laps and walks to the whiteboard. She grabs a blue marker and scrawls: "The mind is its own place, and in itself can make a heaven of hell, a hell of heaven." She reads the quote aloud and then says, "Can anyone tell me what Milton meant by that?"

The class goes completely silent. No groans. I reread the quote and the words echo in my head. For the first time all year, I flip open my English notebook in the middle of class. It's mostly empty, except for where I wrote down the homework assignments. On the top of a blank page, I copy down the quote.

"Aysel?" Mrs. Marks says.

I can't believe she's calling on me. She never calls on me. I thought we had some kind of unspoken agreement.

I shrug and quietly say, "I don't know."

"Oh, come on." She taps the end of her marker against the whiteboard. "I see you're writing something down. You must have some thoughts about it. Give it your best guess."

I take a deep breath and read the quote for the third time. The quote makes my brain feel like someone's plugged it into the wall and given it a spark of energy. "It reminds me of Einstein."

After I say that, the class goes back to snickering and groaning.

"Silence," Mrs. Marks hushes everyone. "Go on, Aysel."

I know it's in my best interest to stop talking. A week ago, I would have done just that. But now, I feel like there's something in me that can't stay quiet anymore. "What I was trying to say is that it reminds me of Einstein's theory of relativity. But obviously Milton isn't talking about the speed of light, he's talking about how the human mind views life."

Mrs. Marks is nodding encouragingly, so I continue. "But really, Milton and Einstein were kind of saying the same thing. That everything is subjective in the human mind. Our emotions, our opinions, they're all relative. It all depends on perspective."

"Excellent, Aysel," she says. "You should participate more."

And to my surprise, there are no whispers. No hushed insults. The room is quiet, and Mrs. Marks goes back to yammering on and on about *Paradise Lost*. She assigns us our pages to read for homework and then the bell rings. As I'm leaving her classroom, Mrs. Marks gives me a small thumbs-up. I nod at her, smiling with my eyes. I hurry down the hallway so I can get to physics before everyone else arrives. I'm practically out of breath by the time I reach Mr. Scott's classroom.

"Whoa, Aysel," he says, holding his hands up above his head. "No need to run."

"Sorry," I pant. I catch my breath. "I just wanted to ask if I could still apply for that summer program."

His lips spread into a huge grin. "Yeah. The deadline isn't until May first. There's still time for you to put together your application." He walks over to his desk and opens one of the drawers. He pulls out another copy of the brochure and hands it to me. "Just in case you lost the other one." He winks at me.

I think about telling him that I still have the other one he gave me. That the glossy pictures are smudged now because I've spent so much time flipping through the brochure. Trying to imagine myself as one of those smiling kids, wearing goggles too big for my face, peering into a microscope or building a bridge out of toothpicks.

I still can't really see myself that way, but I can imagine

the possibility of it. Scratch that. I can feel the potential of it, deep down in my gut.

But I don't tell Mr. Scott any of that. I take the second brochure from him and smile. "Thanks."

I'm walking to my desk when he says, "Oh hey, Aysel?"

"Yeah?" I turn around.

"How's your project coming along? I'm excited to see what you and Tyler came up with."

I think back to the trip to the zoo. It seems like years ago. "We'll be ready by the tenth."

Mr. Scott smiles. "Good, I'm looking forward to it."

THURSDAY, APRIL 4

3 days left

I drive to Roman's house. I texted him to let him know I was coming. He didn't answer, but sometimes he's slow to respond.

I picture him in his room. Flopped down, belly-up, staring at Captain Nemo, absently sketching, his pencil making light marks across the paper. I wonder if he and Captain Nemo sit in silence all day or if Roman talks to him. I wonder if Roman ever talks to him about me. I wish I could get Captain Nemo to divulge all of Roman's secrets.

I grip the steering wheel and remind myself that I don't need anyone to tell me Roman's secrets. That I'm going to make him talk to me. Because I'm going to be honest about everything. I take my eyes off the road for a second and glance at the passenger seat, where I tossed a book I bought called *Exploring North Carolina's Beaches*. I figure I'll start by selling him on the road trip to the ocean and hope the rest will come naturally.

Roman still hasn't answered my text by the time I pull into his driveway. I sit in the car for a couple of moments, staring at the familiar butterscotch-colored mailbox. I text him again and when he still doesn't respond, I try calling. No answer.

I jump forward in the driver's seat when I hear the front door of his house open but relax once I see it's his mom. I step out of the car and wave at her.

"Aysel," she says as she walks toward me. She's wearing a pink sweater and her daisy-print clogs. "What are you doing here?" Her chestnut-colored hair is pulled up into a topknot. It makes her look younger than usual.

I give her an apologetic smile. "Oh, I was in the neighborhood and wanted to see if Roman was home. Last week, we'd talked about hanging out today."

Mrs. Franklin frowns, drawing her eyebrows together. "Roman isn't home."

"Really?" I try not to sound completely shocked. I thought he never left the house, unless it was with me.

"Yeah. He told me he was going to your house."

I feel my jaw go slack. "What?"

She wraps her arms around herself like she's suddenly very cold. "Yeah, he asked for permission to borrow my car to go to your house. I'm not sure if you know, but Roman hasn't been allowed to drive for some time. But it seems like he's been getting so much better, hanging out with you, and so I thought . . ." She trails off.

A horrible thought hits me with the force of a tsunami. I feel like I'm drowning as I manage to sputter, "Can I go upstairs?"

She pauses, staring at me, a confused expression on her face. But then her eyes bulge and she runs toward the house. I follow her.

She speeds through the kitchen, pushing a chair out of the way. It collides with the kitchen counter, causing a teacup to fall from the edge and shatter. I hop over the shards and I'm right behind Mrs. Franklin as she darts up the steps.

We race upstairs and my heart lifts when I see the door to Roman's room is open. Maybe he's inside. Maybe he's just wearing headphones, listening to his terrible music, zoning out and forgetting the world.

Mrs. Franklin stops in the doorway. She raises her hand to her heart and lets out a deep wheezing breath. My feet feel like they are two anchors, weighing me down, but I force them to move and I enter his room.

The hairs on my arms stand at attention and I get a

sudden, sinking feeling as I take in the empty room. I turn to look at Mrs. Franklin and her face is neutral, almost relieved. I scan the room, searching for any sign of him.

The bed is unmade, the beige comforter crumpled in a messy pile at the end. There's a dent in the pillow. I walk over to it and press my hand against it.

"Aysel," Mrs. Franklin says, her voice shaking. "Is there something I should know?" She wraps her arms around herself again. "Should I be worried?"

I don't answer her. I check the nightstand and I don't find any letters—no suicide note. I let out a shallow breath. "I'm not sure."

I crouch down and duck my head under the bed. I don't find anything. I stand up and walk over to Captain Nemo's tank. My heart stops when I see it. Another dish of food has been added. There used to be only one, but now there are two.

I bite down hard on the inside of my cheek. It could be a mistake. Maybe Captain Nemo was extra hungry this morning. My mind races with excuses, but nothing is as convincing as the pit in my stomach that is growing wider and wider as I watch the turtle bob up and down in the water.

"We need to find him," I shout, but it comes out more like a strangled whisper. I rush out of the room and gallop down the stairs. Mrs. Franklin follows me and grabs my hand, pulling me back toward her.

"What is going on?" she asks. Her voice is breathless and her face is red.

"I'm worried that Roman . . ." I can't look at her. I fiddle with my car keys.

"I'm coming with you."

It's not a request; it's a demand. I don't want her to come with me, but I don't know how I can tell her no. How can I tell her anything when all of this is my fault? When I should have told her days ago about our plan, our suicide pact.

My car peels out as I back out of the driveway as fast as I can. Mrs. Franklin presses her palms against the dashboard to stay steady, but she doesn't reprimand me for driving too fast. I speed to Crestville Pointe.

Mrs. Franklin begins to sob. She wails. Her shoulders shudder. She pounds her fist against the passenger-side window. "This is all my fault."

It's not your fault. It's mine, I scream inside my head. My jaw clenches and I keep my eyes focused on the road. Roman always wanted me to watch the road. To stay focused.

"He blames himself for his sister's death," she says.

I know. I know everything. I stay silent.

"But it's my fault. I've told him that a thousand times. I'm the one who left him alone with her. That was too much responsibility for a sixteen-year-old. I should have never left her . . . left him alone with her. . . ." She breaks down and buries her head in her hands. "When Roman went to see a counselor, I went with him. And over and over again, we discussed how his dad and I were the responsible ones, not him, but he would never listen."

I don't even nod. I can't say anything. I park the car at the edge of the woods. I scan the area, searching for the Franklins' red Jeep. I don't see it anywhere. Maybe he drove it through the forest. It's not like he would care that that's illegal and dangerous. "I'll be back," I say.

"I want to come with you."

I glance down at her clogs. "But . . ."

She steps out of the car and tosses her shoes to the side. "He's my son, Aysel. I'm coming."

She reaches out and grabs my hand. We run through the woods and she keeps squeezing my hand, over and over again. Her grip is so tight that I feel like any second my fingers are going to fall off from the lack of circulation. Her bare feet crunch twigs, but she doesn't wince. She keeps up with me and we quickly reach the clearing.

The cliff looms in front of us. I want to find Roman here and I don't want to find him here. I want to throw my arms around his neck and pull him close, breathe in his pinewood scent and kiss the splatter of freckles on the back of his neck. And I want to punch him in the gut, slap him in the face, for betraying me like this. For lying. For trying to die without me. But I might not get to do either if we don't find him in time. My knees buckle.

"You don't think he . . . do you?" Mrs. Franklin asks, her voice hoarse from tears. I watch her staring out over the cliff. The Ohio River sputters below us, and I doubt we would even be able to see him if he was in there. In the water. His head banging against the rocks, his spine broken and flimsy. I squeeze those thoughts out of my mind.

He's not dead. He can't be. I wonder if I would feel it if he was dead. If I would know it, understand it at some cellular level. If my body would be able to sense his energy giving out and fading away. For the first time all day, I squeeze Mrs. Franklin's hand back, returning her tight grip. "We need to find him. We're going to find him."

I don't know why I say it. It's more of a wish than a promise. She drops my hand and reaches out to pull me into a tight hug. She smells like cupcake batter and vanilla. "You're an angel."

I lose it when she says that. I am not an angel. I am the opposite. I could have stopped this. Should have stopped this. I'm about to tell her that when a thought hits me. "You said you gave Roman the keys to the car?"

She nods.

I run back toward my car and Mrs. Franklin follows. I don't even put my seat belt on and I slam on the gas pedal. We roar away from Crestville Pointe. The eight-minute drive feels like centuries. When we reach Roman's house, I pull on the emergency parking brake and jump out of the car.

I dash toward the detached garage. I can smell the exhaust slipping through the bottom crack and I hear the faint hum of a car's engine. I pull at the door, but I can't get it to open. I kick it.

Behind me, I hear Mrs. Franklin scream and run toward the house. I keep banging on the garage, but it is useless. Mrs. Franklin returns, wildly waving the garage-door opener over her head. She presses the button again and again and the door lifts and we see it.

The red Jeep is running. The garage is full of exhaust. Through the smoke, I can see Roman in the driver's seat. He is folded over the steering wheel and his big, beautiful eyes are shut. He's not moving.

My legs go weak and something inside me bursts. My heart.

FRIDAY, APRIL 5

''ve been sitting in the hospital waiting room for hours. I stare up at the pulsing fluorescent white light, trying to get the image of Roman's limp, unconscious body out of my head. The waiting room smells like burnt coffee and disinfectant and salty tears. You never think fear or sadness has a scent until you spend a long time in a hospital.

I wonder if guilt has a scent—a stinking, foul odor that Roman's parents can detect. I'm sitting between the two of them and they haven't said anything to me, except to periodically ask if I'm okay. How can they still be worried about me? Don't they know that I was a part of the problem, in on the plan? I'm sure they'd hate me if they knew the truth.

Both of them have been back to visit Roman. Thankfully, he's stable. He floats in and out of consciousness. I guess he hasn't had a chance to tell them what a traitor I am, to him and to them.

I squirm in my chair. The plastic seat is damp from my sweat and sticks to my thighs. I should have worn jeans instead of shorts. As I pick at the skin around my fingernails, I find myself getting more and more angry at Roman. Maybe I am a traitor, but he is, too. He went ahead and tried to die without me.

Roman's mom puts her hand on my shoulder, pulling me back into reality. "Sweetheart, the nurse says Roman should be awake soon. I explained who you are and she said that you can go visit him in a few minutes, if you want." Her voice is soft, almost like a lullaby. "I told her how you are the one who saved Roman's life. If it weren't for you . . ." She pulls me into a hug to suffocate the sound of her own tears. "We're so grateful for you."

She lets me go and gives me a sad, small smile. "How will we ever repay you?"

My breath catches in my throat. I can't find any words— it's like my mouth is full of quicksand and every word I want to say gets pulled back into the pit of my stomach.

"It's okay, sweetie." She pats the back of my head with her perfectly manicured nails. "You don't have to say anything.

I know this is a lot to handle." She tilts her head so she can look me in the eye. "You do want to see Roman, don't you?"

I make myself nod. I want to see Roman. I really do. It's all I want.

But at the same time, I don't know how I can face him.

I sit with Mrs. Franklin for a few more minutes. Mr. Franklin returns from the hospital cafeteria with a coffee for her and a cookie for me. I place the cookie on the side table beside me. I don't touch it again.

Eventually, a nurse with hair the color of cinnamon approaches us. Mrs. Franklin gestures toward me and the nurse nods. As I stand up, my legs stick to the leather cushion of the waiting room chair. It's like the chair is begging me not to go, warning me not to go.

The nurse leads me down the tiled hallway to Roman's room. I study the cards and words of encouragement that have been taped on the other doors. One door has a whole bunch of yellow balloons tacked on it. I wonder if I should have brought balloons. That's probably a stupid thought. This doesn't seem like an occasion for balloons.

Finally, we reach Roman's room. The nurse turns the metal knob and walks inside. I stand out in the hallway for a few moments, squeezing my hands together, taking deep breaths, humming Mozart's Piano Concerto no. 15.

"In here, darling," the nurse encourages. I wonder if she

deals with this all the time. Visitors who can't bear it, who can't face reality.

The sight of Roman lying in the bed makes my heart stop. His tall, lean body is too big for the hospital bed—his toes hang over the edge. The hospital lights make his skin look almost translucent, and there are big dark circles under his hazel eyes. They don't look golden at all now. Just a muddy dull green.

"Aysel," he says. His voice is hoarse and strained.

The nurse gives me a hopeful smile and reaches out to touch my shoulder. "I'll be right outside if you guys need anything."

I look around the room because I can't stand to look at him. I see his mom brought his collection of Jules Verne novels and his sketchbook, and there's a vase of marigolds that's been placed at the side of his bed. No Captain Nemo. I guess that makes sense. Hospitals probably don't let you bring in your pet turtle.

But besides the flowers and the books and the sketch pad, the room is sterile. Nothing like Crestville Pointe. It's not like the place he imagined he'd die in. He can't die in this place. He can't die at all.

"Aysel," he repeats. This time his voice is louder, but it still sounds impossibly sore.

I blink back the tears that I can already feel building in my eyes. "How could you?"

"You didn't want to," he says. "I know you didn't. And I didn't want you to. I care about you too much to watch you die. I want you to live, Aysel. So I did it alone because I wanted to save you."

I jut my chin out and look him straight in the eye. His face is so pale. I can see his veins. He looks too fragile, like any second his body is going to give out on him. "Save me? If you were at all worried about me, you wouldn't have done this."

I move closer to the side of his bed but keep standing. I watch him try to shake his head. He can barely move his neck. As I get closer to him, I can see that his throat is bruised. Purple and swollen. "I had to do it, Aysel. I'm not like you. I don't deserve to live." He lets out a heavy breath. "I can't live with myself. Not when I know I'm the reason Maddie's dead."

"But what about April seventh? And dying in the water?"

This time it's his turn to refuse to look at me. "I didn't want to jump from Crestville Pointe without you. It seemed wrong. And the more I thought about it, the more I realized it wasn't right for me to die on the same day as Maddie. Or in the same way. It would be like I was taking something from her." He tries to shake his head again. "I don't know why I picked the car. I just got this feeling in my stomach that if I didn't do it now, I was never going to be able to."

I lower my face so he can't see my eyes, pressing my chin against my chest. I suck in the sound of my sobs, but the tears still dribble down my cheek in silence.

"Don't cry," he says. "Come here."

I don't move.

"Aysel, come here."

I take a deep breath and sit down in the chair next to the bed.

He puts his hand out and I grab it. His grip is weak and loose, unlike when he squeezed my hand at the carnival. And this time, I can feel my hand. I can feel everything. And I want to keep feeling everything. Even the painful, awful, terrible things. Because feeling things is what lets us know that we're alive.

And I want to be alive.

"I can't lose you," I finally manage to say.

"Don't say that," he whispers.

"No, it's true. I can't lose you. Roman, you have to decide to live. I know that nothing can ever erase what happened to Maddie, but you can't give up."

He moves his face to make a frown. It looks painful. I can practically see his muscles aching under his skin. The skin around his eyes looks so dark and bruised, like someone punched him repeatedly in the face.

"I'm not asking you to live for me. Even though that would be nice because I'm in love with you. And yeah,

yeah, you can tell me I'm misusing that word, but I don't care. That's how I feel. But this isn't even about me, or how I feel about you. I want you to live for *you* because I know there's so much more waiting for you. There's so much more for you to discover and experience. And you deserve it, you might not think you do, but you do. I'm here to tell you that you deserve it. And I know I sound cheesy as hell. Believe me, six weeks ago, I would've slapped myself for saying shit like this, but knowing you . . ." I trail off for a moment. "Knowing you has helped me see things differently. See myself differently. And all I want is for you to see yourself the way that I do."

After I say all that, I feel drained, deflated. I know most people use "deflated" in a negative way, but today, I feel deflated in a positive way. Like I've kept all these secrets inside of me for so long, and now, I've let them all go. I feel lighter. I feel free. I told Roman I loved him; I put that positive charge out into the universe. And now I'm just waiting to see if it sparks—if it puts us in motion.

Roman makes a sputtering noise like he's about to say something, but then his eyes close and his breathing steadies. He's fallen asleep. I sit there for a while, my left hand still holding his right. I feel creepy watching him sleep, but I can't help it. I'm scared that if I take my eyes away from him, he's going to disappear.

His chest rises and lowers. He looks so frail, but he's

still alive. And that's what counts. As I stare at him, I find myself wishing that I could see through his skin, see inside him. See if there's only emptiness, darkness, or if there's more.

SUNDAY, APRIL 7

0 days left

Today's the day: the anniversary of Madison's death. I almost didn't work up the courage to come to the hospital, but I knew that if I didn't come, I'd never forgive myself.

For the first time in three years, I'm wearing something other than a gray striped shirt and jeans. I borrowed a simple black dress from Georgia and washed my hair and pulled it back into a French braid. It's not like I think Roman cares at this point what I look like, but I care. And I'm trying to show that to him.

The silver flats I also borrowed from Georgia make a pitter-patter sound on the tiles as I walk down the hallway.

Once I reach Roman's room, I peek inside and see his parents gathered at the foot of his bed.

"Oh, Aysel," his mom says. She gives me a cheery smile. I'm starting to believe that Roman's mom's warmth isn't a facade like he says; she really has that much love inside of her.

Mr. Franklin has his arm wrapped around her, and when he sees me, he draws Mrs. Franklin closer to him.

"Come in," he says. His voice is less effusive than his wife's, but it's not cold either.

Roman looks at me. He doesn't say anything. Maybe it's my imagination, but I swear that his eyes light up a little. The skin around them is still bruised, but it's less startling than it was on Friday.

"I'm hungry, are you?" Roman's mom says to his dad. His dad looks confused for a second, but then he gets the clue.

"Oh yeah," he says. "Starving."

Mrs. Franklin turns to me. "Hon, do you mind watching Roman for a few minutes while we go get a bite to eat?"

"No problem." I smile at her to let her know I appreciate her kindness. To thank her for letting me still see Roman, for putting me on the approved visitors list and treating me like family.

Mrs. Franklin kisses Roman's forehead, and once both of his parents are gone, I take a seat in the chair next to his bed.

"I should be at her grave," Roman finally says. His voice

is still strained, but it's stronger than Friday. "Today, of all days, I should be there."

"She doesn't need you to be at her grave to know that you care."

He squints at me. "You really believe that?"

I nod. "I do, Roman. She might not physically be here, but she's still here. And she wants to see you happy. I know she does."

He's silent for a few moments. The sheets are pulled up to his chin and he's completely motionless. We stare at each other quietly until he asks, "When I get out of here, will you go with me?"

"To her grave?"

His lips twitch and I interpret it as a yes.

"I'll go anywhere with you." My face burns. I'm not used to saying things like that, but when I see him slowly smile, all my embarrassment goes away. "Look at me, still being cheesy as hell."

He lets out a low, gravelly laugh.

"And speaking of that," I say, and reach into my bag. I pull out the book I bought about North Carolina's beaches. I place it on his food tray so he can see it. "I thought maybe when you get better, we can go here."

He stares at the book and his eyes brighten. They turn from the muddy green to a dark gold.

"To the ocean," I add.

He doesn't say anything. He grabs the book off the tray and thumbs through it. I can tell he's trying to act disinterested, but on certain pages he spends a bit longer staring at the glossy photos.

Finally he asks, "Why?"

"Why what?"

"Why do you keep trying when you know how messed up I am?"

I shrug. I stand up and walk over to the side table where his mom has placed all of his Jules Verne novels and his sketch pad. I grab the sketch pad and then sit back down in the chair. I flip the pages.

"Why?" he repeats.

I stare down at the charcoal drawings and then glance up, forcing myself to look him in the eye. "Because loving you saved me. It's made me see myself differently, see the world differently. I owe you everything for that."

Before he can respond, there's a knock on the door.

"Hello?" a professional-sounding voice says.

The door opens and a woman stands at the front of the room. She's not wearing a lab coat or scrubs but instead is dressed in black pants and a white button-up. "You must be Aysel," she says, and then turns to Roman. "Hello, Roman. How are you feeling today?"

Roman just stares at her.

She reaches out and touches my elbow lightly. "Do you

mind waiting for us in the hall?"

I shake my head and walk out of the room, quietly closing the door behind me. I pace the hall as I try to imagine the conversation that's happening in the room. I picture Roman's stony, silent face and that woman doing her best to pull answers out of him.

I'm about to walk the length of the hallway for the twenty-third time when the door opens and the woman walks out. She brushes a stray piece of her dark hair away from her forehead. "I'm Dr. Stead." She holds out her hand.

I shake it weakly. "Aysel, but you already know that. You're working with Roman?"

She nods. "Yes, that's right."

Good, I think, but don't say anything. "I hope you're able to, you know, get through to him."

She doesn't smile but somehow manages to look friendly. I wonder if that's a skill they teach you in medical school. "I'll do the best I can. You know, I'm pretty good at what I do." She reaches into her pocket and pulls out a small business card. She hands it to me.

The paper is soft, and I run my fingers over the embossed text.

"If you ever want to talk, or need anything, you can reach me at that number," she adds. She looks at me, her light eyes soft and kind. I wonder if she knows about Crestville Pointe, about our pact. If Roman said something to her.

"Thanks," I say weakly, and turn the card over. She walks away and the click of her heels echoes in the hall.

When I walk back into Roman's hospital room, he gives me a cold look.

"What?"

"You aren't seriously going to tell me I should talk to that lady, are you?"

I clutch the card in my hand. "Did you tell her about us?"

"What about us?"

"You know. . . ."

He props himself up so his back can rest against the hospital bed's metal headboard. It looks like it's a struggle, but he makes it. "No. I haven't said a damn thing to her. And I'm not planning on it."

I sit back down in the chair by the bed. "Maybe it wouldn't be such a bad thing."

He sighs and I swear I can hear the muscles in his throat ache. I imagine what the inside of his body must look like— all poisoned and bruised. I try to push that thought from my mind.

"I'm not sure I even know you anymore," he says.

I bite down on my lower lip. "That's not fair. I mean, you don't have to talk to her. But at least talk to me?"

He doesn't say anything. I stand up and walk back over to the bookshelf. This time I grab *Twenty Thousand Leagues Under the Sea.*

I sit back down and open the book. The silken pages are easy to flip. I start reading aloud to him. At first, my voice is a bit shaky, but I soon find a rhythm. Every once in a while, I glance over at him and see him looking back at me, his face relaxed like he's listening to the story.

He lets me finish the second chapter and then stops me. "Aysel?"

"Yeah?"

He scoots to move his body closer to the edge of the bed. His movements are slow and labored. "Come here." He reaches toward me, cupping my face in his hands. I lean in and our mouths meet. His lips are chapped and swollen, but the kiss is soft and light and perfect.

"I'll talk to you," he whispers. "I promise."

As I look into his golden-green eyes, I don't know if I completely believe him. I know he's still broken, impossibly sad, but as he holds my hand, I feel the potential of happiness in his pulse.

"And you know what you said before about me making you see yourself differently?" he asks, his face still inches from mine.

"Yeah."

"Well, that's why I drew you the way I did. To try and show you the person I see when I look at you, not the person you seemed to think you were."

My eyes blink like a bright camera flash just went

off—everything is white and gauzy—and I feel more exposed than I have ever been in my entire life. I know he sees me, every tiny and hidden crevice, but it doesn't scare me. My heart flutters as I realize I'm enjoying the light. I'm done with the shadows.

He watches me, his eyes traveling all over my face. "I guess I want to see the world differently—" He stops and his expression turns sad again. The room is so silent that I can hear the ceiling light buzzing.

"But it still kind of sucks, you know?" he finally adds.

"Yeah, I know." My whole body aches for him and I wish there was something I could do, but I know the only thing there is to do is stay.

"Should I keep reading? This world"—I pick up the book—"doesn't seem to suck so much."

"You say that now, but wait for it."

I look down at the page, an illustrated sea monster staring back at me, and then gaze at Roman. "I'll wait for it, if you'll wait for it."

He takes my hand and squeezes it. "I'll wait for it."

I started to write this book in January 2013 after the death of one of my closest friends. I found myself in a very dark place, and working on this project was, in part, my way of grappling with those emotions. To me, *My Heart and Other Black Holes* has always been a story about the people who understand you, all of you, even the scariest and weirdest parts of you. It is about those people who come into your life when you least expect it, in the strangest of ways, and change everything—it is about the importance of letting those people in, of opening up to them. It is about the people in your life who help you to see yourself differently and the true power of human connection.

Although this story ends on a hopeful note, the road to recovery is long and ongoing. In many cases, the battle with depression is a lifelong one. To those of you who may be dealing with emotions similar to Aysel and Roman's, I want you to know no matter how lost you feel, you are never alone. If you are having suicidal thoughts, you should treat it as a medical emergency. Please, please reach out and talk to someone. The National Suicide Prevention Lifeline is always open, and as scary as it can be to talk about what is going on in your mind, I hope you will find the strength to do so. The most powerful thing we have is our voice. I have listed some resources at the end of this book.

To those of you who feel you may have a friend who is struggling with depression, please reach out to them. I know it may seem uncomfortable, but talking about these things is what will help us begin to erase the stigma associated with depression and suicidal thoughts. The best thing you can do for your friend is to talk with them or an authority figure. By encouraging them to speak, you may help steer them toward the path of recovery.

Finally, I hope this story has reminded you of the people in your life who matter. Hold them dear, be kind to them, and remember life is fragile. I wish you all a very kinetic and beautiful life.

LIFELINES

National Suicide Prevention Lifeline:
1-800-273-TALK (8255)

Kristin Brooks Hope Center Hopeline:
1-800-422-HOPE (4673)

Kristin Brooks Hope Center Teen Peer Counseling Hotline:
1-877-968-8454

WEBSITES/COMMUNITIES

To Write Love on Her Arms (TWLOHA):
www.twloha.com

IMAlive: www.IMALIVE.org

7 Cups of Tea: www.7cupsoftea.com

Crisis Chat: www.crisischat.org

Youth Suicide Prevention Program: www.yspp.org

National Alliance on Mental Illness: www.NAMI.org

The American Academy of Child and Adolescent
Psychiatry: www.AACAP.org

The American Academy for Suicide Prevention:
www.AFSP.org

Acknowledgments

Endless thanks to Brenda Bowen, my incredible agent, who changed the course of my life when she agreed to take on this manuscript and has gone on to make all of my wildest dreams come true. I am forever grateful for your guidance, savvy, enthusiasm, and belief in my work. I will never be done thanking you. Also many thanks to the entire team at Greenburger Associates, especially Stefanie Diaz and Wendi Gu.

Deepest gratitude to my lovely editor, Alessandra Balzer, who somehow manages to deliver the sharpest, most brilliant suggestions in the kindest, most inspiring way. It is a dream to work with you. Huge thanks to everyone else at Balzer + Bray and HarperCollins—I am so lucky to have you all in my corner.

I have been fortunate in my life to have many wonderful teachers. In particular, I would like to thank Chris Lynch and Pat Lowery Collins for their generous mentorship during my thesis semester. I would also like to thank my eleventh-grade English teacher, Connie Smith, who encouraged me to pursue my dream of becoming an author. On a similar note, thank you to all my former students: I am grateful that I had the opportunity to know each one of you.

Thank you to Dr. Anthony Cavalieri at Cincinnati Children's Hospital for lending us his expertise and reviewing this manuscript.

Enormous thanks to Brenda St. John Brown, this manuscript's first reader, who provided invaluable feedback. Love to all the ladies of #twitterbloc, who have been a part of this wondrous journey with me from the very beginning, especially Kayla Olson. Cheers to all my fellow 2015 debut authors—it's been a wild ride! In particular, I want to thank the members of #beckminavidera: Becky Albertalli (Jim), David Arnold (Big D), and Adam Silvera (Kareem)—I am beyond lucky to have friends as brilliant and funny as you. (Becky, I will never stop sending you Sailor Moon gifs.) I also want to thank the Freshman Fifteens for their support—I am endlessly fortunate to be a part of such a fabulous group of ridiculously talented women. Special thanks to Kim Liggett, who answers every email and helps me chase away every doubt—let's build that tunnel? Also, many thanks to Alexandra Perrotti (my forever friend who has been swapping tunes with me since we were fifteen), Renee Sabo, Erica Kaufman, Sara Farizan, and Kristan Hoffman for all of their support—both virtually and in person.

Endless gratitude to my amazing family, on both this side of the Atlantic Ocean and the other. In particular, many thanks to my grandpa (who taught me how to grow tomatoes), my grandma (whose lack of surprise about all of this is the biggest confidence boost), and my brother, Brandon Khader—my bottomless love for you inspired the birthday party scene. Immeasurable thanks to my father, who sacrificed so much so I could chase my dreams.

Mom, you deserve your own section because you are the reason I love stories. You tirelessly read every word I ever write and manage to strike the perfect balance of honesty and encouragement. Thank you for everything.

And finally, a tremendous thank-you to Gregory Warga. Thank you for believing this moment would come, even when I didn't. Thank you for being my floodlight in the darkness. Everything I write is in some strange way a love letter to you.

About the Author

Jasmine Warga grew up outside of Cincinnati, Ohio. Before becoming a full-time writer, she briefly worked as a science teacher. This is her first novel. Learn more about Jasmine at www.jasminewarga.com.